"BLUE MODE!" ST~~URGIS SCREAM~~ ~~INTO~~
HIS HELMET.

Instantly a grid map lit up in a green digitized image on the right side of his visor. The map showed the geometric shapes that represented each of the attacking vehicles. Even as Sturgis watched, the screen began reading out numerous bits of information.

"73 VEHICLES, FIVE FORDS, 2 ISUZUS, 8 BUICK STATION WAGONS . . . RECOILESS RIFLE-50 CAL, BACKARMS MORTAR-50MM, BAZOOKA . . ."

"This looks as close to Custer at Little Big Horn as any of us is likely to get," Billy Dixon said with a dark laugh.

"Yeah," Sturgis grunted. "Except Custer had a hundred more men than we do." Then, "P.D. Mode!"

"PROBABILITY OF DESTRUCTION AT THIS SECOND 95.67%" the grid read back in green digits.

"Cover! Cover!" Sturgis yelled to the C.A.D.S. team, and then turned to Dixon. "Hold those last shells, Billy. I have an idea . . . ."

CADS

#7 DOOM COMMANDER

JOHN SIEVERT

ZEBRA BOOKS
KENSINGTON PUBLISHING CORP.

ZEBRA BOOKS

are published by

Kensington Publishing Corp.
475 Park Avenue South
New York, NY 10016

First printing: June, 1989

Printed in the United States of America

Chapter One

The frigid February winds poured in through the opened emergency jump door of the huge Bear-40 Strato Bomber as it cruised at 20,000 feet, sending papers, blankets, and mechanical odds and ends flying around the interior of the intercontinental jet. The sixteen men and two women who sat inside on gridded aluminum seats that ran along each wall shivered as the outside air slammed through the plane, their eyes wincing from the blast. The opened visors of their C.A.D.S. (Computerized Attack/Defense System) suits allowed the freezing winds to enter the seven-foot-high tech suits of mega-destruction. Their mirror hued visors would have sealed them off completely from the cold if they'd been closed, but the suits weren't functioning quite properly, to say the least. Not since the team's bloody battles in Moscow, where they had used up all their ammunition and run down all the suits' battery charges to dangerously low levels.

It felt stuffy, uncomfortable with the visors closed; none of the warriors could quite get enough air into their lungs. It felt as if it were going through an old and not very efficient air conditioner. Thus they kept their visors up and let the air whip at them with such force that even seated they had to hold onto the curved metal struts that ribbed the inside of the jet as turbulence whipped around the Bear-40. It was like a wild animal testing everything to see if it could be torn free.

5

Every C.A.D.S. trooper stared toward the opened door in the side of the jet, stared out at the black-clouded sky and prayed they wouldn't have to jump into it. It would be like jumping into the abyss. None of them had fond memories of their last jump, onto the polar ice. The weight and bulk of the C.A.D.S. suits—miracles of modern engineering when they worked—were like stone anchors when they didn't. Each trooper hoped Col. Sturgis had opened the jump-door only as a precaution. Even with the heavy-duty parachutes that each had strapped to his back they had their doubts about making it to the ground in one piece if they jumped. They'd much rather make a landing *in* the jet!

Col. Dean Sturgis, commander of the strike force team of Tech Commandos, gripped hard on both sides of the five-foot-wide, eight-foot-high door and tried to see clearly through the visor on his C.A.D.S. suit which he had pulled down to protect him from the slashing ice pellets which pinged against the outside of the Stratojet, and against his titanium suit armor, with sharp reports. *Time versus fuel consumption.* They weren't going to make it. He hadn't told the rest of them yet, wanting them to stay cool until the last second. There was no sense in getting their adrenaline pumping, in giving their minds time to wonder about what it would be like to die in that cold black night below.

Sturgis knew they weren't going to be able to land the jet as he had hoped. He'd kept checking up front with MacLeish and Dixon who were co-piloting the stolen Soviet rig. And the news wasn't good. The fuel was almost gone, the dials actually hovering right on the empty line. They'd already performed their share of miracles just getting back from their destructive mission to Moscow over the arctic icecaps without any real maps. And they'd performed another feat avoiding a squad of MIGs in occupied Canada which had been sent up to see who was invading their air space. Only a thick fog had saved them. But miracles were about to run out. They couldn't make

6

jet fuel out of the icy rain which drove against their cockpit window in an angry cascade of black liquid.

"Altitude?" Sturgis asked the suit computer, having already switched to Internal Information Mode so that none of the others could hear through their helmet earphones. The metal battle-suits were all connected to each other by numerous electro-magnetic spectrums, from radio to sonar to microwave. And it was a cardinal rule of C.A.D.S. warfare, right out of the manual—to always be in contact with all other members of the team. It was one of the aces in the hole that the fighting unit had. For they were like one when electronically connected, able to see the man on every side and whether he was friend or foe. But rules were made to be broken. Sturgis had had his share of broken rules all the way back to when he had been one of the top astronauts in the space program and been bounced for insubordination one time too many. Still, it was one of the luxuries of being the commander of the Omega strike unit, that he could break them.

"18,500 FEET," the suit computer read out in green digital words that ran across the bottom of the inside of the visor. "DROPPING AT 50 FEET PER SECOND, INCREASING BY 2 FEET PER SECOND."

"Estimated fuel in time?" Sturgis asked in a half whisper, realizing that there was no need to talk softly as they couldn't hear his voice.

"APPROXIMATE 10 TO 12 MINUTES FUEL LEFT, DEPENDING UPON RATE OF DECLINE AND DECELERATION. BOTH ARE VARIABLE, UNABLE TO COMPUTE WITH 100% ACCURACY AT THIS TIME."

Sturgis leaned his head down and slightly out of the opened door. The jet had already slowed to about two hundred miles an hour as it descended, the novice pilots searching for a decent flat place to land. The wind pressure even against the heavily weighted suit and the servo grips of his steel hands which held onto both sides of the steel door frame with over a thousand pounds of pressure

7

per square inch, was intense.

"Telemode," Sturgis commanded and instantly the visor went from normal clear vision to telescopic view. It was as if the whole world was shooting up at him and the C.A.D.S. commander had to fight a sudden dizzying vertigo as he had the illusion he was plummeting down through the blackness. He could see the peaks of the Rocky Mountains below, the outlines of the blanketing fir trees. Everything was amber and dark, as if looking through a filter.

"Map I.D.," he said again and this time it took a few seconds for the built-in computer to respond. He could hear the thing humming behind his skull. But then it had to go through about a hundred thousand calculations as the information of the peaks and lakes below was compared to every other possible combination of such terraformation in the US. At last after what seemed like an interminable wait as the wind buffeted against the suit, it began reading out data:

"STATE OF OREGON, SOUTHERN REGION," the green digitized letters danced across the lower part of the visor. "CRATER LAKE TWENTY MILES AHEAD."

"Airfields for possible landing of craft?" Sturgis asked, hardly able to hear himself from the slashing winds that shrieked along the streamlined sides of the jet.

"NO ABANDONED AIRFIELDS WITHIN TWO HUNDRED MILES," the computer read back quickly, now that it had a fix on their location. "OR NATURAL LAND CONFIGURATIONS NECESSARY FOR MINIMUM 3,000 FEET NEEDED TO LAND AIRCRAFT. RUSSIAN AIR BASE OF STRAVNIK FIFTY MILES SOUTH." An amber warning light suddenly flashed in the lower right hand corner of the visor, one of the emergency warning systems of the suit that advised him what was up on its own accord.

"WARNING, WE ARE BEING TRACKED BY STRAVNIK AIRBASE. ACCORDING TO LATEST INTELLIGENCE INFORMATION IT IS EQUIPPED

8

WITH MISHKIN 200 PANTHER MISSILES CAPABLE OF DESTROYING AIRCRAFT WITHIN ONE MINUTE OF FIRING." Sturgis scanned back and forth and snapped out angrily at the suit for telling him bad news.

"Infra Mode," he barked at the machine. It took no note of the emotions, fortunately for it, or it would have gone mad long ago from the curses that had been expressed at it. The C.A.D.S. suits and all the perceptual and weapons equipment they contained made the wearers godlike, more powerful than whole armies of centuries before. But the armor-suits were also possessed of quirks, and something approaching personalities as well. They could function perfectly—and then suddenly just conk out. The infrared mode of viewing didn't go on. The batteries were low though they still read at least twenty percent, which should power all the helmet's functions.

"Infra, you son-of-a-bitch," Sturgis shouted inside the suit, slamming the helmet with the side of his gloved hand. For a moment, he forgot that the servo mechanisms of the arm and hand were up-powered a dozenfold. His head was suddenly ringing like Old Liberty. When his eyes cleared a second later, the infrared screen was covering the whole central part of the visor as letters and readouts danced along the top and bottom of the huge mirror eye peering out upon Soviet-dominated America.

That was better. The infrared cut through the darkness and the dusty haze that seemed to lie over much of the region. Sturgis could see the swirling glows of heat through the night, picking up the patterns of everything down there. It made the night look like a rainbow. His trained eyes tried to make sense of the halos and globs of shimmering red and blue and green and gold that represented all that lay below.

Crater Lake—he could see the smooth outline of the ancient volcanic crater now filled with a five-mile-wide lake raised hundreds of feet above the surrounding land. Suddenly his attention was caught by a long flat patch of land, an even blue in infra, indicating dirt, rather than trees. The grid along both sides of the visor told him the location and he read out the coordinates into the computer, asking for a topographical look. Instantly the computer rearranged the region he was looking at so it was as if he were staring out from ground level. It was flat, nearly. As flat as they were going to find in the next sixty seconds. For suddenly the amber warning light was flashing hard like a Christmas tree bulb warning that Santa was coming.

"MISSILE HAS BEEN FIRED," the suit visor read out. "EVASION MUST BE COMMENCED. WARNING! WE ARE BEING TRACKED BY PANTHER-FIVE AIR TO AIR MISSILE. WARNING!"

Sturgis screamed at the Voice Recognition Command Module to open him to full communication with the whole crew.

"Fenton! Dixon, I'm getting a missile readout on my visor."

"We already caught it, Skip," Fenton spoke back in his clipped British accent. "Wondered where the bloody hell you were. I slammed the decoy switch, figured you'd okay it."

"What *is* it?" Sturgis shouted.

"It sends out a whole load of aluminum balloons, should confuse the hell out of the missiles, Skip!"

"Right," Sturgis replied. "We're getting out of here. See that crater lake down there at fifty degrees? There's a series of flat fields, just weeds and low brush for several miles alongside it. Get us right over it—pronto. Drop to five thousand feet. We'll jump from there."

"All right, you all heard!" Sturgis said, standing in the middle of the suddenly sharply descending jet, as he addressed the C.A.D.S. troopers. His own "Inner Circle" team was nearest him: Tranh Van Noc, Vietnamese fighter par excellence; Mickey Rossiter, his broad face streaked with grease and a smear of blood from their recent battles; Sheila DeCamp, doctor and knockout brunette whom Sturgis had bedded down. They were in good shape— Only trouble was Robin, his wife, sitting next to Sheila, looking peaked and pale. She hadn't been the same since he'd rescued Robin from her Russian brain-conditioning ordeal. She could talk, walk, chew gum. But Robin was different.

Sitting right by the opened door, his wide black mustache hanging out of the helmet, was Wosyck. The Polish-American Solidarity fighter, was the newest member of Sturgis's elite strike force. Wosyck had an ego a little too big for a team, but he was a self-starter like Billy Dixon. On the other side of the door, Fireheels. The vital American Indian was a full-fledged C.A.D.S. warrior, and the scout of the team. On the gridded aluminum seats facing him from across the plane, sat the rest of the C.A.D.S. troopers. Sturgis had selected these men personally from the best at White Sands Base. They were all that were left of a much larger force that had fought hard in Russia, accomplishing the mission.

"All right, we're going down," he said, addressing all of them. Every face looked at him with tight grim lips. "We gotta move fast, and I mean fast. Close your visors, go on full defensive internal systems."

The visors all snapped down hard—even Robin's visor—and in a flash Sturgis was looking at eighteen black armored cyclops like himself, their mirror visors reflecting back images of one another like an endless series of mirrors. "You've all got heavy-duty Soviet parachutes on. For carrying down jeeps, big loads of supplies. So you don't have to worry about that. But they're not automatic—so pull hard on the release ropes."

"Anybody got any Dramamine?" a voice piped up from the suit-speaker; a voice which Sturgis recognized as Dixon's. "We're at fifty-five hundred, Skip . . . Now five thousand, like you said. Putting her on full autopilot, and heading back there."

"Good. Now everyone, line up," Sturgis snapped, waving at the exit door as he stood on the other side of it. They rose up in their nuke-knights suits, and fell in one

11

behind the other. Sturgis put Robin first so she couldn't somehow get tangled up. She looked bad, staring back up at him, her visor on clear-mode, with a pathetic kind of puppy-dog look.

"You'll be okay," Sturgis said, touching his helmet against hers. "Just pull, baby. Pull it *hard*." He pulled her right hand up to the parachute cord. Her thick-gloved hand tightened around the cord. Sturgis could see a dim smile coming from within the visored helmet. She nodded. "I can do it," she said softly.

"FORTY SECONDS TO MISSILE-DETONATION," letters read out in flashing red now across the screen, so the colonel would definitely see.

"See you all down there in Club Med," Sturgis yelled into the helmet mike. He pushed Robin out before she had a chance to think about it all. He could see her tumbling end over end, the immense C.A.D.S. suit turning like some lumbering elephant in the air. Down into the wind-snapping darkness she dropped. *Like a body falling into a grave,* he thought. Then Sturgis canceled all thought and screamed out, *"Next!"*

Chapter Two

One after another they jumped out into the black mists as the jet held its automatic course making a slow circle around the three by four mile patch of flatland below. Sturgis stood next to the door slapping each one hard on the shoulder as they went out the door screaming defiance, or fear, or bravado calls.

"Count three and pull," he shouted as he pushed them slightly to the right or left as they went out the door. Just a helpful nudge, but it would keep them from tangling up with each other. Dixon and Fenton came tearing out of the cockpit and stopped just short of Sturgis.

"Come on, man, you go first, Colonel," MacLeish yelled into his visor mike. "We'll—"

"No time," Sturgis screamed back as the warning light in the visor flashed faster and faster, almost becoming a solid color.

"FIVE SECONDS TO IMPACT," the letters read across the visor. He pushed both of them out one after another, with hard shoves of his thick black-armored hands. And they disappeared below cursing, twisting around like men performing the diving championships at the Olympics, the new, fifteen-hundred meter dive. Better than when there had been such things as Olympics, before the mushroom clouds hit the scene. Sturgis braced himself at the door, finding it a little harder to jump himself than to push them all out.

13

"THREE, TWO—" He could see the Soviet missile now, streaking out of the darkness below and up like a burning spear, a flame of yellow arching out of its cold steel tail.

"Geronimo!" he yelled out with an almost childlike high pitched sound as he kicked out to push himself away from the jet. The force of the mechanically assisted leg muscles shot him out a good fifty yards within two seconds. Which was lucky for Sturgis. For right behind him the Panther Class missile—a cigar-shaped thing eight feet long—lanced into the Bear-40 engine on the right wing of the jet.

The Stratojet went up like a bonfire in the sky, lighting up the American night and the clouds above with a brilliant burst of yellow and red. Sturgis felt the force of the awesome blast slam into his suit even as it spun away from the burning wreckage which was now spreading out above in all directions. The unspent missile's fuel caught and blanketed out in a fiery curtain.

Then he was spinning end over end, the sky above and the mud below just indistinct blurs which buzzed past his visor in half-second rotations. He felt the sound follow right behind the blast force; it was like being in the very machines that made the thunder of storms. The deep grating sound shook the entire suit, rattling things around within it with most unnerving clanking and scraping sounds. Somehow Sturgis was able to read the digital words which scrambled across the visor.

"STRAIGHTEN ANGLE OF DESCENT BEFORE DEPLOYING CHUTE OR SUDDEN WEIGHT COULD CAUSE MATERIAL FAILURE," the computer readout warned him.

"Yeah, right, easy for *you* to say," Sturgis snapped back. He ordered the jetpack on for a quick one second burn, but it didn't put out a match-worth of flame. The thing was dead as a proverbial doornail! If only he were *Peter Pan*! Why not? He held both arms out at his sides like he was being crucified and it helped, slowing his descent and pulling him out of the tumbling spin. Within another second or two he was floating along, gliding down the buffeting air currents like a surfer on the sky.

"CHUTE MAY BE DEPLOYED," the visor scrolled past him, but Sturgis was way ahead of it, his hand already jerking hard on the cord of the bulky package of material strapped with plastimesh holds around his chest. There was a sudden whooshing sound like a hundred sheets were being snapped open at once and then he jerked up hard. The chute billowed out and filled with the frigid Oregon night air. Sturgis's head snapped back and forth on his neck as he grunted hard. Being thrown around inside the suit *hurt,* even if it was lined with all kinds of high-tech shock-buffer materials.

Then he was floating down like a dandelion puff, and everything slowed down real fast like a film dropping to quarter speed. He could see the others all drifting down around him as he switched to Infra Mode again. Bodies floating everywhere, the huge suits rolling slowly back and forth in the wind. All chutes seemed to have deployed well, though Red Mode—which he commanded the visor to switch to—showed only sixteen dropping C.A.D.S. troopers. He prayed hard that two of them had already landed, and that it wasn't defective chutes that were responsible for the discrepancy in numbers.

As he fell, the displays along the bottoms and sides of the C.A.D.S. helmet kept up a steady stream of information, giving him the changing temperature of the outside air, the wind turbulence, his rate of descent, the time, and a hundred other things, none of which Sturgis gave a damn about at this moment. If the suits had any engineering flaws in their information processing systems it was that they thought everything was of pretty much equal importance. Only those adept at the usage of the high tech attack defense system could filter out nearly 99% of the junk. Experience showed it was the other 1% that mattered. The life/death stuff!

Above him the sky was a glowing orange globe of flaming fuel. It was dropping in an ever expanding curtain of fire, like a cloud spreading out to several acres. The jet, or what was left of it, was split up into over a hundred pieces. There were chunks as big as a red glowing wings, to fragments of snowball-sized steel. Each hot fragment was spitting steam as they contacted the heavy moisture in the low mist-clouds.

Sturgis realized with a horror that swept through his entire nervous system that all those flames were basically coming down right over his men and him.

"Heads up," Sturgis screamed into the visor mike built in below the screens inside the helmet. "There's fire coming down." He could hear their expletives and groans come through the radio speakers mounted on each of side of his helmet. They'd seen it. As if it wasn't enough to just be falling into the unknown. He saw a few spurts from jet packs far below but they only lasted a flash and then were out again.

Sturgis saw that a whole detached section of falling jet fuel was coming down fast at him. Again he tried with the Peter Pan-arms trick to get his trajectory changed slightly. And damned if it didn't work! He veered sharply to the right side, the sheer weight of the suit and the thickness of the arms making enough wind drag to affect the industrial-strength twenty-foot-wide chute. The billowing circle with Russian markings all over it glowed orange like a sky-ad for Marx and Engels.

The fire curtain—burning fuel—which he could feel the heat of as it fell, ripped right past him only about ten feet off. It undulated like a thing alive as it kept on heading down, moving at almost double his speed. The missile's burning fuel spread out into a fine spray, which only fired it up with that much more intensity. He saw a chute about five hundred feet below him suddenly catch on fire as the sea of fire swooped over it. There was a harsh scream over his headset and then whoever it was dropped fast. The scream lasted for several seconds and then was gone.

"UNIT 14 TERMINATED," the letters moved coldly across the right side of his visor in red letters. Sturgis saw

16

another chute catch way below and to the right, as the flames came over that group as well. Then he had his own worries, for the gray-black earth was coming up fast and he could see dark shapes piercing up out of the shadows.

"Telescreens," Sturgis screamed and the viewer crackled with energy as the helmet shifted over to close-up. *Trees!* He'd come down off the flatlands in an unfortuitous grove of Hanson's Pines. The screen read out the species name, even giving him the varying heights of the 45 trees. The computer said they were right in the spot he was spinning dead onto. Great. It could identify trees — only it couldn't do a damned thing about avoiding them.

He called for the auto rockets again and this time, for whatever fickle reason, a sputter of white flame shot out the side of the jet pack. That pushed him over perhaps fifty feet, even if he fluttered down faster. Then the ground was right at his face.

He came down hard, trying to stay up on both legs. The C.A.D.S. suit took the impact; the servo-mechanisms that assisted his natural strength and upscaled it a dozenfold tensed and withstood. But the sideways force of the final burst of the jetpack also gave him a sideways momentum, so Sturgis suddenly felt the whole suit starting to pitch over. Sturgus flexed his legs fast, as if pogo sticking, and the suit responded. It jumped up a good five feet in the air and then came down again about eight yards off. This time he was able to stand as the gyros aided him. The huge olive green chute came down just to his side, folding down on itself in irregular swaths of ripstop and metal fibered material. The big chute had held. They weren't fireproof but they sure were strong!

He turned his wrist and an autoknife shot out like a switchblade under the left glove. A good fourteen inches long, it was razor sharp and cut through the quarter inch strands of the lashing to the chute in a few seconds. Sturgis retracted the blade and stood up to the suit's full 7'2" height, turning his big 'eye' back and forth, scanning the nearby terrain, searching for his men.

"Red Mode," Sturgis ordered out and the entire C.A.D.S. team appeared in the lower half of his visor. A computed mock aerial-view, showing their proximity to him. They were spread out over nearly a mile. And only fifteen of the Red triangle shapes showed. That was three too few. Three hadn't made it, or at best were injured.

"Skip, you alive?" Sturgis heard a voice loud over his helmet, as a figure suddenly came walking toward him with wide six-foot strides. The soft Asian syllables told of their owner.

"Tranh! Thank god," Sturgis shouted out as he recognized the man's voice. Sturgis saw his name, unit number, and weapons capabilities display in the lower visor grid too. "We have to check out who's hurt. My screen shows three suits missing."

"Mine shows four," Tranh said back as the two of them started fast in great running strides alongside one another toward the main body of the troopers, who had fallen to the east. Both men had landed just inside the beginnings of a patchwork quilt of rust coated wheat stalks which rose up a good three feet in height. But the suits' legs rode over them like they were low blades of grass, though they could feel the slight spring of the pressed down vegetation beneath the soles of the suit's titanium/plastic boots.

They found two men—Fenton, and one of the new White Sands troopers, Mitchelson—standing at the base of a gnarled oak. It was big enough to show it had been around a few centuries, with wide dark branches which reached out in grasping wooden gestures in all directions. And the oak had managed to snag the two men, who were hanging upside down high up, wedged into the tree.

"Colonel," Fenton shouted excitedly through his mike. "Damned bloody well glad to see you! We've got problems all over. Over to the west, I read two men. They are not responding to my comm signals. Their body readouts are showing a flat signal on three life support modes. It looks bad."

"Over there?" Sturgis asked, sweeping his long black-

18

armored arm over toward some nearby flames where some of the burning jet wreckage had tumbled. He could see chutes tangled up in trees on the other side of the flames.

"That's the place," the Brit commando acknowledged. And without jet packs it isn't going to be an easy job to get to them! To get Fenton and Mitchelson down, the two C.A.D.S. troopers started climbing the tree, kicking off small branches with super-enhanced leg muscles to make room to go up the side of the thing. Their gloved hands grasped firmly around each trapped trooper and pulled them loose.

"Stay here!"

The colonel and Tranh had hardly gone fifty yards toward more chutes. The Rocky Mountains were reflecting the first pinkish rays of dawn from the eastern horizon when the colonel saw another chute spread out against some rocks ahead—in ashes. It was no doubt one of the men he had seen catch fire on the way down. He followed the ropes to a fallen trooper. Sturgis tapped hard on the side of the motionless suit's helmet, but nothing stirred.

He slammed the emergency clasp on the visor and it flew open. A babbling brook of blood poured out, drenching the dented metal suit and the ground around it in a flash. There was nothing inside that was recognizable as a man anymore, nor as a woman. Can't help this one.

Sturgis tore around the makeshift landing field, Tranh at his side, following the computer readouts of Red Mode. He didn't let himself relax an iota until he found his wife Robin sitting against a tree. She was not able to stand up even with the servo system. He held her de-gloved hand, trying to calm her down. He was putting her through too much. Not that it was his fault that she'd been captured by the Reds. Still, he knew with what she'd been through in the last month—torture, brain-washing Kremlin-style—and now fires and parachute jumps and God knew what all! She was heading toward a permanent check-in at the funny farm. Unless things got real slow and safe. Her eyes looked funny. Glazed over. Still, he left her, once he saw that she was basically unhurt, and headed out to aid the others. Duty. The next set of spider-web-branched trees had caught some lucky soul whose chute looked like Swiss cheese. Both of his legs were tightly entangled between two crisscrossing branches as if it had him in some exotic wrestling hold. Fireheels was standing at the base of the tree, his hands on his wide black titanium hips. The guy jammed up there was actually laughing.

"Hey, Chiefie," a voice drawled down from above in a deep southern accent. "Thought I'd do some tree climbing as long as I was up here. I'm not hurt a bit. I'm enjoying myself here. You should see—there's squirrel eggs and all kinds of neat stuff up here."

Fireheels chuckled as Sturgis came up alongside. "Dixon's having a swell time up there, observing nature. I don't have the heart to tell him squirrels don't lay eggs," the Indian said with a onesided grin.

"Let's get him down," Sturgis ordered.

"I'll set up a pulley system on top," Fireheels grunted, as he started up. "We can wrap some rope around the legs and we'll lower him down. Like a stuffed steer," he couldn't help but add. Dixon didn't get himself in too many awkward helpless situations like this. It was a picture the Apache trooper would savor for a long time.

"The hell you will, boy," Dixon snarled down, hanging by his legs like a high tech steel bat asleep in his aerie. "Get that damned Mohawk or whatever he is out of here!" Dixon demanded. "I can handle this. You too, Sturgis, step back! I think my LFP tank still has some burn left in it," he said. He was referring to the Liquid Flaming Plastic flamethrower system built into his suit. Only a few of the C.A.D.S. suits had the equipment as it took up room for other valuable firepower. Billy was an expert at LPF-mode.

"Don't be a fool," Sturgis started to say, as he realized what Dixon had in mind. But the platinum-haired southerner had a mind of his own.

Dixon raised his right arm and sprayed out a sudden

stream of flaming plastic hellfire. It landed on the branches that were encasing him along with the chute. The whole tree above him suddenly burst into flame like it had been doused with nuclear lighter fluid, and the men below jumped back. Just in time, as the intense fire quickly burned through the branches that were imprisoning Dixon. He fell free, smashing down through branches below which snapped under the weight of the armor-suit. Screaming out a rebel yell as he dropped, Dixon twisted and tore through everything in his way. He landed right on his armored ass in some bushes that surrounded the tree.

"Damn, that was fun," he spoke up, as a suited hand reached down to help him up.

"Now I *know* you're crazy, Dixon," Fireheels said as he reached out and broke a whole branch off that had lodged itself in the chute's back webbing, which was still latched around Dixon.

Sturgis, Fireheels, and Dixon went on and helped others who were stranded up in the pines, or had landed and needed minor suit-repair. It took nearly an hour to get them all down and count up casualties. Five were dead, their chutes having caught on fire high in the air, dropping them to the ground below. Even the well cushioned C.A.D.S. suits without jetpacks couldn't take a half-mile drop. None of the dead men were pretty sights when their visors were opened. All things considered, though, it could have been a *more* disastrous jump.

Chapter Three

"I said strip them!" Sturgis commanded through his radiomike, as the surviving C.A.D.S. troopers stood around the line of dead they had set down side by side, sitll wearing their bloodstained suits. "We can't be sentimental out here in the middle of nowhere. We're somewhere in wilderness-Oregon with over a thousand miles between us and White Sands base. God knows what kind of natural obstacles, mountain bandits, and over-toothed creatures we'll have to deal with. We're going to need every damned bit of working C.A.D.S. material we can get our hands on."

The men looked nervously at each other through their opened visors, their pale and sweating faces appearing small inside the seven foot suits.

"Dixon, Rossiter—I want you to go through the dead men's C.A.D.S. suits," Sturgis ordered. "Take anything that works, and any spare ammo as well. Also see if you can rip all the batteries out and get some juice out of them. Maybe we can all charge up a little. God knows how long these battered suits are going to function, even minimally."

"Will do, Skip," Dixon answered, resignation in his voice. He and Rossiter began unclasping the C.A.D.S. suits holding the dead. It was a grisly sight for all concerned. But the men had to be buried, not the suits. They dug some graves quickly using the servo-powered arms.

and makeshift jet-debris shovels. Then the broken bodies, which looked as if they had been put in a dryer on full spin for about a year, were placed into the cold earth. Sturgis said a few prayers over the dead men as snowflakes began falling, coating their faces and crushed bodies with a layer of white.

"Lord, take these C.A.D.S. troopers into your cloudy arms. I can't quite figure out why you're putting us through all this—but we'll assume it's for the best. And is going to work out for the best."

"Amen to that," MacLeish blurted out as the troopers stood in a circle around the five graves. Tranh added a few sentences in Vietnamese and then made a motion with his arms over the earth seven times.

"What does it mean?" Sturgis asked softly as the Vietnamese-American finished the hand motions.

"Means, may your souls not be attacked by demon ghosts, your bones not eaten by monkeys. Ancient Asian prayer. Very powerful. Must be said. Must be said," Tranh trailed off as if a little embarrassed. The Asian, who had fought alongside Sturgis years before in Vietnam, felt self-conscious about his religious superstitions, his endless litany of ghosts and ancestors who could come back from the grave with vengeance on their minds if not prayed to properly. But it was his ancestry. His whole culture. He'd rather look a little demented in front of the others than let the dead wander in burning clouds of darkness for eternity. He made another set of hand motions furtively as if hoping no one would notice and then stepped back away from the snow-covered burial site. The troopers filled the graves in with the mounds of dirt alongside them. It took only minutes to fill and stamp down with the heavy boots of the C.A.D.S. suits.

Rossiter and Dixon set up a mini work camp, enlisting the aid of some of the others to break the dead men's suits down into spare parts. Some were so smashed they just had to be torn apart to salvage what little was inside somewhere. Rossiter was mainly after working computer

23

chips for replacement in the circuit boards. Whole boards were great, but he didn't expect that after a five thousand foot fall. And working power-pack batteries, at least partially juiced, were most important.

But after five hours of hard labor they hadn't gotten a whole lot. A mile is a long way to fall even for a C.A.D.S. suit. He had the rest of the team come over two at a time and juiced up their failing battery packs and replaced what busted units they could with parts from the dead men's suits. It still barely got many of them functioning and charges up to what read .23 percent of capacity.

"Which isn't a hell of a lot no matter how you twist the numbers," Rossiter said to Sturgis as the last of the suits' external battery inputs were snap-loaded. "These babies tend to start having real problems below twenty-five percent charge. We're heading into Nineteenth Nervous Breakdown territory here, Colonel." Rossiter stood there, his suit visor in open position so his full ruddy face seemed to fill the whole inside. "You know, once the memories start to go on the software, even our hardware, when we get down into the teens in power-charge, and the suit has to switch to sheer life support systems. When that happens, we'll lose all the sensors, all perceptual modes. The damned thing won't know what to do, it will have no sense linking it to the outside world or to us. The HCI network, Human Computer Interface, will be kaput. Might as well be stomping around in two hundred pounds of dead weight."

"Tell me about it," Sturgis snapped. He'd seen more than one suit go loco. At extremely low power situations the suits could do almost anything crazy—just start running off, the legs moving automatically, or throwing on their back jetpack as if trying to perform independent aerial maneuvers. Men had died that way. It wasn't a laughing matter. And yet they *needed* the suits to have even the slightest chance of getting across this sunbaked hell, the wasteland of all wastelands in nuked-America.

"Look, you heard what he told me," Sturgis addressed

them all through multi-link, which they would keep on at all times now. "These suits could suddenly be a hazard to your health if we're in any kind of dangerous situation. We've already basically run out of ammunition, but for a small amount of low-calibers. But the suits' mode systems and servo muscular mechanics seem to be functioning. I've ridden in these suckers down to ten percent power-charge and lower, so I know it *can* be done. But it's not always easy," he admitted softly, "things get weird."

"So what do we do if the suits start getting ideas of their own?" one of the troopers asked, his face visor sealed shut as he clearly didn't trust the rad readings and the air around these parts.

"Just get the hell out of it, use emergency deplode. Then you'll have to go on foot, or maybe we can rig something like a semi-suit. I don't know. But don't worry about it. Get out, that's the main thing. If it starts sparking inside or if it asks you funny questions, or makes weird propositions—just say you're married and throw the emergency ejection on."

The quick eject was a special charged set of carefully placed explosives packets which could blow the C.A.D.S. suit apart into four equal sections, pushing the force of the small blasts in an outward direction so no harm would come to its occupant. It meant the suit was shattered, destroyed; its brain functions and physical structure useless but for scrap. So they rarely did it that way. But it could mean the difference between life and death if it were ever needed.

"Now, we're moving out," Sturgis said sharply. He was in a bad mood, and getting worse. "So if anyone has to empty their wee-wee bag, better do it now or forever hold your peace. For we gotta head into *that*—" he pointed at the land to the south and east. It looked harsh, almost moonlike, not like the Oregon they had all known and loved from picture postcards of pre-war America. Before the burning hell fell from the skies, this wasteland had been the best part of the U.S.A.

They formed up and moved out.

"Keep suits on full internal systems," Sturgis addressed them as he took the lead. "I don't like that greenish glow ahead. It's like the whole territory has been irradiated at high levels. The molecules of the entire ecosystem could be radioactive; from air and rain, even the mists, passing over it."

He didn't like the looks of the sky above. It was churning with blackness as if preparing to release a load of hail or snow or maybe radioactive cats and dogs, for all Sturgis knew.

"Switch all but minimal life support systems to power in the legs and servo mech's," Sturgis ordered his computer, passing the command to the rest of the men via the comm.

"SWITCHED," the computer read out in flashing digital green letters along the bottom of his curved, tinted, bulletproof visor. It showed him the entire energy distribution pattern of the suit in a grid display to one side, what systems were being browned out, what given more energy. Displays within displays.

The sun became a burning hot tormentor. They moved over the prairie land in great running leaps assisted by the sophisticated gear, steel cable, and diode system of the legs. All a man had to do was tilt his foot in a certain direction and press down with his thigh and the suit would gear up the motion mechanically from ten to a hundred fold—at full power. Of course you had to know how to use it. The slightest push off angle could send the suit plummeting.

Sturgis ordered up Retro vision and saw in the lower quad of the visor the view behind him. A mini video camera whirred its lens out from the back of the helmet and sent back the images. His fighting team, Tranh, Dixon, MacLeish, the 'Inner Circle,' were striding along with their huge armored arms swinging back and forth right behind him. But Robin and some of the newer recruits, although making a brave attempt at it, were

26

lagging farther behind every minute.

Sturgis slowed down, not saying anything to them about the lag. A man—or woman—just had to learn how to operate the suits. There wasn't a whole lot to say. It was a *feel,* more like playing music, than driving something. Sturgis was a master-suitman. He had been the so-called "test pilot" for the things when they were just a glint in the Air Force's eye, way back in the experimental, controversial C.A.D.S. Development Program, CDP. Sturgis had been one of five original testers. The other four were dead. Horrible deaths in the very suits they tested. Sturgis had been the best, and the only one to make it. Though how much longer that fact was going to remain true was highly questionable.

He dropped speed by fifty percent, and then even more as large snowflakes started to fall. They were wet, and heavy and seemed to coat the suits almost immediately as they gathered on the shoulders and tops of the helmets. Normally the suits would just have sent out current into the heating coils built in beneath the titanium plastic armoring, but they couldn't spare a drop of energy in that direction. They'd have to rely on the inherent heating ability of the layered suit itself, which was designed to protect them down to sub zero temperatures, like heavy arctic gear, and against extreme heat.

As the storm intensified and the icy winds increased, they began feeling really cold, cold enough so that their muscles and joints tightened up, their breath rose into their helmets in steam. But everyone wanted to keep up, to not lag. The snow seemed attracted to the suits, seemed to have almost a charge to it, a magnetic charge—although it registered no rads on the C.A.D.S. geiger counter readings. Within minutes, they were all nearly coated in white and the snowfall had become a blizzard with flakes as large as lily pads, slamming down with increasing wind-driven force.

Sturgis could hardly see ahead. The infrared didn't work in these blizzard conditions as it just bounced off everything, reflecting back a pattern, like snow on a TV screen.

"Link up with cables," he commanded them suddenly, slowing them down before they got totally isolated from one another. Even the visor-screen's red mode, which gave troop placement, was going a little dim. Might easily lose each other on electronic links. And it would mean *good night* if someone stumbled into a chasm or off into the frigid night alone.

It took several minutes for them to pull out the mini steel cable from their lower back units and feed it to the man behind them, so he could snap a small eyehook through a corresponding link on his suit.

Once linked, they headed on into the ever-darkening snow which fell in angry jagged curtains, slamming into them with fifty and sixty mile an hour winds. They could hear the flakes pounding against the visors and Sturgis knew already he had made the right choice by not chucking the suits. They'd be dead by now out in that, their bodies flailed to pieces as if ice-sandpaper had gone over them.

He moved slowly, one step at a time. Even then, the heavily armored suits rocked back and forth from the winds which blew from every angle as if trying to take them down into hell. With Sturgis's systems going out and some of the inner helmet grids flickering wildly, he headed into the fathomless grayness ahead. In multi-million-dollar ultrahigh-tech fighting suits, it was still nothing more than the blind leading the blind. . . .

Chapter Four

Some of the C.A.D.S. heating systems started to fail. That was a disaster not just for the comfort and survival of the men — but for the computer and mechanical functions of the suits as well, particularly the sensing devices along the outer edges of the titanium flesh. They just iced up, got electronic frostbite. The men began losing the servo mechanism link-up. The HCI, Human Computer Interface, wasn't interfacing.

When the servos went out, the C.A.D.S. troopers had to raise their seventy-five-pound legs with everything they had in human muscle power as if they were moving through quicksand. The legs still swung freely on their super lubed gears, but a lot of force had to be expended to move them. Some suits were holding up, though. And being linked up by cable enabled them to pull each other along, each man adding to the strength the others lacked. Once they found the pace, it seemed to take only half as much effort to move the suits and they made a slow but steady march right into the darkest part of the storm system. All the communication and sensing systems went out. Then the grid screens on every visor. They were — most of them — deaf, dumb, and blind.

They were into it about five minutes with the light totally gone and the whole world nothing more than the middle of a snowball, when Sturgis heard a scream over the static riddled almost inaudible radios in the helmets. The scream pierced the ether and he felt a tug behind him. He stopped, realizing that somehow the cable had broken.

29

Sturgis jumped a single bounding step back and drained power into his helmet light—and saw a wide crevasse which seemed to have appeared out of nowhere. For just an instant he thought he could see the beacon light on the top of another man's helmet flashing on and off automatically. *Below.* But then it was gone, smashing against the hard ice walls as the suit just kept falling down a bottomless crevasse that had appeared from nowhere. Poor Nichols! Sturgis knew the trooper didn't have a chance. Say another silent prayer and move on. And don't stop or he'd start crying for all the men who had died like flies around him. Some smart leader he had turned out to be. He couldn't help but feel responsible for the deaths of every man who fought beside him!

Sturgis had them all bunch in even closer so they could actually see the man in front of them, pulling their cable distance in from ten feet to about five. They'd have to move like snails now. He put one foot down at a time and got his sonar working slightly on the grid by dropping all external readouts from the power grid. They didn't mean anything now anyway.

The small green readout from Sonar Depthfinding gave the colonel a crude geotopical configuration of the land for a few hundred feet ahead. It was enough. Enough to barely make their way around soft spots—hidden crevasses. They moved on, blowing from side to side like palm trees in the eye of a hurricane. Somehow they pushed on like this for nearly three hours. They grunted and groaned and slammed their way through the falling sheets of ice heading straight toward the south-south-east.

Robin was having the worst of it and MacLeish and Wosyck held her up between them, big men that they were and very proficient in use of the suits. They half carried her along. If anything, the cold inside the suits, which Sturgis estimated to be about -10 degrees, though suit temp gauges were not functioning, kept him awake and alert. He had to stay in front, not treat Robin as more important than anyone else, though of course she was.

MacLeish and Wosyck understood.

At last Sturgis couldn't go another step himself as the suit's very jointworks seemed to freeze up, getting harder and harder to move as if it had rusted. If he couldn't make his relatively solid suit go, then the rest of them would be feeling even worse. He stopped, and found the radio comm — by cutting other modes — to be working enough for them to communicate. They stood in a tight circle, nearly helmet to helmet.

"We can't go on and I don't see a hell of a lot of cover, other than these drifts on each side of us," Sturgis told them.

"Mounds of snow nearly ten feet high have formed as windblown build-up from the storm," Rossiter added. He was the only one who had any I.R. mode function and could 'see' that.

"Maybe we could dig in, like the Eskimos," Tranh suggested from inside his frosted visor. They were all coated with the strange clinging flakes, which had iced over on some parts on the suits so it was a good inch thick. They looked monstrous, the cyclops eyes of the visors clouded over with veins of blue ice, shoulders of the black C.A.D.S. suit covered white like some Neanderthal snowman.

"We haven't enough power to dig shelters," Sturgis replied as he bent back and forth to gauge the nearby depths of the snow. Didn't want any crevasses opening up under them as they conferred!

"Maybe ah could do y'all a favor," Dixon shouted out in his thickest drawl as he slammed a button and unhitched the LFP nozzle. "Stand back friends, ladies, gentle souls, it's time for some blizzard roasting," Dixon laughed into the air.

"Wait a minute," Sturgis screamed as he suddenly realized what Dixon had in mind. A huge spray of burning plastic came gushing out of the nozzle which the southern boy pointed at a ten foot high dune of snow some twenty feet away. The plastic hissed through the air, sizzling the

31

snowflakes into a funnel of steam. The flames ripped into the side of the ice hill, fiery napalm-like plastic tearing right through it. It quickly dug deep into it, making a tunnel, but some of the flames as well shot back off the surrounding ice. Sheets of flaming plastic nearly got a few of the C.A.D.S. troopers, who fell back stumbling. Two sets of the mens' boots caught on fire and other troopers quickly put it out with pounded handfuls of snow from the ground.

Sturgis was both annoyed and glad to see that the insane idea was working. For, as Dixon poured on the fiery plastic for another twenty seconds or so, he carved a whole little instant hole, an igloo right out of the hard ice pressed hill. Satisfied, he shut the thing off.

"There, Skipper," Dixon said, turning his helmet to the side. "How's that?"

"I'll talk to you later, pal," Sturgis exclaimed. The blowing flakes from above seemed to intensify as if they knew that escape of its would-be victims was near. The flames quickly died out inside the new ice-cavern and Sturgis led the way in. The maniac had dug a tunnel that appeared to be opening wider as it got deeper, about twenty feet in, five to six wide. It wasn't the Taj Mahal, although it had a crystal brilliance sparkling from all around them, like a cave of diamonds.

Within a minute they were all inside the melted-wall cavern, though it was a tight fit with the bulky suits. Dixon was the last one in and he gave the LFP a little squirt behind them, getting pretty handy with the thing. A little wall of ice came cascading down from the melting flames and the troopers were suddenly sealed in. They stood around in the darkness, not an infrared mode working. "Temperature is going up," said Fenton. Then MacLeish broke the darkness by telling a very dirty joke about an Irish milkmaid and a Rabbi. Then they all started singing "Bang Bang Suzie" of which every man knew at least one verse, even Fireheels. Singing in the pitch darkness over the crackling radio units.

"Suzie had a boyfriend, her boyfriend had a truck," MacLeish started.

"He put her on the back seat to see if she would—." Billy Dixon added.

"Bang, bang Suzie, bang bang Suzie," they *all* sang the rousing chorus with gusto, "Bang bang Suzie, 'cause Suzie's back in town."

Another man yelled out the next verse:

"Suzie had a boyfriend, his name was diamond Dick, He never showed his diamond, but he always showed his—"

"Bang Bang Suzie, Bang Bang Suzie, Bang Bang Suzie, 'cause Suzie's back in town." the troopers joined in unison. Suzie had an infinite number of verses. And they tried to sing all of them. Even Sturgis got in with a few nasty ones of his own. It was sure better to sing in here, sheltered and warmer, than to stand freezing outside, thinking about one's imminent death.

And in the darkness smiles broke out on their thawing lips. Even on Dr. Sheila DeCamp's trembling features. She had always wanted to hear what the men said when they were totally, completely on their own. When they let go. In a way, it was an honor for her as she had always strived to be a real trooper, not just some dame in the way. She felt for the first time that she was one of the guys. When a split second lull came after the hundredth repetition of the obscene song, DeCamp herself threw in a few lines that made the suits all shake in the darkness with laughter.

Robin stared into the darkness, neither laughing nor not laughing as the ice-cavern shelter and its inhabitants were covered ever deeper by the raging snows. She was just staring. Though there was nothing to see but total darkness. The darkness was like that of her cell in the Kremlin. Her mind was elsewhere. In that Never-Never Land of pain from which—just maybe—she was never coming back.

33

Chapter Five

Hundreds of miles to the southeast, far past the reach of the mega-snow storm, a group of bizarrely garbed men stood around in the moonlight as they carried out ritual ceremonies to their gods. They danced around a bonfire with vigor; sweat covered bare skin, blazing eyes, their long black hair flapping around their shoulders. Their faces were covered with streaks and ashes of bright color, giving them demonic, frightening appearances. Behind them stood a towering sandstone mountain into which they and their ancestors had handcarved their pueblos. A labyrinth-city of rooms and levels rising up the whole side of the mesa, rising up out of the flatness of the prairie land of Utah as if reaching toward the nearly full moon above. Rising to try to touch that silver orb which lit the wild scene with a harsh illumination, bathing the desert in its neon white glow.

Along a ledge about twenty feet above the prairie ground sat the elders of the Naqui tribe, an offshoot of the joining of two small bands of Apaches and Hopi indians. They had combined 100 years before for their mutual protection against an exceedingly hostile post-war world. And flourished. For on their land, they discovered when they drilled for water around the mesa, was black gold—oil. It came bubbling up from several underground lakes in the earth. The smell of the stuff permeated the Naqui land, not a pleasant smell, but they didn't complain. For the black liquid meant they could run generators, drive diesel cars, small machines. Their crude refinery plant purified the stuff at least to its minimal combustible state. Even as the Naqui braves circled the fire made of dried cactus coated with the oil, they could hear the chugging of the oil pumps and the small purification plant some five hundred yards to the south. But it was a familiar sound to all of them and was filtered from their ears even as they heard it.

They listened instead to the chants of the Old Ones, the dozen Shamans, medicine men, who shared responsibility for the nearly thousand strong who made up the tribe. There were hearty men, wives, and their children, all spread out in the complex of pueblo tunnels, man-made as well as natural. Rooms that ran inside the half mile long, thousand foot high sandstone mountain rising above them. The Shamans were decked out in their finest tonight, for it was a night of talking with the gods. And the gods noticed everything, particularly in rituals and sacrifices. Even down to the smallest feather, the dullest gilamonster tooth necklace. Thus they had on their best, all of them wearing brilliantly feathered headdresses, vests made of bison skin and wolf hide with mountain lion teeth ringing their sleeves and chests.

Some had hand-wrought armorings and decorative workings made by using artifacts of the industrial America that had once been. Hammered beer cans had been turned into bracelets and necklaces, computer chip boards, car mirrors, even a can opener here and there, hung from their hide jackets, their shoulders, and legs. Every one of the Indians was trying to outdo the other on this Night of Appeasement. And in the moonlight, they seemed to shine with a supernatural shimmering, adding to their otherworldly appearance as the rays of the white moon, and the dancing light of the great bonfire, reflected off their myriad jewels, decorative teeth, and body armor.

Below them the Naqui braves, nearly a hundred of them, also in their "Sunday best," though not of the level

35

of the Shamans, danced and sang out the songs of redemption and expiration, life and death, pain and bravery. They stamped down and raised their hands and heads to the sky in a constant moving circle of undulating, glistening copper bodies. The dancers wore deerskin vests and loincloths and small leather aprons with the fur still on from beavers, elk, other creatures of plains and nearby mountains. Brightly colored paints and dyes decorated their chests, arms, and backs. Broad slashes of reds and greens, purples and yellows, all signifying their bravery, their powers among men.

The medicine men watched with approval as they chanted ever louder, each one banging on some sort of drum, made from either hide, wood, or even made of empty metal cans that had once held the produce of America on supermarket shelves. The larger tin cans especially made a loud ringing sound and were much prized by the Shamans. They chanted as the flames burned ever higher in the cactus-stem bonfire.

"O buffalo gods, cloud gods, gods of death and life, hear we Naqui as we sing to you. Hear our prayers, hear our obedience to your ways. See that we have carried out all the rituals to appease you." They held their hands out over the people, showing that all were obedient to the rules of life and death. They knew that peeking from behind the moon where they slept and hunted, the gods could see them all, every one of them and all that they did.

The dancing braves went into a frenzy as under the influence of mescal-laced beverages they grew wilder and leaped up into the air, through the smoke of the fire trying to jump the highest. And the Shamans' voices as well rose. The drumming grew ever louder as if every man was trying to outdo the other, trying to capture the ear of the moon gods, so as to shine in their presence.

The women and children were not permitted to attend the sacred ceremonies, but their eyes watched like burning coals from safe within the pueblo rock dwellings, faces just inside windowless frames, noses peeking from around yucca-wood doors.

At last, as the moon twisted across the sky and finally seemed to rest for a moment atop another sandstone mountain some several miles off, the top witch doctor, the Blue Shaman, Urdun, stood up and held his hands out, far apart. He let out a piercing scream that would have made a wolf cower with its tail between its legs. The frenzied dancing of the braves below suddenly stopped in their tracks, frozen where they made their last leap.

"The ceremony must begin. It is time," the Blue Shaman shouted out in a deep guttural singing voice. The other Shamans echoed his words behind him as they all rose, their metallic, feathered, and toothed vestments jangling and glinting like they were sewn with tongues of silver fire.

"It is time," they all sang, standing just a few inches behind him, "it — is — *time!*"

"Bring out the first sacrifices," Blue Shaman intoned and instantly a group of six braves came rushing out from the shadows. They were covered in stark geometric patterns of red pigment, as if blood had been carved from their flesh, but it was not their own blood. Each carried in his hands dangling, and still living rattlesnakes, which squirmed wildly as they were carried along.

"O Plains Gods, sky gods and oil gods — we of the earth give these to you for your feasting —" the Blue Shaman screamed out the words to the sky as he beat on a faded empty can of "Giant economy-size kidney beans" from the Brigham Young Mall, a place now in ruins miles off. As he and the other Shamans made their chants and bangs, the braves holding the snakes reached out with fast motions and bit off their reptilian scaled heads. They spat them right out again and then threw the whipping snake-bodies into the bonfire, where the wet dripping red meat sputtered and crackled loudly. One of the Indians wasn't fast enough. He took a set of snapping venomous fangs into his cheek just as he went to bite the snake-head. He

37

fell silently to the ground, going into spasms within seconds. The snake men threw all their snakes into the fire and then dragged the stricken one off. He was not of the Chosen. There was no room for such. The gods removed the unworthy.

"Oil gods," Blue Shaman went on when he saw that the last snake had been thrown in the fire. "We of the land, give you meat from the land." At the word "meat" several braves pulled an immense live bison out from the darkness and up to the fire. Ropes were all over the thing, around its neck, legs, so that it could be dragged, manipulated, forced to move in any direction by the slightest pull on a rope. The huge beast with tufts of dark fur rolling off its back was terrified and made bleating sounds that mixed with the chants and drumming. It had been beaten for hours, weakened.

There was a loud engine sound and from out of the shadows walked a large Naqui brave, a good seven feet tall and naked except for a strip of mountain-panther hide around his loins. He too was covered with the blood red streaks and geometric images. And in his hands he held a chain saw. It was on, spurting smoke as it let out a tremendous sound.

The giant bison was tied to stakes driven into the hard earth on all sides of it. The brave approached with the saw. The animal knew something was up. It didn't take an Einstein to see that. The Blue Shaman held his hands out to the sky again and the chainsaw reached out. The chainsaw teeth bit into the bison's right shoulder and within seconds the leg was cut through. The animal had let out with a horrendous bellow that could be heard for miles and made the children's eyes peering from inside the sandstone pueblo's windows wince in fear. As the bison jerked and screamed, the brave walked around it, cutting off the other legs as well. As each was severed it was picked up and thrown into the fire by other dancing Naqui.

Within a minute or so the creature was a quadraplegic,

with every appendage gone. It lay there, blood pulsing out of the opened wounds, still alive, still bellowing for all it was worth. Then the saw descended to the dying creature's neck and with a great sound of ripping bones and a final scream that dwarfed the others, the bison was suddenly silent as its entire bulky head, horns and all fell from the body.

The Blue Shaman looked down approvingly as the bison's bloody head was lifted and two men heaved it into the fire to join the snakes which were already burnt down to charcoal sticks of flesh. The rest of the bison's body, which weighed a good twelve hundred pounds, was untied and rolled and tugged by over a dozen braves. It couldn't be cut up. That was not the way. The gods who lived on the moon's ghostly surface wanted the main section of the body to be whole. The meat had to be unspoiled, undivided.

The braves grunted as they rolled the bleeding carcass over several times and with a final great heave sent it into the great fire. It didn't get in very far but it sent up a shower of sparks which spiraled up into the sky. Within seconds the plains bison's flesh was burning brightly, its thick mat of fur catching like kindling. The smells of the burning hide and the meat wafted over to the Shamans.

"Oil, give us oil as we give you the food that your ghost mouths may eat," the Blue Shaman intoned in a growling chant to the clear sky which writhed far above in high rad Aurora Borealis, in curtains of shimmering color. The sudden appearance of the glow was a good sign. The colors were the jewels of the gods. They were dancing now, as they received their meals. The oil would flow.

For the moment, the Naqui were safe. At least from the gods, if not from men.

Chapter Six

The C.A.D.S. troopers were suspended in a world of snow-bound darkness for what seemed like an eternity. After several hundred verses of "Bang Bang Suzie" even the most gung ho of them shut up and they just stood around inside the cavern Dixon had melted for them, each lost in his own thoughts. Even though it was a waste of precious energy, Sturgis, who could hear the men humming and breathing hard inside their suits, decided to throw a little light onto the affair. All of the C.A.D.S. suits had searchlights built into them, small tubular shaped lights which could throw a powerful beam. Sturgis commanded his suit, which barely responded, to shut down heat for a moment, use that power to throw on the light at quarter strength. There was a dim whirring sound as a small metal flap opened in the helmet. Then a low yellowish light was cast over the ice cavern.

"All right!" a voice piped up and then a few more. There is something inherent in man that doesn't feel secure in the darkness. He is braver in the light, thinks better, fights better. The little bit of dim illumination that Sturgis's helmet threw out seemed to help their morale a lot. And paradoxically, some of them were able to sleep once the "night light" had been thrown on. Setting the suits on auto lock, the legs just froze rigidly in place, so they could sleep standing up as if in steel cocoons.

They were protected from the murderous thirty below

40

temperatures outside, sheltered from the snows and the driving winds, but not, definitely *not warm*. It still felt like a refrigerated meat room in the C.A.D.S. armor.

After eight hours according to Sturgis's inner-visor grid clock, which would be the very last thing to go if the battery got down to zilch since it operated on about a trillionth of a volt, Sturgis decided it was time to get out of there. Or try. The oxygen supply inside the ice-cavern was getting low and he could feel his lightheadedness as well as the gasping air intakes of the others. The storm would surely have blown past by now.

"Rise and shine all you C.A.D.S. heroes," Sturgis yelled through the helmet mike. That shook them up and groans issued forth all around him.

"Hey, easy on the decibels, okay?" Rossiter piped back as he unlocked the suit's freeze position and rose up straight as an arrow next to Sturgis.

"Damn, I was having the best dream I ever had in my whole life," Dixon spoke up. "Me and Marilyn Monroe was under a truck—and both of us naked as—"

"Can it, Dixon," Sturgis commanded. "There's *ladies* present. A breed you doubtless wouldn't know diddly squat about." The troopers cracked up from around the ice chamber.

"The only *lady* I ever knew was my mom," Dixon rejoindered.

"Shut up, *pig*," DeCamp hissed out. Her voice was shrill; it had a hysterical edge to it. Now that they were all safe from the storm, their thoughts started making the rounds about whether they were actually going to get out of there again. Sheila's voice betrayed that tension.

"What do you think, Skip?" MacLeish asked as he tried to jump up and down to get some blood circulating through his cramped muscles inside the suit. It was virtually impossible as there was about an inch clearance between the men. They were stuffed in tighter than a tin of Portuguese sardines, with a few extras thrown in for good measure.

"I think it's time to get out of this Eskimo graveyard," Sturgis replied. "Before we lose whatever oxygen's left in here and don't even have the strength to get out. Who's up front? Use your Systems Blade and poke a hole out there."

The nearest was Fireheels and he pressed the button on his suit so a long, spinning steel blade whirred out from the right arm, just alongside the gloved hand. He pushed it into the dense wall of snow and ice that had sealed them in. And pushed some more.

"I'm not reaching anything but more ice," the Apache trooper replied in his laconic tone.

Sometimes Sturgis wondered if the guy actually cared about it all. It was as if Fireheels could just stay in the cave and watch them all turn into ice cubes—or make their way out and fight another fifty years—And it was all the same to him.

"I think the storm must have dropped a buffalo herd's load of the white stuff on us," Rossiter suggested. "Once a dune is formed, it just builds up, you know. We could have twenty feet of the white stuff around us now."

"Well that's great, that's just damned great," Matherson, one of the newer and younger recruits, starting shouting in his helmet. "Now, we'll never get out of here, we'll freeze and they'll never find us—and—"

"Trooper, *shut up,*" Tranh yelled into his mike, not sure just who was making the baby sounds. "We *are* going to get out of here, and soon. And we don't need bullshit like that floating around the airwaves. I won't even ask your name. But let's not hear that kind of talk again."

"Sorry," the voice muttered back, but they could all hear the man's breathing, hard and labored as though he was going to crack at any moment. Sturgis couldn't blame him, or any of them. Especially the raw recruits. They weren't afraid to die or they would never have joined up in the toughest detachment of fighting men the US had ever seen. But it was another thing altogether to see your death coming at you, freezing your limbs one digit at a time.

42

Not like dying in battle. The battle was over.

"Billy, how much fuel is left in that overgrown weinie roaster of yours?" Sturgis asked as he moved his fingers and toes inside the suit trying to get his blood going faster. His red stuff needed anti-freeze; everything inside felt like sludge rather than nice warm liquid blood.

"Not a hell of a lot, Colonel," Dixon replied after a few seconds of checking the readout dial. "Maybe ten seconds at full blast, double that at low strength."

"Well, looks like we're going to have to get out the same way we got in," Sturgis addressed them all. "Pull down your visors, so your faces are protected. I know there's no internal air supply anymore in the suits—so just hold your breath." The visors dropped down and locked into place. "Fireman, do your thing," Sturgis said softly, hoping he wasn't putting them in mortal jeopardy.

The C.A.D.S. troopers pulled back as far as they could into the cavern, although there wasn't much room to maneuver. The suits were protected by a shield of synthetic plastisteel-asbestos, ten times more resistant to fire than the natural stuff, woven into one of the outer layerings, only microns thick, but—But it didn't help still their pounding hearts when Dixon turned on the faucet and let loose with a burst of LFP!

The initial surge of flame ricocheted off the wall of ice that had sealed them in and the flames washed back over the C.A.D.S. team. There were a few stifled screams as the flames engulfed their suits. But within a second, the ice was melting and the flame had enough room to dig forward into the snow wall, so that it left the human meat alone.

Dixon let out with a wild rebel yell as he sprayed the LFP plastic flame ahead. The man was clearly never happier than when wreaking havoc—even if just on snow. It was a pretty frightening experience for all of them with the sizzling ice sending up layers of steam so that it filled the cavern. "Anyone for lobster? Steamed C.A.D.S. lobster?" Fenton quipped, his voice cracking.

"Easy, easy," Sturgis kept intoning over his suit mike, hoping the words would keep the most nervous of them, and particularly Robin, from totally bugging out. He sure didn't need any of them to start running around the place. The suits still packed plenty of punch with just their servo mechanisms, and an unthought-out motion, especially a fast one, could severely damage another suit—and the trooper within.

It took only about eight seconds, though it seemed a lot longer than that, for Dixon to empty out the plastic contents of the flamegun. Then the thing just sputtered out a few drops, and it was out.

There was a still steaming tunnel ahead of them about a yard wide, two yards high. And you could see a faint light from the outside at its end, through the ice. But they still weren't quite through. The snow had really fallen out there. Thirty feet of tunnel and still no exit!

"Shit," Dixon muttered as he lowered the smoking muzzle of the flamethrower, disappointed that he hadn't completed his little ice highway.

"Let me get in there and take a look," Sturgis said as he elbowed his way through the others.

"Let me go in there first, Skip," Tranh suddenly shouted out, hurting all their ears as he saw Sturgis bend down and start to step through the opening which was smooth as glass around the edges and quite slippery. "We can't afford to lose you if the whole damn thing should come down."

"That's exactly why I'm going in," Sturgis whispered without looking back. "I can't let any of you take the risk. Dig me out if this damned hallway collapses. If you can't find me, just put a stick over my grave and write—'Here Lies a Frozen Fool' as my epitaph."

"A real bloody comedian," MacLeish snorted as some of the troopers chortled. MacLeish, who had just recently come over to the C.A.D.S. training center in White Sands before the Nuke War, had been a member of her Majesty's Black Guard, a spit and polish, do-it-by-the-book kind of

44

guy. He still couldn't get used to the kinds of chances Sturgis took, or the fact that he didn't delegate these sorts of dangerous jobs to underlings. He *was* too valuable to lose. It was just a bloody fact. The muscular Brit fumed within his suit, but didn't say another word.

Sturgis had to crawl along the cramped carved out tunnel of ice on his hands and knees, no easy task in a high-tech seven-foot marvel of engineering—especially when most of its functions were out. He was suddenly thankful for all those training sessions years before when the suits had been in testing mode. He had hated having to do just this sort of maneuver. Now, though he was glad, for it all came back to him: Move right hand and back left leg together, opposites, and slowly. The way the suit was designed and weighted, any other sort of motion might easily topple him over. And in this slippery hole he might go over on his back, and, like a huge sea turtle, not be able to right himself again.

The flame-built tunnel was about 30 feet long, and when Sturgis reached the far end he could barely see light. He prayed that the storm was over and that he wasn't looking out into a darkness of wind and mega-death. But he reached the end and pressed his suit glove against the wall and found it solid. He pushed hard again and the thick plasticized-steel hand glove dented the snow wall, but didn't go through.

It was punching time.

He braced himself, setting his boots against both sides of the tunnel and dug their cleats into the ice. Feeling secure, he pulled back his right hand and let go with a vicious punch right into the ice wall. It sank in deep. He pulled back and let go again, then again. Within seconds, as he felt sure of his angle and happily nothing was fizzing up in the suit, Sturgis *really let go*. It was like a Sonny Liston, or a Mike Tyson, doing their heavy bag work. Punch after punch slammed into the snow, and each shot dislodged whole sections of ice.

It didn't take all that long. Perhaps twenty punches,

aided by the C.A.D.S. servo mechanisms which amplified his arm power dozens of times. Suddenly he struck out and Sturgis felt the fist go right through and out into the open. He widened the arm-size opening by ripping backward with his splayed fingers and soon created an opening big enough for him to fit through, though it felt like a worm going through a snowman's intestinal tract.

Then he was outside, falling suddenly through the end of the tunnel opening into soft snow. And it was *beautiful* out there! As black and churning and angry as the sky had been when they went into the cavern, now it was sparkling, sunny, a day like the good old days. A day of hope.

He stood up and took a few seconds to take in the beauty of nature when she wasn't trying to kill man. The snow blanketed everything, the ground, the pines that rose up off in the distance, crowning them with an adornment of glistening icicle jewels. Animals rushed here and there through the covering of white, excited by the snow.

"What the hell's going on up there?" a voice suddenly piped up over the helmet radio. Sturgis recognized it as Tranh's.

"Sorry; everything's okay, just got a little hypnotized by the sun and snow. Come on out, the weather's fine. The blow has blown."

There was a muttering of suddenly cheerful voices from within the ice-cavern. Within five minutes the entire C.A.D.S. unit, amidst much slipping and sliding, had emerged and were standing on the pristine snow. The suits slid down a good six inches into the fresh powder and Sturgis reminded them all to be careful. There were chasms all over the place, after all.

They walked around testing the suits on the shimmering surface and breathed in the glistening morning as Sturgis had. He checked on Robin, walking over to her, putting his metal arm over her suit-back. He could see through the polarized visor that she was totally out of it, her eyes "pinned" in shock. But she managed to flash him a quick smile which cheered him up immeasurably. If you could smile, even grimly, Sturgis reasoned, you were still on *this* side of the pale. At least that's what his mother had always told him.

"I'm—I'm all right. Don't go out of your way for me," she said in such a soft whisper that only by touching his helmet to hers could he even hear her. "You've got the whole team to be concerned about, getting us back to White Sands. I don't want you worrying about me. I mean that, Dean. You've got enough problems. I'm okay."

He knew she wasn't okay by any stretch of the imagination. But she could walk and she could talk so she was at least functional. And in the post-nuke world, that would have to do.

Chapter Seven

They started ahead cautiously, Fireheels in the lead as his scouting abilities and his knowledge of this entire region—what had once been Utah—made him an ideal forward recon. Sturgis had the women and the two troopers who had been slightly hurt in the parachute drop set in the middle of the force. The whole unit moved ahead as one, arranged in a rough sort of phalanx, spread out over about a hundred feet. The suits were all still functioning, at least the servo-drive mechs. Everything else, including the computer readout systems, were spasmodic, shutting off for hours at a time then suddenly slamming on again so that all of a sudden digital readouts were winking on all over. Then just as suddenly it would go out again. Sturgis didn't even relate to his computerized info center anymore. There was no way of knowing if the thing was making sense, or was totally bananas.

"When are we going to eat?" Rossiter piped up after they'd been marching for hours toward some low mountains ahead.

"Yeah, food, boss," Dixon piped in, making an obscene sound over his mike that brought chuckles from some of the others.

"Ain't got no candy bars, pal," Sturgis replied. "Tranh, you got any secret appetite-suppressing Vietnamese powders hidden away in your suit?"

"I wish," Tranh replied. "I got powder, but it's flea powder to keep the damn desert mites out of the suit. They seem to like to gnaw on the wiring."

That brought a few more chuckles but no chow. No one else commented on it, but Sturgis knew they were all just toughing it out. They couldn't go very far without something to put in their stomachs. They hadn't eaten for days now, and he knew that couldn't go on, not with the amount of energy they were all putting out. Keeping the suits moving along, even with the aid of the vaguely functioning servos, they would run out of human fuel by the end of the day. Might not even be able to march tomorrow.

Fireheels—who could spot any sign of life—scouted around. Except for some poisonous snakes scuttling over the melting ice as the sun rose higher sending down raw heat, and a heavily armored armadillo with two little duplicates of itself marching along fast behind it, there wasn't a lot out here. And none of it stuff that one would want to put in one's mouth.

"When we get to those mountains ahead boys, there's bound to be some game there," Sturgis said, not knowing himself if he was lying. But the words seemed to motivate them to move a little faster; got their spirits up. The idea of food ahead has pulled men forward into danger and the unknown since caveman days. The need to fill the stomach has been the motivating factor in all evolution, maybe. Sturgis just prayed that there would be something bigger than a hummingbird to make soup out of ahead. Or the men might start looking at him and each other funny. It can happen.

The snow melted completely by the time they'd marched on for four hours—always toward the White Sands base. The ground grew soggy, making it hard-going. But the troopers kept their spirits up with some dirty jokes, two complete rounds of "a hundred dead graysuits on the wall" sung down numerically and then back up again—plus a number of Rossiter's recipes of how he'd cook gila monster's rattlers, any living thing they saw.

At last they reached the low hills that ringed a range of mesas ahead. Immediately the terrain changed dramatically with shrubs, and huge fir trees covering the slopes in a green blanket of life. A pleasant relief. Sturgis made a quick scan of the slopes, now that his systems were up again, searching for the best way up. Much of the nearby pine forest was a thick tangle, and looked even thicker higher up. There was no way around it all without detouring for many miles. They'd have to do some heavy bushwhacking. The day had just a few more hours of light, so Sturgis decided to push it.

"These suits weren't made for forest travel," Dixon complained as they started up the incline of the first hills.

"They are now, pal," Tranh answered back sharply, irritated at the southerner's constant griping about this and that.

"Just lean slightly forward," MacLeish commented dryly from the back of the phalanx. He was rear guard, strutting in his extra large C.A.D.S. suit on the right flank. "I did my training in the English woods in a suit that was shipped over there years ago. It's a little tricky at first, but I discovered that if you lean slightly forward at say a ten-degree angle, you'll see the suit will almost pull you forward."

A few of them nearly fell straight forward on their helmeted faces trying out the instructions, but after a while everyone seemed to get the hang of it. The slightly bent forward high tech commandos made their way up the first few hills.

They got up about five hundred feet above prairie level without too much difficulty. Then they spotted Fireheels, who had scouted on ahead, slamming his suit knife which poked out below the gloved hand right into the base of one of the towering pines. Sturgis tensed up for a few moments as he wondered if the Indian was attacking something that the colonel couldn't see from his angle. But as they headed up another fifty yards he could see that the Indian trooper was actually digging right through the bark, collecting a thick amber syrup that dribbled out.

"What the hell—" Sturgis began as he reached the

C.A.D.S. suited Apache.

"*Sugar* pine," Fireheels answered before Sturgis could even ask the question. "Biggest pine tree in the world, up to three hundred feet. But its fame—at least to the Indians—is as a source of food energy. This sap is almost pure energy, *sugar*. Sugar pine—get it?"

The others caught up and they gathered around in a circle crowding in. With their visors open they could all immediately smell the sweet-scented odor of the sap as it drifted on the breezes.

"Here, have a taste," Fireheels said, taking his battered canteen from the hole where dripping sap had nearly filled it and handing it to Sturgis. He tilted the canteen back to his lips and slurped in what immediately tasted like maple syrup but much thicker. The texture was somewhat hard to swallow, catching along his tongue and throat. But the relief of eating *anything*, even syrup, was heaven. He handed the metal canteen to Tranh who took his slug and handed it on to the next man.

"This stuff is packed with pure energy," Fireheels explained as he gathered the canteens from the men. They all flipped the levers on the sides of their suits allowing the inset metal containers to pop free. "Indians knew for centuries to drink this sap, it's in many of our legends. This way, a man could walk days without game or any other source of food. It's all here for us, man," Fireheels said with a peculiar look. "Nature provides all we need, and us Indians knew how to use it." He said this with more than a trace of bitterness: "It was the white man who loused it up." He looked at Sturgis who was still licking his lips in happiness and amazement. "White man was indifferent to nature."

"I'm not going to argue with you on that one," Sturgis replied, knowing the Indian brave had very strong feelings on the subject of what "western civilization" had done to life and to his Indian culture. "We took out a lot of our own as well," he added. "Trees are mostly gone, but so are a billion people."

"I'll need some men to go gather some of the berries up the hill there," Fireheels said, suddenly changing the subject. He didn't want to get in any deeper. It was all blood under the bridge. "The dark brown berries, when crushed, form a mild acid that breaks down the syrup, makes it easier to swallow and digest."

"Tranh, Rossiter, Wosyck, go do some berry picking," Sturgis said.

"Only the darker ones," Fireheels yelled out as they started up the hill about fifty yards farther where there was a mini jungle of the yard high bushes. "They have the most acid." With the C.A.D.S. troopers standing around amazed, as they found it hard to believe that an old gnarled pine tree could produce such tasty syrup-delights, Fireheels scored three more trees and filled up every canteen in the unit.

When enough berries had been gathered he crushed them up in one of the all purpose soup/stew bowls that they all carried hidden away in one of many inset chambers of the suit. He mixed it with a little snow that hadn't melted underneath the nearby bushes. The whole operation took just over half an hour. Then the berry juice was poured into each trooper's canteen and then shaken for three minutes. The C.A.D.S. troopers then took deep drinks from the nature-made milkshakes.

"Goddamn, this is good," Dixon hooted, as he wiped his lips and tilted the canteen back for more.

"You could open a restaurant, Indian," MacLeish said in amazement. "This is bloody good. Better than most English cooking, which as we all know is among the best in the world." All in all, there were few comments, just happy faces and moving mouths.

When they'd had their fill, Fireheels filled up each canteen again to the top, so they'd have some to get them through the next day or two, and added more berry juice. With thanks and slaps on the back from everyone the Indian headed back up the slopes. Fireheels once again was moving fast ahead and disappearing among the trees.

The man was half mountain-panther, Sturgis had already decided. He seemed to love to stalk, to move like a breeze even in the huge C.A.D.S. suit through the forests.

Walking seemed a lot easier now to all of them as they felt the pure energy of the sugar pine sap surge through their veins.

They made good time up the first of the steep wooded slopes that led to the mesa lands and mountains, along a ridge with more of the sugar pines. Then up a second wooded mountain, this one reaching up a good six or seven thousand feet.

The sun was starting to head toward the far horizon and Sturgis debated whether to camp out on the flat strip they had reached—but then decided they'd better push it. The western forests were not a place to dawdle in.

They'd gone perhaps another thousand feet higher when he started hearing ominous sounds in the distance. It was a sound unlike any that Sturgis, or even Fireheels—who had spent his young life out in the wilds—had ever heard before. It was a howl, deep and predatory. At first, just one, then several, and within a minute or two, as they continued a little more quickly up the mountain, many of the howling animal voices. *Way too many.*

"What the hell are they?" Sturgis asked as the Indian trooper came into view. Sturgis hunkered down beside him, keeping low.

"Could be wolves! There's sure to be some around here," Fireheels answered nervously, which was unusual for him. The Apache rarely displayed much emotion of any kind. "But they don't sound like any wolf I've ever heard. Not even like those mutated wolves we encountered in Siberia. Maybe we should—" He didn't get to finish the thought when they heard a rustling sound in some bushes about a hundred feet off and an immense head appeared, pushing its way through.

"Jesus H. Kee-rist," Dixon muttered, as similar expressions of fear were whispered in every helmet. It was a dog, but a dog like none any of them had ever seen. Clearly some sort of Doberman-like mastiff, but larger, with an impossibly long set of jaws which were opened, tongue hanging out. The sharp canine teeth were clearly visible—and glistening with saliva even from a hundred feet. Then another head appeared, and another. Until the troopers' whole left flank was suddenly filled with the lion-sized heads. The dark red eyes of the dogs zeroed in on them, staring at the feast of humanity that lay before them. Sturgis counted several dozen of the creatures and he knew there were more behind them. A lot more. This was a huge hunting pack. And from their eyes and the way they didn't look away from the men, he also knew they were flesh eaters.

"It's a damned army of the bastards," Wosyck muttered beneath his thick handlebar mustache.

"Oh Dean, I'm—I'm scared," the C.A.D.S. commander suddenly heard Robin's terrified voice coming over his helmet radio. She'd had a run in with dogs before, nearly been torn to pieces. And those had been mere puppies compared to the nuke-spawned monsters facing them now. More of them than they had bullets.

"Let's move out fast, but no sudden motions," Sturgis ordered them sharply. "Go straight to the right. Tranh, MacLeish, Dixon, take up the rear." The troopers headed a little too fast away from the dog-pack, and the movement pulled the animals out of their green cover. They showed no fear, just followed. Perhaps they had been studying the humans to see just what danger, what weapons they might possess. Apparently they decided the humans possessed none. Or they would have used them by now.

The mastiffs came walking across the slope as if in no big hurry. Their huge black and brown bodies, with great muscular legs and necks, looked even larger as they issued out from the bushes. And the C.A.D.S. team could see, to their dismay, that there was a virtual invasion force of the meat eaters. Fifty, maybe sixty. The pack spread out as they came out of the bushes in an uneven line that quickly extended hundreds of feet along the mountain, then headed forward moving faster as they got their hunting unit in the right formation to cut the humans off from escape.

Sturgis didn't like that either. These overtoothed sons-of-bitches, seemed to know what they were doing. It wasn't an ordinary bunch of mutts looking for an easy meal.

"Keep your 9mm. modes operational," Sturgis ordered them all. "But don't for God's sake fire, until I give the order. Maybe we can just bluff our way out of this." He dropped back with the three men riding shotgun as the troopers moved at a half-run right across the slope, darting through the trees.

The sun was sinking fast now, throwing the whole slope into long shadows which didn't help the human side of the equation all that much. Sturgis was sure the dogs could see a lot better than they could in the twilight. As the troopers moved, the dogs increased their motion. But still they didn't charge. It was as if they were in no great rush to take them down, but wanted to savor the hunt, savor the chase.

"That huge mother in the middle," Sturgis said, "the one that's bigger than these other sabre toothed muskrats or whatever they are—you see him?" Sturgis asked softly.

"Affirmative," Tranh replied.

"Yeah," Dixon and MacLeish echoed in whispers through their retracted visors.

"So what?" asked Rossiter.

"I think he's the leader, let's take that one out, maybe it will scare them." They had only small caliber Soviet pistol ammo, and not much of it, in their Multi Mode firing chambers. It was a system that could take almost any caliber of slugs and automatically alter its muzzle and other variables for firing. They raised their right arms and sighted up the advancing monsters, now only seventy-five feet away.

"Ready—Use only one and two round bursts—Now . . .

fire!" Sturgis yelled out. The four troopers turned their wrists slightly to the right and the slugs barreled from the muzzle beneath their glove hands. A dozen .22 cal slugs ripped right into the lead creature's belly and, as big as it was, it went down peppered with red holes.

The other dogs pulled back and once in the underbrush set up a howling. But within not more than ten seconds, another of the mastiffs—the one that howled loudest— seemed to take control and snapped its head at them letting out an unearthly bellow. And with it in the lead, the dogs started forward again.

"Uh, I think they operate like us," Tranh said nervously. "When the top man goes down, the subordinate takes over."

"You're right," Sturgis said, his lips growing dry as he suddenly had the terrifying image of the entire C.A.D.S. unit ripped to shreds by these mongrels. The suits would protect them up to a point. But if the dogs knocked them down and just started tearing away at every part of the suits . . . The units were strong—but they weren't miracles. And even if they held, sooner or later, you needed *air*.

The four of them sprinted along the slope toward the rest of the C.A.D.S. team which was a hundred feet ahead. And as they moved, the dogs as well increased their speed, some of them breaking into runs. The four troopers caught up to the rest and as Sturgis searched around for any cover, and saw none, he suddenly had an idea.

"Rossiter, do we have enough juice for the S.S. Mode?" Sturgis snapped out, referring to the Siren and the Searchlight capabilities of the suits, built in devices which could create intense beams of light strobes, and sirens which could be activated. Primarily the system was meant for use as warning or tracking beacons for downed troopers.

"They don't take much juice," the suit mechanic screamed back, his voice filled with tension as the moving wave of mastiffs came charging in, the line circling around them. "Won't get more than a half minute, before we all lose total power but—"

"Everyone gather in a tight circle—fast," Sturgis shouted out. "When I say go, hit the Emergency Signaling Switch—that'll set the whole thing off. Got it?"

"Got it," every voice whispered back in sweating fear. They put their backs together like Custer and his last troops as the Indians had closed in, stared out at the avalanche of fur and teeth which was coming full charge.

Seventy feet, fifty. They could see the dark eyes of the creatures in the final violet rays of the sun. Like shark's eyes, they were without a shred of mercy or warmth. Just pure predators, ready to take down anything.

"Now!" Sturgis screamed out. In unison they all slammed the SS buttons and suddenly the whole mountainside was lit up with flashing strobes and piercing sirens going off with sharp ear-splitting, high-pitched sounds. The dogs went crazy. They stopped in their tracks, let out involuntary squeals of fear. And turned and ran. They didn't even know what it was they were running from, just that it terrified them. By the strobe lights, flashing every twentieth of a second the troopers could see the pack turn tail and run right back into the woods. As the last one yipped and disappeared Sturgis yelled out to turn it all off again, praying he had saved enough juice to keep the suits moving.

The entire C.A.D.S. unit let out cheers and gathered around their commander, slapping him on the back. They acted like teammates who had just won the World Series, the Superbowl and the $64,000 question all rolled into one.

Dixon laughed so hard, he fell right down in a patch of snow and sat there for several minutes shaking his head from side to side. It was apparently just about the funniest thing he had ever seen. Or maybe it wasn't laughter. Maybe it was the sound of uncontrolled *relief.*

Chapter Eight

The C.A.D.S. troopers weren't bothered again by the pack. They camped out on a high slope that night at the top of the mountain on which they had battled the mastiffs. They didn't take off their suits, preferring to sleep in the uncomfortable confines of the battered high-tech wonders. Only Fireheels shed his, unclasping the front holds and stepping out in his grimy rawhide outfit. He parked the C.A.D.S. suit against a tree in a half-sitting position and then climbed up fifteen feet of the fir to a stretch of three thick branches. There, the isolation-loving Indian bedded down and quickly fell asleep.

Sturgis made sure there were two guards on duty at all times, changed at two hour shifts. God knew what else was out there in the darkness. But even then Sturgis got only brief dozes as he kept ripping open his eyes every time he sank down into dreams.

Bad dreams with too many teeth, dreams with the suits filled with blood, just blood.

When he awoke, after many fitful tossings and turnings, there was a ghastly green dawn. The chartreuse sun had an ultra-violet sheen around it like a halo as it came through the brownish tinged clouds. The skies were getting worse these days, Sturgis thought darkly, worse than ever. The colonel wished he could just fall into sleep, a real sleep for about twenty years. Or at least just hole up. Being a leader, though, meant getting the others going when they all wanted to do the same thing he did—sleep and dream. Dreams were a lot more peaceful than the waking world.

With a groan he sat up and then pushed hard with the suit's balky arms to get the thing upright.

"All right you rusty Sir Lancelots, let's get these mechanized mamas moving. And I mean now, let's move it." Sturgis walked around banging at the chest levels of their suits, jolting the exhausted troopers awake with sudden wide terrified eyes. Might as well get their blood going from the start. Adrenaline would keep them more alert. From full lying position, it was hard for some of them to get up. Some flopped like fish. He went around and lent a hand, reaching out and pulling them up. They helped the others.

Within five minutes the nuke-troopers had broken camp and it was once more "hi ho, hi ho, into the upper oxygenless slopes we go." Sturgis had to slow down once they got up a few thousand feet along the increasingly barren slopes. Without internal oxygen supply, it was rough going. With the batteries dying, the amount of energy they had to pump out was growing each minute. If any of the suits went down up here, they'd have to abandon them. Take a chance on just coveralls and ragged sweaters.

And one suit did die then. All of sudden, DeCamp's suit just stopped dead in its tracks, frozen like a black sculpture, with one arm reaching forward and legs apart. It just jammed as she'd taken a step. The doctor couldn't stop herself when the C.A.D.S. suit started toppling over sideways, heading straight for a slide down a graveled slope that stretched down at a fifty degree angle for a thousand feet.

Tranh was nearest her, just behind Shelia DeCamp in a double line of the troopers. Seeing the problem, Fireheels, with cat-like speed, leaped forward, grabbed her belt, cutting off her fall. He pushed her upright hard, as he planted the wide booted soles of the C.A.D.S. suit into the side of the mountain for support.

She went sideways now though, tumbling to the left, sliding on the suit's front. Sturgis and Wosyck, who were ahead, turned and caught her from each side.

Sheila was none the worse for wear inside the protective armor of the suit. But the technological marvel was dead as a doornail. Sturgis had Rossiter inspect it after De-Camp had unlatched it and stepped out. The female medic looked frazzled; her inner clothes, sweatshirt and camouflage painted jeans were coated with sweat and grease from drippings of the unit's gear and pulley systems. Still the brunette smiled.

"Ain't worth shit," Rossiter scowled after a few minutes' exploration. "I'll just salvage some comm and chip junk. And then we can heave this sucker down the hill. Better for it not to be found whole, anyway. Shall I cannibalize it?"

"You better believe that one," Sturgis said, giving the thumbs-up for Rossiter to proceed. He turned to Sheila, said, "I'm sorry."

"It's no problem," DeCamp said softly as she stood there, arms over her shoulders as it was cold on the high slope even in the middle of the day, with the radioactive smog covering the pale yellow sun. "I can make it without the stupid suit." The statement was a bad joke as far as Sturgis was concerned. She wouldn't last two hours up here without the suit's many protections.

"I don't need my suit," Sturgis began, "you can—"

"Take mine," Fireheels spoke up as the rest of the troopers gathered around, their boots planted firmly in several inches on the dirt and rock, taking a breather. "I don't like wearing the damn thing half the time, to be honest," the Indian said, looking at Sturgis.

Before the C.A.D.S. commander could even give it a rejection, the Apache was stripped out of the thing. He stood there in deerskin pants and jacket with several US Army sweatshirts thick and bulky on underneath. He wore Nike Air Float cushioned sneakers, thick things filled with bubbles, and carried the pistol from the suit.

The emergency firearm hung on his hip. It had no ammo at present, but who had to know? The Indian liked the feel of it. And the size. Something you had to *hold*; not a high-tech self-activated weapons system!

Fireheels helped DeCamp into the suit and once she was all latched in she formed up with the others.

Robin was his biggest concern. But, despite her mental weariness, she kept up with the rest of the men easily. Maybe the movement, the sheer physical exercise would help her, be good for her, get the blood moving through her still reeling brain.

"I know this area well, from these Mesa-Mountains all the way back to White Sands," Fireheels said. "My grandfather used to run through these hills when young, moved fast as the deer himself. How do you think I got my family name—Fireheels?" the Indian smirked at his commander.

"You sure it's not fire-up-your-ass?" Dixon chortled, bringing guffaws from some of the others who felt a little alienated from the Apache trooper. Fireheels never played cards with them, or seemed to be quite like them. His eyes were in the stars and the wind. "I'll move faster than any of you." With that he turned and started fast up the side of the mountain. He moved with the grace of a mountain goat and even as the rest of the troopers got themselves moving, Fireheels had already vanished onto an inset part of the slope several hundred feet up. Most of the terrain wasn't on the computer maps—all post-nuke earth-changes. Earthquakes had made this warped land.

They climbed for hours, then went down into a valley that dropped a good thousand feet. Then back up yet another rise that seemed to go up into the clouds. Sturgis's altimeter wasn't functioning, but he knew it was at least ten, maybe twelve thousand feet. This crew couldn't go on much more.

"What is this? Bloody Mt. Everest?" MacLeish gasped. Suddenly Fireheels came back down, moving in great strides down the hill, surefooted in the way of the original Americans.

"Town ahead, not huge, but got stuff for sale. Looks okay. No cannibalism, or poles with skulls that I could see. Smelled meats and potatoes, and I think, some home brewed beer."

That list brought smiles to the men. The sugar pine's nectar was strong, but it was like eating candy bars all the time, liquid candy bars. Their teeth and throats felt coated, saturated with sugar.

They followed behind Fireheels who headed up another six hundred feet, moving slowly as they reached the highest part of the slope. The trees were much more scraggly up here and all bent slightly to the east as if praying to Mecca or away from the western winds which blew eternally.

Sturgis saw the town, a few clapboard shacks, light bulbs—or more likely oil lamps—flickering on and off. Half the hovel towns that passed for villages out here didn't even have electric light. Much of the US had fallen into rapid centuries of de-evolution. They'd have to be on guard, for people had become suspicious, defensive of all strangers.

"Watch your step, but act friendly," Sturgis said to the others. "I'm sure we're about to scare the daylights out of these townsfolk." He had his visor retract all the way into the helmet as did the other troopers so their faces showed. At least the citizens here wouldn't think they were all monsters!

They did anyway. Two ragged children peered from a rock then started running off screaming wildly as the C.A.D.S. troopers came stomping into the west side of the two block long town.

"Howdy neighbor," Sturgis said as he turned his head from side to side leading them all down the narrow dusty street. Men and women peered suspiciously out from low narrow windows and out of what looked like junk stores with various pots and pans, pieces of machinery, all kinds of used goods stacked. Maybe the C.A.D.S. troopers could pick up some needed repair materials. If they could show their peaceful intentions.

"Howdy, just here to buy things, don't want no trouble," Sturgis addressed one and all. The furtive watchers looked skeptical to say the least, terrified was more like it. None of them withdrew completely, but none stepped forward either.

"You can hardly blame them," Tranh spoke up through his opened visor. "I mean imagine if you were just sitting around and a spaceman crew from Mars shows up. Even if they did have big friendly faces like us." The C.A.D.S. troopers laughed at that one. Friendly, they didn't exactly look. They had forgotten how, if they ever knew in the first place. Their huge black metal armor coated with grease and dirt, their faces stubbled to the point of rough sandpaper, their mouths hewn into semi-permanent scowls, they looked menacing. It wasn't exactly fun to be moving around in the suits, but if someone took a potshot . . .

Sturgis knew there was a way to men's hearts beyond the fear, the suspicion. He reached around the side of his suit and slammed a small latch which didn't open at first but after a couple more hits did. He didn't know if the suits were rusting or what, but everything on them seemed to be getting less functional by the day. He gripped two small objects within with the thick black gloves and drew them out, holding them up in the air.

"We've got something here you all might be interested in," Sturgis bellowed out, turning his hand back and forth so they could see. *Gold*. It glistened even under the violet tinged skies. Men had pursued it, wanted it since the dawn of time. It was a strong persuader and caught their attention. Dollars were worth toilet paper. But gold—

"Who are you guys?" one brave shopkeeper asked, his sudden greed giving him the courage to step forward and take a closer look at the proffered coins, thick and heavy looking, to see if they were real. "You look like you just landed from the moon or something. You sure you all are earthlings?" He tried to smile as he asked the question to show he wasn't being hostile and had nothing against moonmen, but there was a quavering in his voice. "Ain't that a US flag on your weird outfits' shoulder?"

"Human as you are pal," Sturgis replied. "We wear these suits to protect us from the mean world. We're C.A.D.S. troopers, officially sanctioned and mandated combat forces of the US government."

"There *ain't* no US government anymore," a voice bellowed out behind the standing troopers. They all turned, startled at the hostility and loudness of the voice. Standing on the far side of the dirt street about thirty feet away was a big grungy fellow in army fatigues with a face full of scars and a body full of fat. Around him were a half dozen other unappetizing looking lugs who for their sheer ugliness must have been the speaker's brothers.

"You heard me, I said there ain't no US government anymore," the man echoed. "There ain't nothing except power and strength. And you know what I think? That them suits youse is wearing ain't diddlyshit. I think they're just pieces of tin hammered together—and if me and my boys walk over to you, we can knock you right down like pieces of rotted wood." The man laughed and his compatriots joined in, amused by the "tin men" who stood before them. "Hey look, there's a long-haired Injun too!"

"Careful," the shopkeeper near Sturgis whispered out of the side of his mouth as he was only a few feet away, having edged close to see the gold. "That's Matty J., they calls him. He's the scumbag of the town, him and his bullyboys. We all pays 'em 'protection,' and even then he busts things up pretty bad when he gets the mood. Careful stranger, *careful*." The man kept looking at the gold which vanished agonizingly as Sturgis slammed it back into the small compartment on the side of the suit and turned around to face the town thug.

"You talking to me?" Sturgis asked with a smirk as he walked around to the front of his men, waving his hand in

64

the air, the signal for them all to simmer down as he could sense his men were ready to dump the crud.

"If you speak English, yeah, I'm talking to you, tin-head," Matty J. laughed, rubbing his big gut which hung out of a torn sweatshirt under the open surplus-jacket like a rotting whale carcass on a beach. Two ancient six guns hung at his sides, knives and other deadly half-rusty junk ringed the fellow like a walking armaments convention. His fellow travelers sported the same basic garb. He walked forward, stepping off a wood splintered sidewalk that ran along the stores on that side of the street. Heads peered nervously out of every window and door, but none pulled away. They wanted to see this particular confrontation. Best thing since the cable went dead, Sturgis supposed!

"Take off them suits," the man demanded, reaching fast for one of his pistols. The C.A.D.S. troopers whipped their visors down so any stray slugs wouldn't make their way into their faces. Fireheels jumped behind the protective wall of suits that stood like frozen robots just staring through the tinted visors at the slime.

The man drew fast and let loose with a whole chamber full of .45 calibers right at Sturgis who was walking slowly toward him. The bullets ricocheted right off the suit and backward, striking one of the other thugs in the stomach so he let out a loud hissing groan and collapsed to his knees.

Sturgis reached forward and grabbed the pistol, squeezing it hard with his gloved hand. The six gun bent in half like it was made of paper. Sturgis threw it to the ground twisted up like a pretzel.

As Matty J.'s expression suddenly went from nasty to frightened, Sturgis made his gloved hand into a fist and slammed out into the bullyboy's huge gut. The man went flying backward with tremendous velocity, ripping right through a set of rusty hinged wooden doors. They heard all kinds of sounds, like he was taking out half the furnishings of the store as he crashed around inside. His pals quickly went in after him, dragged him back out. Whatever ideas they had held about taking out the high tech battle troopers vanished as quickly as the cloud-covered pale sun far above. The entire crew of thugs took off down the street, Matty J., half bent over coughing and wheezing like an elephant with asthma, being supported between two of the fleeing men.

Once the crew had vanished around the corner, looking back with angry glances, the storekeepers, women and children who had seen the entire confrontation let out a chorus of cheers, whistles, hoots, and yells of happiness. The gang had been the town's nemesis for years. And just like that these men from Mars had walked out of nowhere and kicked butt.

The townspeople surged from their hiding places and surrounded the C.A.D.S. troopers thanking them profusely, offering them food and water, trying to get them to come to *their* store. And begging for another look at that gold. Plus of course, they wanted *news*.

Chapter Nine

In the half caved-in Town Hall, all the townsfolk treated them to some delicious squirrel and rabbit and "other stuff" stew. Then, much restored and happy, Sturgis and about half the men unsuited and left their C.A.D.S. equipment guarded by the others. Even with but a few rounds of ammo, they were more than a match for anything this town had to throw against them. Sturgis had clearly demonstrated that. As long as the batteries held out, even a little, they were like super-men. When the juice ran dry—that was a different story.

"Let's split up and check out what this backwoods mall has got to offer," Sturgis said as Fireheels, Rossiter, MacLeish, Dixon and Tranh split up into three groups of two each and went out in different directions to scout up whatever repair materials they could. Sturgis and Tranh headed off a block to the left where the largest of the "stores," if they could be called that, stood. It was a two story affair positively bustling with all kinds of junk set in an ordered tumble out front, and in dusty rows inside. Machines, appliances all broken or in pieces. Never had Sturgis seen so many diverse things. Phones, generators, fans, wheels, gearboxes, even a few car engines sitting like the metal mastodons they were, inside a wooden overhang to protect them from the periodic rains.

"Nice stuff," Sturgis said to one of the storekeepers. This was an old man with veined, ruddy face who looked to be in his seventies if he was a day. The oldster looked down at the two of them, chewing hard on a long piece of brittle straw.

"Seen what you done over there, mister," the man commented, letting loose with a gob of brown spit down into the dirt on the floor. "Was real nice. But you better be careful now, hear? Hash, that's the boy whose belly you busted up. He don't like that. Him and his boys been taking provisions and silver money from us for years, 'cause they're tougher than we are. He'll be looking for ya."

"Thanks for the warning," Sturgis said as Tranh leaned down and looked closer at one of the car engines. "I'll file it away in the what's-trying-to-kill-me-now department. Like I said, you got some nice-looking equipment out here. What's this town about? What's the story?"

"Story is we's the biggest trading post for miles, make that a hundred miles in any direction," the man went on, smiling broadly with pride so Sturgis could see his toothless mottled gums. Radiation poisoning. Sturgis had seen it take every hair and tooth out of a man as if he'd been hit with a sledge hammer. But the old codger was hanging on.

"Lot of this stuff actually works too," the ruddy faced oldster said, leaning down and kicking at a few items with enthusiasm. " 'Course you gotta tinker with them to get it going just right. But there's lots of good tinkerers in these parts."

"Skip," Tranh said, looking up at Sturgis. "I think this old V8 engine here might actually be functional. Everything looks in working order, no rust. Let's get Rossiter and Dixon to take a look. Those two know motors like the backs of their greasy hands. If we could get this damn thing moving—maybe we could actually rig up some sort of transport."

"I hear you pal," Sturgis said, his eyes widening. It would make a big difference to have a vehicle, even a makeshift one. "What's something like that go for? You got any car frames to go along with it? Or any motor vehicles in *one* piece?"

The old man said, "Got some cars in pieces, that's all. Don't know what to charge . . . well, exact price, that we'd just have to see," the man said. He was looking sort of sideways at Sturgis's metal pocket, as if he was hoping some of the gold might fall out. "Far as car frames go, we got some wrecks around back. Come on, check it out, fellow. Nice to meet a man with actual spending money. Mighty nice indeed." He let out a high pitched cackle apparently over how much money he suddenly saw himself making and held out his hand for a shake.

"Name's Kinniston. Me and my brothers run this place, Ethan, Rip, and me. Call me Spit, 'cause everybody else does. Don't know why." He let loose with another gob that went a good twelve feet and hit the side wall of the porch he was leading them down. For a seventy-year-old plus he moved pretty spryly on his thin chicken legs, around which, Sturgis noted, the too-big pants he wore billowed out as if they contained only emptiness.

"Holy rusting Americana, Sturg," Tranh exploded with a loud laugh as they came around the back of the place. "Look at all this stuff." It was like a graveyard of cars, truck frames, even an old school bus, all lying around in mostly small broken pieces.

" 'Course you can't jes' jump in and start up the motors," Spit said, which was the understatement of the century since most everything was pretty much on the far side of functional. "But there's good parts, lots of good parts." Sturgis's eyes swung back to the bus, once he had made a quick perusal of the several acre field covered with the debris of a lost, once technologically functioning America. It looked the least broken down.

Sturgis walked over with Tranh and Spit following right behind and around the bus several times. It actually looked solid other than being covered with graffiti and bucketfuls of paint where someone had doused it with a dozen different colors. A layer of grease and dirt coated the thing, and it was not exactly the award winning sports coupe of the century. But after he and Tranh kicked the flattened tires, tested the rims and went inside finding a lot of it in manageable condition—real pedals and a steering wheel too—he grew interested.

"What's the story on this one?" Sturgis asked the old man, whose eyes were twinkling with dollar signs. He looked as if he was about to have a stroke as his face grew red, but he tried to maintain his cool at the same time.

"Now that one's, that's the best thing on the lot," Spit said rubbing his chin with his spidery hand. "Was still being driven up to just six months ago—"

"And then?" Tranh asked, as he started to open the hood.

"And then the motor blew up," Spit replied quickly, like that wasn't important.

"Oh damn, Sturgis, check it out," the Vietnamese said as he propped the hood up with a long rod. Sturgis moved back around to the front and stared down. It was charred and burnt, melted rubber and metal fused. It would have to be replaced.

"Tell you what," Sturgis said, making a decision. "How about we make a combo deal? I'll take the bus and the V8 motor, and whatever odds and ends I need to get the whole project together. And in return—" Sturgis reached in his pocket as Spit's eyes grew wide. "I'll give you four pieces of gold. Each weighs one ounce." He withdrew the gleaming, fine-condition coins of the US Mint and handed them over. Spit began breathing hard the moment the coins touched his hand. They seemed to burn him, as he grew dizzy and sat down fast. Sturgis guided him down on to a rusting fender so he didn't go over.

"All my life, all my life," Spit said, with a dazed smile on his face. "Been waiting for the big score. And now? This the real thing?" he asked, putting a coin in his mouth and biting down on it with his wet gums. "Used to be able to use my teeth to test it—but now ain't got any teeth."

"It's real, all right," Sturgis laughed as Spit gnawed on

the government issue coins as if trying to taste them. Spit got one of his brothers to come out of some shack out back. This guy *did* have teeth to test it and his eyes lit up too.

The brother led them personally back though the store, anxious for even more gold. Sturgis picked out some 30 cal. and 12 gauge shells, about sixty in all which could be used in the C.A.D.S. variable-ammunition-mode chambers. It was *something,* not a hell of a lot. They had Rossiter look at the engine and the bus. He groaned and mumbled to himself, finally saying, "Needs a load of cleaning and taking every damned thing apart down to the bearings. But — *maybe* I can interface it with the — "

"But how long?" Sturgis asked as Rossiter and Dixon looked at each other.

"Two days," Rossiter said, "and we'll need more batteries. We can strip a few suits and power it with that but — I'd rather keep all the C.A.D.S. units functional."

"Even if we get juice we're still going to need gas," Dixon pointed out.

"Got some of that too," Spit said, limping inside to follow the action. "Twenty barrels of it, in fact, hidden away like the precious wine that it is. Just use it for our own private generator on special occasions — like Christmas."

"I want it," Sturgis said, "a full tank's worth anyway for the bus and a few barrels for carrying along."

"It'll *cost,*" Spit answered, his eyes getting watery and pale again. "Mebbe . . . Let's see . . . Ten more coins?"

"No way," Sturgis said with a firm expression. "You've already made a small fortune with the junk we bought already."

Small wasn't the right adjective. The old man smiled. Why this deal would make Spit the richest man in town. Already he was planning how not to share it all with his two brothers, since he had lied and told them Sturgis had given him only two coins for the vehicle and parts.

"Oh, all right," Spit said, waving his hand in disgust.

"Take it all, take us out of house and home, for five more coins!" He led them, as he jangled the gold pieces Sturgis handed over in his hands, fascinated by their sheer essence.

"Back here, under these doors," Spit said, pointing to a pile of torn off Chevy and Ford doors all atop one another. Sturgis and a few of the troopers pulled them off. Lo and behold, a wide trench filled with the still sealed metal barrels stood side by side like time capsules in the sand.

Dixon jumped down and opened one of the caps. He stuck his finger in, got a good coating of the liquid within and pulled his finger out popping the dripping forefinger into his mouth. The master mechanic licked the liquid off like a child and his popsicle and then seemed to roll the substance around in his cheeks.

"It's the real thing," he said, swallowing it after a few seconds, making a thumbs up.

"Does that guy always drink the stuff," Spit asked, half gagging.

"It's his vitamin therapy. Contains vitamin G—gas. If you don't get enough of it—all your teeth fall out."

"No wonder I lost mine," Spit said with enlightened shock. "Well you gotta leave me at least one barrel—so's I can start growing my teeth back again!"

Chapter Ten

Dixon and Rossiter went crazy for the next solid 24 hours. Commanding the suited troopers around like slaves, they managed to get the bus all the way up on posts set in the ground so that they could work on it from underneath. The axles and wheel rims were actually in good condition, they discovered, after testing it. But two of the wheels were ripped apart pretty badly. Apparently someone had been using it for axe and knife practice. They searched around and found two truck tires that were only about six inches bigger then the ones on the school bus. They moved the smaller tires to the front and loaded the big diesel-rigs rubbers onto the back.

The whole front of the chassis had to be sanded out as the charred remains and the plastics might melt once the thing got going and would clog up even a pristine engine. Then the Ford V8 was carried over by two C.A.D.S. troopers and set into place. While Dixon welded the thing, using one of the still functioning laser torches on the suits, and made an attempt at matching spare gear boxes, Rossiter got a load of car batteries and started juicing them up from a small electricity generator, now gasoline powered. To Sturgis, it was a wonderful 24 hours!

Then they went crazy armoring the strange new Road-thing, figuring without much fire power and shielding they'd be sitting ducks for any bandits out there waiting on the still eight hundred miles to White Sands.

The basic frame of the bus was kept, but the windows were sealed up with long slabs of quarter-inch-thick steel, and four-by-eights, dozens of which had somehow found their way into the car dump. As Rossiter and Dixon worked by floodlights, ordering everyone assigned to work like dogs, half the town turned out to see the madmen working, to see the suited C.A.D.S. fighters carrying their immense loads around like crazed manic robots.

As the welding sparks flew like fireflies Sturgis set up some C.A.D.S.-suited guards at the ends of the single road. He stationed them a hundred yards down the dirt road just inside the woods. *Just in case.* The activity might well attract attention in these parts. It was the ideal town to work in. For whenever the bus surgeons needed a wire, or a catalytic converter or whatever it was, someone could run off and find it in one of the fifty trading posts of machines, metal, tin, furs, etc., etc.

When they all finally stood back and examined the monstrosity that had been wrought, Sturgis let out a long strange sound. It looked . . . *Weird* was the only word that came to mind. Extremely weird. Both sides of the "bus" had been covered up with the long steel slabs, the roof too. But not particularly neatly, as the thick pieces of steel had been laid over one another like bad plywooding on a floor and welded right there. The front of the bus had been made to resemble the front of an old time steam locomotive with a long scooping bow of metal which had spikes and points coming out all over it, giving it an almost dinosaurian appearance. A machine gun, 50 cal. jutted from the front of it, on a swivel, and loose as a goose. It was in good order, as it had been stored in sealed oiled paper inside a wooden box. Plus two lunchboxes of ammo, nearly three hundred rounds that had been dug up after much scouring.

"What do you think, Skip?" Dixon asked, wiping his hands of grease and then smearing the filthy rag across his face leaving wide broad stripes of oil and sludge on his cheeks. Rossiter's feet stuck out from under the lopsided madman's Road-Weirdie. He was still working.

"I—I—," Sturgis stuttered as he walked around the armored behemoth. "Won't the extra steel plates slow her down?" he asked, slamming his steel-gloved hand against a shield-panel and feeling the bus shake slightly.

"We ripped out the whole inside of the bus," Dixon said leading Sturgis to the front set of steps that led up into the bus. Every seat in the thing had been torn from the floor. And in their places, steel poles a good inch thick had been bolted in floor to ceiling, seven on each side of the bus, running down the length.

Sturgis nodded, peered inside. Why, it looked like nothing more than a totally vandalized subway car, with hardly a trace of light coming through the slits in the armor.

"So I don't think we've added any more overall weight than we took out. Rossiter's the math freak, he can show you on computer grid, I think he got himself juiced up enough."

Tranh tapped Sturgis on the shoulder. "Batteries are up, Skip. They're juicing up all the suits. Go get a jolt." Tranh told Sturgis to go around back of the store. "Actually they've got enough of a power station going that we should be able to get all the suits back up to forty, even fifty percent."

"What about a hundred?" Rossiter asked bitingly, having come out from under. "Can't we get the suits back to the shape they're supposed to be in? All systems go and functioning, on full interface?"

"No can do," Tranh said. "We can get enough juice out of the generator, but we can't get the power, the voltage needed to really ram the juice into these suits. Back at White Sands, you know, or if we had one of the Rhino's nuke generators—we could do it. But we can't. This stuff just ain't got the macho to do the job."

"Hey, I'm not complaining," Sturgis said, holding up his hands. "You guys are performing miracles. Rossiter: once the suits are juiced, are we ready to pull out?"

"Give me another twenty minutes. She had a new second emergency tank. I want to get that filled, the regular tank is ready to overflow."

Sturgis smiled and went around to the back where the generator was set up.

"Here for the full wash—or just battery recharge?" DeCamp asked. "No one's wounded or sick, so I'm doing tech-duty!"

"Battery and wipers," Sturgis replied. He stood there frozen as DeCamp—never noted for her electronic wizardry—connected up two jumper cables to opposite sides of his neck.

"Okay Frankenstein," DeCamp said standing back. She flicked a switch on the generator and Sturgis's suit seemed to jump around and quiver a little.

"What the hell's going on? I'm getting a mild shock through my whole body," Sturgis barked out.

"Relax," DeCamp said. "You heroes, I swear, you're all babies! So it shocks you a little loading up. Didn't you ever get a needle at my doctor's office?" She flipped another switch and the voltage hit into Sturgis even harder. He gritted his teeth vowing to get even with the medical genius the first chance he got. It took about ten minutes and at last Sheila yelled out.

"All loaded pal." She slapped Sturgis's helmet hard and the C.A.D.S. leader's brain reeled from the sound. "Move it out. Your computer grid and all that junk should be coming on again if you test them. I'm sure that'll make your day."

Sturgis tried to unclench his muscles from the electric bath and noted with satisfaction that green digital lights were popping on all around the inside of his visor. Readouts of temperature, location of his men, mode checks, all dancing out with a kind of delight their messages of electronic fact.

He waited as all the rest of them got charged, then it was time. "All units, go to full auto link-up," Sturgis commanded over the helmet to helmet. "Let's move 'em out boys," he shouted over the radio.

The townspeople, who had been watching the whole 24 hour operation with awe and fear, were now truly frightened as they saw the visors all click down. With the men's faces gone, and the suits giving off a subliminal hum, a crackling of nearly invisible electricity coursing around the black titanium frames, even the bravest of them looked on in real fear. They weren't human after all!

"Full link," Sturgis shouted again and this time he got back fifteen quick beeps that rang out in number and location on a small grid map. Red Mode was working again. Thank God. He always felt at least a little more in control when he could read out on his own men any time he wished. "Check all systems and see if there's any major problems," Sturgis ordered them. "Primarily the unit's human-computer-interface. We don't need these things suddenly having nervous breakdowns." They checked and checked, but all came back positive. The suits were strong. But then, they had been designed to be. Had been designed to be able to walk through a nuclear blast site minutes after detonation with the radioactive winds still blowing. What was a little 20,000 mile round trip to Russia, a parajump and some funky weather.

"All right, load up into the bus," Sturgis commanded. "You're not going to like it in there but we'll save time." Even though the suits were partially powered again, jumping along the 800 miles to base in the long running strides that the C.A.D.S. units were capable of, would use up too much power, too fast. For the time they'd have to tone down their acrobatics and ride the *Road-Weirdie* if they were going to make it back to White Sands in one piece!

The troopers got grumblingly onto the bus, not liking the claustrophobic feel as they had to duck down to get through the inadequately widened doorway. They walked down the bus aisle to the back, taking their places next to each one of the two lines of poles that ran from front to back.

Dixon shouted, "Don't you all start shouting over these radios now that they're working all nice and loud again.

My ears need a rest from being next to that goddamn motor all night, trying to seduce it back to life."

"Ignore the southern ignoramus. You hold onto these poles here," Rossiter said as he stood at the doorway letting the men all pass. "That's why I put them in, since this is going to be bouncy ride. I don't want you all banging away into each other like cans of Vienna sausages so you get all squashed in there."

It was like a troop of clowns going endlessly into a Volkswagen, but somehow the entire unit got in. Fireheels, who was by choice suitless, sat up front on the steps as Fenton MacLeish took the wheel. As the best driver of the unit, a Rhino-ATV trainer for years, Sturgis knew that the Brit was the only one ready to handle this strange metal mutant.

MacLeish turned the key and started the thing up, pumping hard.

There were tremendous backfires.

"No, no, you don't have to pump her," Dixon shouted from the second pole back as he eyed the Brit driver suspiciously, not knowing if he wanted to let him take the controls of his prized co-creation. "We made her real fast. So all you gotta do is touch her, and that engine will take off like its having multiple orgasms." Rossiter vehemently agreed.

MacLeish didn't hear or didn't want to, and believing that all good motors need a good jolt of gas to get them going, he slammed his foot down again as he shifted into gear. The bus suddenly shot forward like a Mack truck at the Diesel Olympics.

Every man in the vehicle was thrown around, slamming and bouncing into each other as the Brit twisted the wheel this way and that. The bus surged forward weaving wildly for several hundred feet, bowling over three small storage huts and a few small trees, then straightened out.

"Sorry, sorry about that," MacLeish said into his suit mike. "Just getting the gears' *feel*." He released the foot brake and touched at the pedal and the bus purred and moved smoothly ahead. "All *bloody right!* That's more like it," MacLeish roared, as he headed the bus down the main street and toward the south. The townspeople gathered around and waved goodbye, sad and yet relieved to see the "spacemen" leave. None of them had quite figured out just what Sturgis and his crew were up to. But the gold spoke wonders. So they waved and tears glistened in the eyes of those who had made money and those who hadn't. They had been told that America still lived, and was still fighting the enemy!

MacLeish drove the bus slowly out of town, making sure of the feel of the vehicle. It shook slightly above fifteen, but above thirty it seemed to stabilize and the whole crew settled down.

The Brit felt like he was driving a mountain. The sheer mass of the thing, which he could feel swaying beneath him, was immense.

"It's too dark in here," Robin suddenly spoke up, her voice nervous, on the edge of hysteria. Sturgis, who had managed to find a pole near her, touched helmets with her. "Just tell your suit, one and two lights on," Sturgis said reassuringly. His tender comments came direct from the contact, not over his mike.

She did as he asked, and two small lights suddenly appeared from indents on the shoulders of her suit lighting up the men around her.

"No one else put on lights," Sturgis added. "We're still on full energy-starvation diets. That's enough. I don't think we're going to get much time to do any reading."

"How do we get out of here, if we have to?" Tranh asked with a strong edge in his voice as well. He didn't like being inside the bus. It was like a tomb. "The living should never ride in a coffin," an ancient Vietnamese saying went. He pushed one of the steel bus walls, but it felt solid even against his servo strength. Couldn't break out that easily if there were any problems.

"The whole top comes off if we have to blow it," Rossiter spoke up from the third pole back where he had

79

secured himself. He was hanging on for dear life with both gloved hands. "Some dynamite we dug up in the back shelves of one of those stores is wired to our roof. It will blow the whole top off in a flash if we have to. Charges go off along both sides and boom—"

"Let me get this right," Tranh said in disbelief. "If there's trouble, you're going to set off explosives *inside* the bus? You sure you're not working for the bad guys?"

"Relax, relax," Rossiter cajoled back. "Our suits can take it. We'll tell you when we're going to blast, you just have to look away. Look down at the floor. Your suit can take it. I promise. If I'm wrong—sue me." That brought a few laughs but only angered Tranh more.

"I won't sue, I'll come back from the grave and haunt you, Rossiter. I'll be a skull hanging over your shoulder twenty-four hours a day. A bloody dripping face, screaming out your name. 'Rossssiitter, Rossitterrr.' How would you like that?"

The mechanical-whiz blanched at the words. Tranh wasn't very nice anymore, was he? He had always had a fear that he would be haunted, having read too many horror comics when an impressionable child. Rossiter shivered in the semi-darkness and prayed that the Asian-American wouldn't die and come back dripping. But he prayed even more, that if and when they had to blow the roof that it wasn't *his* ass that got fried.

Chapter Eleven

It didn't take a long time for the "bus" to start developing trouble. They'd gone perhaps fifty miles over a county road that still was in decent shape when the vehicle started knocking like it had a terminal case of gaseous indigestion and then shook violently, making the C.A.D.S. troopers reel around inside hardly able to hang onto the poles. Dixon got out and cursing madly, made some adjustments in the engine and diddled with some junctures here and there. After that the bus ran smoother, though it still made noises like it was constipated whenever they hit a bump.

"Where we heading?" DeCamp finally blurted out into her suit mike after they'd been on the road a good three hours. To her mind, they were seeming to just head ever deeper into darkness, swerving wildly.

"Home, Sheila," Sturgis, who was hanging onto the pole just behind MacLeish, who drove like a maniac, answered. "We're following the C.A.D.S. compass, and I'm double-checking that with Tranh's and Fenton's every half hour or so to make sure there's no malfunction. If it seems like we're zigzagging a lot, it's because whoever built this road must have consumed several quarts of gin first, it curves around like a snake."

"What do you reckon our ETA for White Sands?" Tranh asked.

"Oh, somewhere between five days and eternity,"

Sturgis replied.

"I gotta take a leak," Wosyck shouted from midway down the aisle. "And I mean *bad*. The damned pump on the suit's tinkle-vacuum ain't working no more."

"Leak time's in half an hour," Sturgis declared coolly. "We gotta make more time, and higher ground as well. Because, if my eyes aren't deceiving me, it looks like we might be in for some heavy leakage from the sky." He'd been keeping an eye on it for the last hour out one gun-slit and it was definitely getting worse out there by the minute. The sky was darkening up with thick brown and greenish clouds which swooped down ever lower. Sturgis knew that the clouds portended big trouble. The storms of post-nuke America could be vicious, releasing waterfalls of liquid. They made cloudbursts of the old days mere leaky faucets by comparison. The weather was warm— rain, not snow.

They drove, heading into a steep uphill grade which only slightly soothed his anxieties about a flash flood or road washout, until they reached the scenic overview.

Beyond their position, prairie lands extended as far as the eye could see. Flat, except for some mesas.

"Rest stop," Sturgis exclaimed over his mike. Fenton hit the brakes.

"Take care of your bodily functions, get a few sandwiches and candy bars at the Howard Johnson, maybe some souvenirs for the kids. We'll be departing in ten minutes."

"Right on," Wosyck shouted out, his huge handlebar mustache visible through the upraised visor of his C.A.D.S. helmet as he nudged past Sturgis.

They all made their way to various bushes, trees and boulders, the two women going in one direction and the men in the other. It was impossible to take the whole suits off, as that was a fairly time-consuming operation, but the miracles of modern technology had emergency latches that opened up the vital areas so relief could be obtained quickly, and directly; or "storage" removed.

They had barely taken care of business when Fireheels, who had climbed to the top of the bus, let out with a not-too-loud war whoop.

"Trouble coming, Skip, and *big*. We got a mechanized war party bearing down from the east." Sturgis rushed to the bus and leaped up on the roof with practiced servo-assisted legs. With the suit not quite at full power, he barely made it to the top of the bus some ten feet above and had to reach out for Fireheels, whose strong arms gave him just enough of a pull to keep him from going over.

"There, you see them?" Fireheels asked as he pointed off about two miles away. There was an obscuring cloud of dust and Sturgis at first had a hard time really seeing much of anything. He was always amazed at the Indian's powers of perception—and he wasn't even wearing his suit, nor did the redman have binocs.

"Macro view," Sturgis commanded the suit verbally and the right side of his visor seemed to telescope his view forward as if he was being shot from a rocket. The recharge had given the visual and most of the electromagnetic perceptual modes enough juice to function. The zoom-view cut through the dust cloud. Sturgis could see them now—a dozen or so motorcycles with nasty looking dudes atop them covered with rifles and belts of slugs. They were clearly heading straight for the bus which was visible from their line of sight. They were right on the road too.

"Son of a bitch," Sturgis muttered, wondering why the gods would allow men to be attacked while they were relieving themselves. But he didn't wonder too long. He had to plan.

"Back to the bus," Sturgis shouted over the suit-to-suit radio. "We got company." The C.A.D.S. troopers came tearing back to the school bus and scrambled on board.

"What do you have in mind, chief?" MacLeish asked as he stopped at the door of the bus and stared hard at Sturgis.

"We'll smash right through the bastards," Sturgis answered with a cold edge in his voice. "We can't stay up here, there's no maneuverability for the bus. And we can't go back 'cause there isn't room to turn this big bad bus. And I don't want to lose time. So—"

"I hear you," MacLeish said as he climbed up and got into the driver's seat. "We'll bowl the bloody bastards over," he spoke enthusiastically, seeing that he was going to get a chance to show off his real driving skills for the first time.

"Dixon, Tranh, Wosyck," Sturgis yelled out, snagging the three men as they started up the stairs. "I want you men up on top of this blunderbus. Lay down a line of fire as we go through them. Now *move*." The commanding tone of his voice sent them leaping up one after another right to the top of the bus where Sturgis and Fireheels reached out and grabbed hold of the troopers. As soon as they were all lying flat Sturgis ordered MacLeish to take off down the slope.

The bus flew along like a wild mustang out of control, weaving from side to side, rolling along on its springy shocks. The motorcycle brigade continued on its course straight toward them. If they didn't get out of the way of the bus—so be it!

"Dixon, Tranh, cover the right side. Fireheels, you and I will handle the left flank. Now hold your fire until the last possible second, because with all this dust and darkness we just can't afford to waste ammo."

They slid around the top of the careening vehicle though luckily for the troopers there were luggage racks encircling the roof which they could use as handholds. They literally were pulling themselves around on their stomachs. They raised their arms for the approaching attackers. Fireheels, who was down to his buckskins, had detached the 7.2mm pistol from his suit before he turned it over to DeCamp. The long almost tubular shaped weapon—looking like something between pistol and rifle—was cradled in his hands as he sighted up on the unexpected guests.

"Jesus," Sturgis blurted out as he switched to infra red and saw their faces clearly for the first time through the rising dust. Robes? Bald heads? Strange blank expressions?

It was the remnants of the Army of Anetra! He had nearly wiped them out months before, after having been taken captive by the mad woman Anetra, who ran the bizarre drug-controlled cult. She had plunged to her death in flames. But clearly some units of the cult were still functional. Damned if the front cyclist didn't look like his old "friend" *Disciple B.P.!* And these looked like they wanted nothing more than to take out the bus and everyone in it. Sturgis could see as he zoomed in on their screaming mouths and wild eyes as they waved shotguns and submachine guns in their hands, increasing their speed every second. Probably high on that goddamned "white powder" hypno-stimulant.

Suddenly the bus was heading down the sharpest part of the descending road as if they were on a roller coaster. It seemed an impossibly steep angle and Sturgis prayed that MacLeish could keep the bulky vehicle under control.

"Ready, steady—" he commanded the others as he felt their tensions rising. The Anetra-bikers were now within a quarter mile and already unleashing a barrage of firepower straight toward the oncoming bus. A wasteful display of firepower. But then they clearly had plenty of firepower to play around with. The C.A.D.S. troopers didn't.

Just as the bus reached the bottom of the hill the two forces seemed to slam into one another, everybody firing up a storm. Two of the bikes went flying as the front end of the schoolbus ripped into them. But as MacLeish tried to plow right through the thick of them, the rest of the army of Anetra bikers veered to each side of the vehicle and let loose with a fusillade of slugs from their rapid-fire automatic weapons.

Bullets pinged into the front and sides of the bus by the

hundreds as those inside could only bite their lips hard and pray they didn't have a bazooka or two. Or think about tires. Their prayers didn't seem to be answered for suddenly the front right tire of the vehicle exploded. A grouping of .45s found it all at the same time. There wasn't time for MacLeish to do a lot at 40mph. And before any of them even had time to get scared, the entire bus went careening over on its side in a dust storm of screeching metal and the screams of the troopers trapped inside. The roof *didn't* blow off.

Sturgis found himself flying through the air and instinctively lifted his arms up to protect himself from the imminent crash. He hit the ground with a jarring shock and was knocked senseless for a few seconds even within the cushioning of the C.A.D.S. suit. When he came to, which he knew was almost immediately, as the bus was still grinding along the ground sideways, all hell was breaking loose. The air was filled with screams and the cracks of numerous guns going off simultaneously. Maybe trying to take the bus through the enemy force hadn't been such a good idea after all.

A grinning genie-sized biker came bearing down on him, his SMG strapped to the handlebars, blasting out a barrage of whistling white hot slugs. Sturgis felt a whole migration of the bullets rip into the suit and he knew that but for the thick armored covering he would be a dead man. The biker, seeing the suit take several direct hits, turned sharply just a yard or so from his supposed victim and started off in another direction. Sturgis saw that he spotted another figure lying prone some twenty yards off.

Which was his last mistake. For just as the bike slid past Sturgis, the C.A.D.S. commander kicked up from the ground with the servo-assisted leg. The thick titanium/plastic boot caught the slime from the army of Anetra dead center of his chest. The blow sent him flying right off the bike, his rib cage crushed in like a pile of broken pick-up-sticks. Blood spurted from the shiny pated biker's mouth and ears as he slid some twenty feet along the ground and smacked head first into a tree, cracking his skull like a rotten cantaloupe. The black cycle went over sideways digging a plowed path into the dirt as Sturgis jumped to his feet and quickly surveyed the situation.

It was worse than he dared imagine. The bus had just stopped on its side and as it came to a grinding halt, small trees went flying in broken splinters. Sturgis could see that the exit door was facing the ground. They were trapped inside, not even able to blow the charges on the roof because of the angle of the fallen vehicle. And the drugged up, robed Anetra bikers were closing in, forming a circle around the bus and opening up with heavy slugs from every side.

Even with their suits and armor and everything, the troopers inside were sitting ducks. Already there were flames; once the fuel tanks went up—it was all over. The Model 2 C.A.D.S. suits could take fire for a short period of time, but after twenty, at most thirty seconds, they could ignite internally. He had seen the fire tests, had seen the outer layers start to melt, shrivel, then the wiring inside explode, ripping the wearer to shreds before he could burn to death. Small comfort. The image of Robin's face turned to charcoal black suddenly filled his vision and it fueled him with a mad fury not to let them die. Not like this.

He ripped his right arm up and sighted up the nearest biker, letting loose with a stream of his recently acquired junk store special's .22 slugs!

The man went down hard, the whole front of his stomach and face mowed open as if he'd been caught in the propeller of a ship. Suddenly Sturgis spotted Fireheels, his deep tan face bleeding from a nasty gash that ran from ear to chin. The Indian trooper saw him at the same instant and came flying over several small boulders to his side.

"We gotta do something, Skip, and fast," Fireheels said as he ducked down as a biker tried to get a bead on him. Sturgis raised his arm and let loose with a burst. They missed. And he knew he was dangerously low on ammo already. They'd hadn't gotten a lot of the useable stuff at the town. Sturgis glanced around for Dixon and Wosyck, who had been up on top of the bus too but he couldn't find a trace of either.

"We need something big, something to really rip into the bastards," Fireheels said with a snarl as he raised his pistol and let off with a few single shots of his own. A cult-biker some thirty yards away took a hit in the shoulder but just grunted and didn't go down. That was the problem with small caliber slugs; they were meant for deer and rabbits, not for 250 lb. plus fanatical cultist biker slime. The druggies could take such lead in their teeth and spit them out again.

Whump!

Sturgis saw the whole bus going up in flame and for a second he could hardly tell if it was real or another nightmarish vision. His eyes cleared and he saw that it was real. He could hear the screams and shouts of those trapped inside over his helmet radio and ordered the thing to shut off, as he couldn't stand to hear it.

Fire. Suddenly he had a flash of brilliance that made his heart beat faster.

"The fallen bikes, Fireheels," Sturgis shouted as both men ducked down from firing back from all the bikers trying to take out the annoying metal fleas who were daring to stop their fun. "We can make mobile Molotov cocktails out of them and send them right into them. I saw it once at an Evil Kneivel show."

"There's another one on the other side of those rocks," the Apache commando warned, firing another slug.

"Okay, Fireheels, you got thirty seconds to get that bike to your left upright—stick a rag in the fuel tank, light the thing after you head it into them. You got me? I'll come around from this side, you take the right flank."

"All right, Skip," Fireheels said with a hard look at his commander. They both knew how dangerous the plan was, not just for themselves but for the troopers trapped inside the bus. If the burning bikes ran into the already burning vehicle, it was all over for everybody.

"Move man, *move*," Sturgis screamed out as they both jumped to their feet and rushed off in opposite directions. The instant they made their moves, slugs whizzed everywhere, slamming off rocks, ripping into trees. Sturgis felt pings off his helmet, but he wasn't worrying about suit-damage right now. He shoved aside a crushed cultist, lifted the bike he wanted to ride up in a flash with the servo assist arms, and mounted. The weight of the suit made the 1200cc Harley drop down a good eight inches as the shocks went to their limits and the tires themselves bunched up like balloons. It started with a cough.

He ripped the cap off the tank and stuffed a rag from the dead man's shirt into the tank. Then Sturgis floored the bike to wheel back about twenty yards, so he could get some speed up.

He had just made his turn, aiming back toward the circling bikers who were clearly having fun as they let out screams of bloody merriment, when he saw Fireheels coming in through the black smoke from the far side. The C.A.D.S. trooper was screaming a blood curdling Indian war cry to catch their attention, and he succeeded. They broke from their circling of the bus to ice the challenger. The bikers spread out into a line about twenty yards long to concentrate their firepower on the mad Indian.

As Fireheels floored his bike and came charging toward the bikers of Anetra from about two hundred feet off, Sturgis floored *his* machine and flew toward the bikers from their back. He waited, waited until he was within twenty yards and then used his butane lighter, lit the gas wetted rag that disappeared up inside the fuel tank. The thing started burning down fast and Sturgis had to use all his willpower to keep the bike aimed at the firing bikers until the last second.

Just as he dove off, he saw Fireheels take a hit from the far side and go flying off himself. But his bike *and* Sturgis's kept going straight ahead. Then all hell broke loose as the riderless bikes tore into the line of firing killers. They went up in a ball of orange a second after one another. The other bikes — and bikers — caught as well, as the wall of fire spread out in all directions a good thirty feet, even brushing momentarily against the bottom of the bus. Sturgis closed his eyes as a wall of fire swept over him, moving about three feet above the ground. He heard the screams of the bikers through the roaring flames and exploding engines and fuel tanks.

When he rose up seconds later Sturgis could see the desperate move had succeeded. The screaming cult-bikers were rolling around the ground engulfed in fire; those who weren't already dead. The bikes burned in flaming pieces all around the orange-lit charnel ground. He rushed over to Fireheels who was lying on the dirt.

"Fireheels, you — there man? You alive?" Sturgis screamed through his opened visor as the flames stopped just yards away. The Apache opened his eyes, hiding the pain that was ripping through him from the slug that had grazed along his shoulder.

"Yeah, I'm still kicking, man," the Indian trooper managed to half grin, half grimace as he let Sturgis help him to his feet. "But son of a bitch! Bullets *hurt!*"

Chapter Twelve

Sturgis and Fireheels ripped a pair of non-burning robes off the cultists who had died under the bus-wheels and used them to smother most of the fires.

"You all right in there?" Sturgis screamed as he rushed to the side gun-slits of the bus. He shouted in from the front through the narrow opening where one of the steel panels on the hood of the bus had come free and lodged into place covering the windshield so they were totally sealed in.

"Yeah, just fine," Rossiter's voice bellowed back over the comm. "Only I'm upside down with my right foot up my ass and somebody's helmet in my eye. Just fine." The rest couldn't be too mangled up if Rossiter was still ticking.

"All right, *push* like mothers, *everybody* in there!" Sturgis yelled out as he and Fireheels got a grip on the four hundred pound metal plate covering the windshield. "We're going to pull this sucker off here." They gripped and strained, pulling with all their might and with the effort aided from inside, slowly the piece of steel plate came free. The rescuers dragged it back a few feet and then returned to the windshield where they helped the first of the troopers out. They had to slide through on hands and knees because of the 90 degree lean of the bus and some had trouble, forcing Sturgis to reach out and literally drag them through. "Careful of the hot metal! Good thing most of the flames stayed outside!"

Within five minutes they were all out. Everyone was

shook up but just one of the troopers, Sarington, was really hurt, with a broken arm. He had somehow twisted his suit arm around and it had snapped under the falling weight of the entire C.A.D.S. suit above it. Sheila, though woozy, began to examine the break.

"What do you think, Skip?" Dixon asked as they all stood in front of the bus looking over at it, like it was some sort of downed African animal.

"Think we gotta get this thing up and moving. Come on, everybody with functioning servo mech's," Sturgis commanded. "We're going to lift her." Ten of them got along the roof edge and reached their gloved hands underneath gripping anything they could find.

"One, two, three—" They all lifted as one, and the entire bus rose up from its side and headed upright. They got it to chest level and raised their arms, then with a heave pushed together as the bus slammed over onto its wheels, sagging down on the front right side where the tire had been shot up.

"Well?" Sturgis asked as Rossiter and Dixon bent down and looked around the wounded rubber. "Can it be fixed?"

"It's pretty messed up," Rossiter muttered, slapping at the gaping hole in the edge of the wheel. "Several slugs must have ripped into her at once, you see—the whole side's blown out."

"Couldn't we take some pieces of those tires from the bikes for patches? There's a few not burning," Dixon said with a sly smile. They looked over toward the field some thirty yards off where the bikes lay sideways burning, charred smoking riders lying by their sides, arms stretched upward frozen in agony forever. Some of the bikes hadn't fully caught fire and lay there shining in the midst of the charred bodies and blackened motorcycles. "We melt 'em right down onto the hole," Billy continued, "you know, like taffy or something?" Dixon had a weird smile on his face. Sturgis looked skeptically at Rossiter as if wanting a second read on the idea. Dixon, he just didn't fully trust, the platinum-locked southern man had some *mad* ideas.

"Ordinarily I'd say, forget it," Rossiter said. "But we do have one of the small laser torches and the temperature it can generate is probably enough to do some serious rubber melting. We'll give it a try. That there tire's useless in its present state."

"Where's Wosyck?" DeCamp suddenly piped up. She had splinted the injured trooper's arm. Sturgis noted her suit was covered with dirt and dust — even dents — from the spill.

They all looked around and realized they hadn't accounted for everyone.

"Last time I saw him he was flying off in that general direction," Tranh said, remembering seeing the big Pole moving like a meteor as he went off the other way.

Sturgis and some of the others headed off that way, as Rossiter and Dixon grabbed a few of the bike tires and rolled them back to the leaning battered bus. They made a makeshift jack from some spare parts within minutes and got working on the repair-project. Soon the smell of burning rubber filled the air with a sickening acridity.

Sturgis and three others headed out looking for Wosyck, scouted around the area to the far side of the heavy line of bushes, looking through dense undergrowth and low trees beyond.

"Here, commander," a voice suddenly came over his helmet radio. It was Tranh who had found something. "Over here.".

One of the suited figures some thirty feet off amidst some trees was waving his arm and Sturgis made his way over with sinking heart. Tranh's voice sounded funny. And he saw why as soon as he came up alongside him. Wosyck had bought it, and nasty too. Somehow, an armor-piercing bullet from the bikers had found its way through the back of the neck armoring, between the spot where helmet and suit meet. One of the few Achilles heels of vulnerability on the C.A.D.S. armor.

Wosyck had, perhaps in a death-spasm, leapt upward.

He was suspended several feet off the ground, his boots dangling down, still moving slightly, as the suit was shorted out by the damaged circuits.

Sturgis reached out and pulled him off with a wretched gurgling sound coming from the opened wound. Once Wosyck was down, Sturgis turned him over. Inside the helmet it was only red as the bullet had been thick and gnarled and had pretty much blew apart after it hit, taking out everything between head and shoulders. Only the suit itself was holding the two parts of him together. One eye dangled on an optic nerve.

"Put him down over here," Sturgis said softly. They carried him and lay the Polish fighter down in front of the beautiful rising fir tree. "He loved trees. Let this be his natural tombstone."

"At least he went fast," Tranh said.

"Too fast," Sturgis replied, knowing that Wosyck had been the kind of man who would have wanted to see death coming at him so he could give it a good smack in the face before it took him into the gray land. "We'll bury him in the suit. We're not going to be able to use this one."

A crew of four raw troopers dug a shallow but service-able hole about eight feet long, four wide and two deep. Wild animals, vultures wouldn't be able to get into the suit. Worms and bacteria, that was another story. Eventually, with their visors up, they gathered at the gravesite as the rubbery smell of the work back at the bus increased, adding to the sickening sensation in their stomachs. The black smoke rose up into the increasingly clouded heavens, into the thick cumuli with purple veins and dark around the edges as if they were packing poison. Too bad there were no funeral flowers to hide the scent.

"Lord, take this Polish-American hero up into your soft clouds," Sturgis intoned. The C.A.D.S. unit except for Dixon and Rossiter who knew their work came first, stood silently, their eyes wet, and not from the smoke. "God knows its *not* soft inside these suits. He was a brave and a good man and helped accomplish our sacred mission. He

94

deserves mercy."

"Amen" DeCamp said with a soft tone. Robin looked stunned, just staring down at the earth-covered hole as if she was staring into the void. Sturgis walked over to her.

"You all right, baby?" he said putting his huge suit arm around the back of her C.A.D.S. unit.

"Yeah, sure—I'm all right," Robin smiled through the open visor. He knew she was lying again. She was white as a sheet.

"Over here," Sturgis suddenly heard over his helmet speaker. It was Rossiter's voice. "We got this damn piece of tire back together though it don't look like it used to. Awaiting further orders."

"I'm coming," Sturgis replied and walked quickly over to the bus, leaving Robin standing looking up at the dropping green clouds as the C.A.D.S. men dispersed from the gravesite.

"Jeez, what the hell do you call this?" the C.A.D.S. commander asked, as he saw the patchwork mess that they had melted into the opening of the blasted tire. It looked like a candle had melted down on it, only this was black and made of rubber. The new coating bulged out from the surface of the tire and sort of coagulated all around the sealed sides of the holes.

"Well, she's filled up and holding," Dixon laughed. "Even if it looks like a whore's fanny, I'm telling you it'll hold."

"He's right," Rossiter added as he kicked the thing hard with his boot. It bounced right back. "At the temps we melted the bike tires and the bus wheel together, it literally forms a molecular bond. That stuff ain't coming out, even if it don't win any beauty contests. We're damned lucky we bought that old pump too!"

"MacLeish," Sturgis bellowed, "get in this schoolbus and make sure everything is still running. We're getting out of here before those clouds fall any lower."

"You don't have to bloody well yell," MacLeish said as he turned his cyclops C.A.D.S. helmet eye toward Sturgis.

He got into the seat and banged his suit bottom up and down a few times to make sure the tire wasn't going to just pop like a weak balloon below him. Then he started the engine and drove ahead several hundred feet, testing the seal. Then backed up again.

"Let's move it," the Brit yelled through the now unplated windshield, no glass either. Just open to the world, to enjoy the air, and the bullets of any further attackers. But they didn't have time to do any more repairs. They'd just have to shoot first.

Sturgis had them gather any surviving weapons and ammo from the dead bikers. Which wasn't a lot. The fire had ignited most of the slugs and belts of bullets. But they managed to snag two small Uzi SMG's and a Browning 12 gauge shotgun that were useable. Each had several full loads worth of shells. But it was still all a child's play armory. They needed heavy duty replacements for their big suit-guns, and for the electromagnetic E-balls which could take out a whole tank in a single strike. They would need heavy ammo before Sturgis would feel even remotely comfortable. It was still 700 miles to White Sands Base.

He got Robin and DeCamp in the very back so they'd be a little more protected if the shooting started up. And then grabbed the pole behind MacLeish as the man closed the bus doors which grudgingly obeyed and the bus started forward. They drove through sparsely vegetated areas and then right out onto the grassy prairie.

The big lumpy wheels kicked up sand behind them making a dust cloud which rose for miles as the clouds dropped lower, growing greener and darker by the minute.

"Move it, man," Sturgis ordered MacLeish once he saw that the guy was driving okay and that the patched wheel was actually going to hold. "Taker her up to fifty, then try sixty, I want to get out of this area."

"Fine by me, Skip," MacLeish said, flooring the pedal.

Chapter Thirteen

Four hundred miles to the south-east, black oil pumped up from the earth like lava. Five Naqui Indians stood around the pit, dropping metal buckets into the flow and dragging them out, then emptying them into an angled pipe which twisted off toward a long, low aluminum shed.

"It's good, a good flow," Natassak commented in his deep voice, feathers and animal teeth hanging from his neck in thick abundance. He stepped down and tasted the flow with his finger, licking it twice. His dowser stick and "magic" shovel had worked miracles again. "This oil is very thin, easy to refine," he went on, smiling with good cheer at the other four. They relaxed, as the head oil man approved their strike. It meant more prestige for all of them in the tribe. More oil for them all to run their generators and power plants, and to earn extra to support their village. There would be enough excess now to sell again to passersby traders, for furs, weapons, countless items normally unavailable in the post-nuke world.

"You have done well, all of you. You are of pure spirit. Come to my council chamber tonight, we will talk of compensation." Natassak walked lumberingly away like the big bear of a man that he was, as the other four, stripped down to their deerskin loincloths, kept at their digging work, moving even faster now, widening the dip-pool, now that the site was "officially" approved.

Their coppery bodies were quickly smeared with the blackish liquid. It wasn't of course gasoline, but several textures thinner than most out-of-the-earth crude oil. It was an excellent strike. Natassak hadn't told them as he didn't want them to get greedy but they had noticed: His tastebuds told him it was perhaps the purest strike in the last few years. It would power their station wagon engines like days of old.

As he walked from the oil dig at one side of their mountain village, he heard a sudden chugging of what sounded like many engines. He stopped in his tracks and looked to the east and even his battle-hardened heart grew faint as he saw the mini armada that was coming over the rise like ghosts out of a fog.

Killboys, he knew instantly. They were the only ones with such forces. And they had made smaller strikes before, trying to steal oil, trying to take over the Indians' reservation. This time they'd brought a whole army to do it.

But then his people weren't exactly unprotected, Natassak thought, with a sudden bolt of strength, of his warriors' fearlessness. He walked quickly back toward the pueblo mountain a hundreds yards off as others of the tribe came rushing out from their cliff dwellings, around which their oil refineries and ground digs were all arranged. They had barbed wire barricades that ringed the entire mile-long by quarter-mile-wide encampment. In the center of it, the Great Mesa, a sandstone mountain, rising up a thousand feet above the prairie like a pillar erected to praise the wind-gods.

Natassak moved fast as he saw an advance squad detach itself from the enemy armada which sat, engines purring at the top of a long sandy rise about a thousand yards from the reservation and the cliffs. The army was composed of cars, trucks, tractors, bulldozers . . . The leader of the Killboys, the so-called *Macro-Kill,* must have stumbled on an entire pre-war trucking lot and armed the things. There had to be at least three hundred of the trucks, not to mention assorted cars, motorcycles and motor-driven contraptions that defied description.

As the first assault detachment of perhaps thirty vehicles came tearing forward right at the outermost barbed wire perimeter, Natassak screamed out loud toward the cliffs, though he knew he was too far for anyone to hear. He had yelled, "Set off the charge, ignite the oil."

As if someone else was having the same thought, there was a sudden sound of rushing liquid, as oil came bubbling up right in front of the attacking vehicles. The defensive system of oil to be fired was hidden in small concrete troughs.

Suddenly just as they rode over it, igniters sparked all along the petroleum aqueduct. The stream of high-test went up like a bomb, and the attackers were suddenly engulfed in flames, those who couldn't stop in time to pull back. The entire Indian reservation was ringed by a sheet of fire, some twenty to thirty feet thick as the fuel bubbled out of pipes they had wisely dug into the ground months before.

The many-vehicle army stopped and pulled up along the flame wall, surrounded them, staying back as the flames rose in orange sheets. Half the advance squad was burnt to a crisp. But the generals of the Killboys set themselves in for the long haul. They left the trucks and set up tents. And even Natassak could see the truth from his vantage point. Though they'd kept back the enemy's initial thrust, they were under siege. They could keep the white bastards out for now. But they couldn't move an inch from this burning hellhole, even to get water. He prayed they'd stockpiled enough. He could feel the presence of Macro-Kill out there guiding his forces. They'd met before. Natassak had almost killed the "n'kici"—vulture's anus. He should have finished the job.

There was no question of surrender. For Natassak knew above anything that if Macro-Kill got into the camp and overran them, he'd kill every man, woman and child. He wouldn't let a stone lie unharmed. Macro-Kill wanted their oil, their refinery too. He'd do anything to get it!

Chapter Fourteen

The C.A.D.S. troopers' weird bus came to another set of low hills and then beyond that Sturgis saw a nuclear bomb-crater's wall poking up. It was a doozy of a blast site.

"Must have been twenty or thirty megs," Sturgis estimated staring at it through the open windshield.

"Son of a bitch," MacLeish whistled as he instinctively veered away from the manmade crater. For it was ugly, black and dark, covered with a coating of thick ash. Even from miles off they could sense the darkness, the death, in the remains of the radioactive impact crater.

"What the hell would be out here," Sturgis wondered out loud, "that would get such a load of hot plutonium dropped on it?"

"Las Vegas," Fireheels answered as he stood on the steps leading down to the closed door. "I know this area. Went on hunting parties throughout this territory with some cousins years ago. Las Vegas was just the other side of these hills. Right where the crater is."

"Maybe the Ruskies wanted to put an end to all the decadent capitalistic gambling," Dixon commented as he spotted the crater from his pole spot about eight feet back.

"We've got to go by it, sir," MacLeish said as he scanned back and forth ahead. "The mountains get too high on each side of that pass for the bus to navigate. We'd stall out halfway up one of those slopes." Sturgis made a quick check with the binocs and agreed.

"All right, go forward, but as soon as there's any leeway to the side, head for it. We're going through a high rad-field," Sturgis warned the rest of them. "So close all visors and other opened parts. Fireheels, I think you'll be okay in the bus — but — "

"Don't waste the words, commander," Fireheels said, "I've been exposed to so much radiation out here over the last years that I should be dead. Indians are strong." He pounded himself hard on the chest. And then mock-coughed, sucking in air hard.

The bus hit thirty and they moved quickly through the pass that rose up to about a thousand feet. Suddenly, with the sun beaming brilliantly down lighting up the whole scene, sat Las Vegas. Half of it anyway, for the other half was now the crater. It was like the biggest advertising billboard that had ever been erected, advertising the city with all its glitter and fast lane life. And to Sturgis's amazement it appeared that there were still buildings, casinos with signs out front. Buildings in good shape; that were open for business.

"Macro view," he ordered the suit-computer and it zoomed his view the mile and a half to the phantasm-city, though more slowly than it should — the charges were starting to ooze down slowly again.

People were walking around and there were casinos open, men in 10-gallon hats, and women, going in and out of them. Everything wasn't as neat as it looked from far off. Indeed it all was in a state of severe disrepair.

"Head toward that — whatever it is," Sturgis said to the Brit. "If the inhabitants can take the rads then we should be okay." The bus came down out of the bumpy slope and hit a sturdy gravel road. Apparently the Las Vegans liked to treat their potential customers with the royal treatment. For after the bumpy prairieland, even a two bit, two lane hard packed gravel road was like a superhighway to these battered high-tech commandos.

Chapter Fifteen

They drove into the bizarre gambling city which stretched off for blocks in every direction, much larger than just about anything Sturgis had seen on his travels through the post-nuke world. And it was all built right up next to the crater, as if it were just some errant bump on the face of the world, and not a quarter mile high mound of oozing radioactive hell.

The makers and shakers of what had been Las Vegas, gambling capital of the world, were still pulling in the suckers as if nothing had ever happened. Everything was in ruins, or half ruins, but still semi-maintained somehow.

Some of the insane allure of the old high-roller days was evident. Neon, billboards, even a few flashing lights here and there, though most everything was half hanging off its hinges and the lights sputtering. Still, Sturgis was impressed. And mystified.

They were stopped by a roadblock as they reached the outer block. There were two armed guards, and a steel pole that could be raised, laid across the road. One of the men was wearing a turban with large fake red jewel in the center. He walked up to the front of the bus as it came to a halt.

"Well, just what do we got here?" the blue-sequined jacketed man asked with a friendly enough smile. His Uzi was slung around his shoulder hanging down the back so he clearly wasn't alarmed by the bus or its suited occupants who he could dimly see holding onto their poles all the way to the back of the bus.

"A bus," Sturgis answered inanely, realizing how dumb an answer it was as it left his lips. "Well, a slightly amended bus."

"Can damned well see that," the man laughed. "And from the looks of it you had some pretty unfriendly encounters. This thing looks shot up to within an inch of its life. But hell, I ain't criticizing no one's looks," the guard went on, "seeing as how we Vegans get just about the strangest assortment of men and ve-hicles you ever laid eyes on. Welcome to Nuke Vegas, ladies and gentle-men — if there be any ladies in that there bullet-riddled piece of tin. You all here for gambling, sex, drugs . . . ?"

"Well, huh," Sturgis said, not sure what he should answer to that one, as it was, to say the least, a loaded question. "Just in the neighborhood, thought we'd drop in —"

The guard winked hard. Apparently he had run into these types before who didn't want to admit their de-bauched fantasies.

"Well, whatever you want, friends, you'll find it here in Nuke Vegas pal. You and all of your friends are welcome. We got every drink, drug and kind of sexual experimenta-tion known to man, not to mention casinos and tables galore. Whatever needs you got — you come to the right place to fill it. Now, if you'll just park your sieve of a bus over here to the right in this parking lot . . . We got too many customers roaming the streets in inebriated states to have a big metal monster like this rambling through. If you want it near you — once you check into a hotel they'll have the valet come bring it around for you."

He motioned for the other guard to lift the pole which he did by hand, cranking a manual handle which lifted the barrier on a long steel cable.

"Move her on in," Sturgis chuckled to MacLeish, "you heard the man." The Brit slowly eased the pedal down and turned the bus around in an almost ninety degree angle over to a large parking lot. Rubble strewn field was more like it. There were already scores of vehicles parked around the thing, as many as five hundred spread out over the acres. And they were all as bizarre looking, beat-up, and makeshift in their own way as the bus itself. Toyota-pontimobiles; Cadisuzufords; the works in improvised transportation.

"All right, everybody, last stop for the tour bus," MacLeish announced over his helmet mike. "Women, gambling, home cooked food. You heard the man. Now remember, the bus returns home promptly at five, so be here. And don't lose your balls."

The crew laughed as they disembarked with eager expectant eyes. Sturgis was undecided at first about whether they should keep the suits on, or store them in the bus. But since this could easily be a violent, shoot-em-up kind of town, and the men weren't armed other than in the suits, he decided that even with the hassles, they should remain on. Besides, it might all be an hallucination.

The C.A.D.S. team walked out of the parking lot and back to the main gravel road that led through the center of the gambling resort. They walked a little unsteadily at first, having been shaken and bounced around the bus so much, and couldn't help but cast constant nervous glances up at the crater wall which loomed just a half-mile away. But once they got their sea legs they all brightened considerably. The city was a miracle of madness. From everywhere, sequin-jacketed hawkers were shouting out their particular brand of human addiction.

"Gambling here, we got roulette, poker, blackjack . . ." one man yelled. He was dressed up as a magician with long black cape and magic wand which he waved around with dramatic gestures. He ended each one by pointing inside the half collapsed building behind him called the Magic Garden. A large billboard showed lots of happy young red-cheeked people throwing money in the air.

"Bingo here," another barker shouted out on the other side of the street as they passed by, "and *working* slot machines. We got lots of winners. Come on in, you tin men," he shouted good naturedly. Sturgis and his crew walked along slowly looking around like gawking tourists in from the sticks. "We got a free first drink, and even oil lubes for robots." He cracked up with those words, thinking it was just about the funniest thing that had ever been said, evidently.

"Girls here, all kinds of *girls,"* the next barker announced as the troopers looked at the immense sequined billboard of a nude woman doing unusual contortionistic things with her body. Sturgis blushed inside his suit as he knew the women were seeing all this. "You boys look like you need a girl," said the barker. He looked like nothing more than a pimp of old days, with flashy purple suit and greased back hair. He addressed them as they slowed down slightly, trying to see inside the half-opened doors that led into a two story cinderblock affair. From small windows here and there, they could see women parading their wares, wearing veils, feathers or nothing at all.

"I bet you ain't had any for a long, long time," the man laughed lewdly. "Why, being inside those suits of yours don't look like too much fun. Come on, lighten up, robot men. We got women to make your diodes pop. If you can pay the freight."

"Thanks," Sturgis said, reaching out and pulling back two of the younger recruits as they started walking right into the place. "We'll check it all out later, promise you. But let me ask you, in this town of pleasures — is there a hotel, a place we can rest up, get a shower, even some decent chow?"

"You want the Le Crater Hotel, it's at the far end of town, about a half mile, right down the main road here. The rest of the hotels are for scuzz, they got bedbugs and lizards crawling out of every nook and cranny. But the Crater, that's the class joint, if you can pay." He eyed them significantly at the last words, wondering if the tin men actually had any cash or were just trying to look tough. "And tell 'em Julio sent you, they'll give you a twenty percent discount on your meal and bed. But now, I helped you all out — come on back later. We got a strip show tonight that will blow your brains out. You hear me?"

"Absolutely," Sturgis answered. "As soon as we're all freshened up, this is the first place we'll head back to." He turned and started forward again with the rest of the troopers falling into ranks somewhat unhappily behind him. Their eyes kept rising to the upper windows where women were waving and jumping around like they just couldn't stand that such a fine brigade of hunky men was leaving without giving them a chance.

Sturgis who had been wondering just why they weren't getting more of a rise, or fear, out of the barkers and hawkers, since they were wearing their suits, soon saw the reason. Everyone they passed looked mucho-bizarre. There were mountain men with long grease-coated beards and bearskin coats that came down to their ankles. And cowboy-types with ten gallon hats and six guns; debonair types with full suits and ruffles, silk neckerchiefs poking out of their chest pockets. Everyone they passed had their own trip going, from scuzzball to high fashion, even a few with crude metal armor themselves, slammed together with rivets and chains all around them.

These gave a friendly hello to the C.A.D.S. troopers, apparently believing them to be some long lost cousins or relatives of their own armored-clan back in the hills. The troopers were just another mass of madness on the streets of Nuke Vegas. It left them feeling a little chagrined.

"I *like* this town," Billy Dixon said, coming up next to Sturgis as the rest followed behind. "But that crater, it's giving me the creeps." They looked up at the towering bomb monument which seemed ever larger as they headed deeper into the gambling metropolis.

"Yeah, I hear you," Sturgis said. It belied the general aura of fun and festivity that everyone was trying to put out amidst the collapsing debris of their clubs and casinos. "It's soot-dark, has an almost palpable presence, a personality of something that doesn't like living things."

"I feel the ghosts in there," Tranh said almost in a whisper as he didn't like to talk about the denizens of the netherworld. "Moving, crying out in pain."

"Rad readout," Sturgis commanded his suit and the digital readout scrolled across the inside of the visor.

"100 PICA-RADS PER MINUTE. AIR DANGEROUS IF PLUTONIUM PARTICLES ARE BLOWN BY WESTWINDS. URGE CAUTION IN BREATHING AND DRINKING WATER," the grid advised him.

"Great," Sturgis spat out. He knew it would be almost impossible to prevent the team from wanting to sample some of the town's wares. They'd just have to check everything before taking it into their systems.

"Careful with the food and water," Sturgis told them over intercom link-up. "Check your geiger systems on everything—and I mean it."

"Even the *girls?*" Dixon shot back with a lascivious tone in his voice. "Are they high rad too, Skip?"

"Well, you'll bloody well find out, won't you?" MacLeish bellowed. "And probably end up with your unquenchable organ shining like a glow worm in the night."

They walked for another five minutes, the men and both women glad to have a chance to exercise their cramped arms and legs. If they could get out of the suits for a breather, things would almost be okay.

The hotel, Le Crater, that the barker had mentioned, came into view. It was clear that it was a better class of establishment than most of what they were passing. For one thing, it stood ten stories high, and aside from some broken windows here and there looked quite structurally sound, other than blackened bricks on the side facing the crater.

"How all this survived at all is beyond me," Tranh commented as they stopped in front of the entrance of the place. "The atomic blast should have taken out everything and reduced it to charcoal."

"Nukes are funny things," Sturgis replied. "A hill here,

or a windshift there, can make a big difference in just what gets destroyed and what doesn't." He started up the alabaster stairs that were only slightly cracked. The rest of them followed behind him, everyone looking this way and that as if trying to take in all the colors, decay, and action at one time.

"Ah, welcome to Le Crater," a man dressed in a pink tux and hat addressed them as they walked past two armed guards into the main lobby of the place. "We are so happy that you have chosen *our* establishment to stay." He looked them up and down, seemed to sniff his nostrils a few times as if smelling the air for money and then looked them up and down again, unsure of their exact social status.

'You really have full hotel facilities here?" Sturgis asked as he glanced around at the shining and for post-nuke America, relatively clean and undamaged decor. There were huge purple curtains hanging down walls, chandeliers dropping down from the immense curved ceiling. And ahead of them two sets of sweeping marble staircases that looked like something from "Gone With the Wind" that Clark Gable and Vivien Leigh should walk down at any minute.

"We have *everything* at Le Grand Crater," the man said, slightly miffed at the question. "Private rooms, baths, meals in the grand dining room—or served privately in your boudoir for those little tête-à-têtes. Your—uh—entire entourage will be staying with us?" the man asked as he saw the other grease coated C.A.D.S. suited troopers continuing to gawk around as they stayed close together, a little nervous about the riches and the swank attitude.

"Yes, if it's possible—we don't have reservations," Sturgis said, making a sudden decision to let them all rest up for a night. After what they'd been through in the last week, they damned well deserve a break, or they might break themselves. For he knew he was pushing everyone to their limits.

"Possible, possible," the greeter laughed. "All things are

possible—providing there is the capital to back it up. You do—have money I presume?"

"Of course," Sturgis replied a little frostily. He motioned to Tranh and MacLeish who were standing on each side of him. They deployed their gold contents from the emergency packs on the sides of their suits, as he had spent his back in the junk-town. They handed him five gold coins each. Sturgis reached out and dropped four of them into the man's hands, stopping when the man smiled.

"I trust this will do for any initial payment," Sturgis said as the man suddenly lost his airs and bit hard into each one of the coins checking their authenticity. No one seemed to trust anyone these days, Sturgis noted with bemusement.

"Yes, yes, this will do just fine. Fortunately, we just had a cancellation for a group of drug businessmen, a dozen of them—who met with an unfortunate accident—an ambush—on the road, so there are some rooms empty. If a few of your crew can double up in the suites, I think we can accommodate all of you. Willson, Feders!" He shouted out in a snarl, dropping the obsequious image completely for a second. "Show these fine metal-folks up to the third floor, suites 13 to 22. You have no baggage?" he asked, looking around as if half expecting little armored suitcases.

"No, just what we carry," Sturgis said. "We're our own baggage."

"And him too, he's part of your entourage?" the greeter asked, suddenly noticing Fireheels, without suit, standing at the edge of the steel plated crowd. He didn't seem to like the idea of an Indian being among them, putting on a heavy, disapproving scowl.

"Damned right," Sturgis replied irritated. "And if *that's* a problem, you can just hand me back those shiny coins and we'll be on our way!"

"Oh, *no* problem, *no* problem," the man replied, not able to bear the thought of parting with the coins now that they were firmly ensconced in his pocket. Again the smile. "Now, I'm Tip, Tip Anderson, the concierge of this grand luxury hotel. Anything you need at all, don't hesitate to ask me. Especially those *private*—needs." He winked so hard Sturgis thought the man's eyeball might fall from his head. "I'm here to help you be happy, men. Now, if you'll just follow my boys here, they'll escort you to your rooms. I do hope you have a pleasant stay." Evidently the guy thought they were all men. Sturgis didn't enlighten him about Robin or Sheila.

Then they were being led up the sweeping marble stairs, their heads spinning at the sheer accumulation of wealth and rich fabric and gold trimmed ropes that hung down from everywhere. It seemed more a place fit for a king, than for a bunch of oil-dripping C.A.D.S. troopers with the sand and dirt of half the prairie coating their battered metal bodies.

Chapter Sixteen

The hotel really was beautiful if you didn't look too closely, Sturgis noticed as he led his men up the marble stairs preceded by the two room stewards. If you didn't look at the cracks in the walls, or the fact that some of the stairs had pieces of wood hammered into place where the original stonework had collapsed, or that the chandeliers were cracked, replaced in parts with pieces of glassware glued together. Still, it was a hell of a lot better than the inside of the weird bus they had been riding in for days.

"This way, gentlemen," the head bellboy said. Like everyone in town, he was wearing his own bizarre outfit. His costume was a yellow vest and greenish pants, with sneakers and a little fake bellboy cap cut out of satin which looked more like some mutant yamulka than the hotel caps of old, the caps that Sturgis had seen before the war. But they were *trying* and that was what mattered. The place wasn't packed to the gills but they passed a few, mostly older men well dressed in western leisure suits. They hardly blinked an eye as the C.A.D.S. troopers walked by on the stairs. Everyone, it would appear, had already seen everything. In the land of the jaded, even giant semi-robots were commonplace.

"This way, sir," the bellhop said when they climbed to the third floor. "You and your men have this whole section of the floor," the hop said, sweeping his hand down the corridor which had doors on each side extending down about a hundred feet. "I'm afraid some of the help is out today, we had some — accidents — the other day." He didn't elaborate but Sturgis had already noticed what looked like mopped up blood stains here and there on the lime green carpeting. Something nasty had gone down. "So, I can't show every man his room and fluff their pillows — but I'll open all the doors and if you need anything, just ring. There's a buzzer in all the suites."

He turned the key to the very first door and Sturgis looked in. It was big, and well appointed with wide antique bed and chairs and rugs set around the place. Better than any Howard Johnson he had set foot in.

"This will do just fine. I'll take this one," he said, glancing around at his men challenging them slightly. "Robin, why don't you head on in and freshen up, I'll join you in a minute." She walked straight into the room and seemed to relax just a tad. The hop looked confused, just now realizing that there was a female inside one of the suits. But he didn't say a word. He continued down the corridor opening each door as the troopers filed in to their various suites.

Sturgis stayed with him, to the end of the floor, making sure everyone got settled in okay, DeCamp had her own room, and she looked a little forlornly at Sturgis as if she wished he would be joining her instead of Robin. But though he had slept with her, and though he liked Sheila DeCamp, Robin *was* his wife, after all. Even if there were problems, to say the least, between them. "Come by later, if you want," Sheila whispered, and shut her door.

"This is all just fine," Sturgis said when they were all inside and he walked back down the aisle with the hop. "Now, if we could just get some water, *hot* water so we can sponge bathe ourselves, everything will be — "

"Oh, you don't need sponges, sir," the hop said with real pride. "Le Grand Crater has actual *running* water, we pipe it in from a nearby spring, using gas powered generators. You pay a lot here — but you get your money's worth. People come from miles just to take a bath, if I dare be so blunt about it. Save up half a year for the luxury of spending a single night here."

"Did you hear that," Sturgis said exuberantly, hitting the door to his suite with a few light knocks, "they've got baths here, baby—with real water." A low female sound came from inside and Sturgis grinned at the hop. "She's overcome with emotion at the prospect. You mean— there's enough for all of us—at once?"

"That's correct, sir," the bellboy went on. "That's one of the main points of Le Grand Crater. That, and our world-class restaurant. I'll tell the service people to throw some more hot stuff in the pipes. And will you and the little lady be desiring anything special tonight? Drinks, drugs, whips . . . Le Grand Crater is fully stocked for all pleasures of the flesh."

"I think a bath will be enough for the moment," Sturgis replied with a lopsided grin. "Here, for you," Sturgis took another of the gold coins that he'd grabbed from Tranh. "Don't spend it all in one place."

"Jeez, thanks mister," the bellboy replied, his eyes widening to impossible proportions. It didn't hurt to reward friends. It might come back to help him someday. "I'll get the water crew pumping like whores. Just wait five minutes and then dive in. And dinner's served from six to nine. Restaurant is down in the main lobby where you come in, just to the right, you can't miss it." With that the youth was off tossing the coin high in the air as he ran down the stairs, as if daring the fates to try to steal it away from him.

Sturgis knocked again just in case Robin was doing some mysterious female thing that a man shouldn't see. But her subdued voice answered back.

"Come in, it's all right." He opened the thick oak door with all kinds of junk carved into its surface and walked into the room. She was stark naked sitting on the bed, the C.A.D.S. suit unlatched and lying in two huge pieces on the floor.

Her body was coated with dirt and numerous small

113

abrasions from the rough ride of recent days. She looked up at him, unaware of her nakedness, so tired was she, so filled with pain that he could see in her eyes. He felt like crying that she'd had to go through all that she had endured. Suddenly the memory of their time in Hawaii together, another hotel room, before the war. How wonderful it had been then, loving, open, sensual at all times between them. And now, she was still beautiful, petite, brown eyed . . . but . . . some of the life had gone out of her.

"Oh baby," Sturgis said, going over to the bed and resting a de-gloved hand on her shoulder. "I'm sorry you've been through so much. I — I — "

"The bath, there's really a bath?" she asked, looking up. "I'd feel so much better with — " Her eyes welled up and by her trembling he could see she was on the edge of complete breakdown.

"Yeah, the hop said so — wait just a couple of minutes," Sturgis hit the unlatching mechanisms for the suit. Within a minute he had completely extricated himself from his unit.

"God, it feels good to be out of that damned thing," Sturgis said walking back to the bed. He rubbed his hands which felt cold from lack of blood circulation. "Come on, the water's probably ready by now," he said gently, helping her to her feet. They walked to the bathroom and he took her in. The sink and tub were porcelain with beautiful brass ornamentation, handwrought faucets and sparkling fixtures. He hadn't seen a setup like this for a long, long time. Neither had she for she got a quite joyful expression on her face. He loved seeing some of the old spark.

"Oh, it's beautiful, it's so — *clean*," she said incredulously. Sturgis leaned over and turned the faucet in the long deep tub and lo and behold, water began flowing. Uncluttered, with no rust or bugs. And *hot*. They could both see the steam rising as the water began quickly filling the tub.

"Come on, sugar," he said gently helping her as if she

114

were an invalid. "Just get in there and stay as long as you want. Soak up that heat." She sat down in the tub, her firm pale body settling back against the white porcelain.

"And look here," Sturgis said spotting a few plastic containers. "Can you believe it? Shampoo, and bubble bath." He handed both down to her and stood back beaming, glad that he had made the decision to come to the place. They'd all feel a lot better after a few quiet hours of pampering. Maybe she'd snap out of it a bit. Maybe her eyes wouldn't look so distant, so empty.

He walked out to the bedroom and took his coveralls off, too, then walked to the window naked. The view was quite profound as the crater was only a few miles off, his window high above the wall of the thing. It was hard to see clearly, but it looked like there were figures climbing up the sides. They had to be mad, but he wasn't going to go out and tell them. He hoped it was rad-resistant mountain goats, not humans that he was seeing. He'd seen what heavy rad damage could do. It made death a many-monthed painful affair, with hair falling out, teeth dropping like popcorn kernels onto the floor. As much as he loved the room and hot water and even all the overdone accoutrements, he couldn't stand the sight of the crater and pulled back the curtains, blocking out the circular vision of hell.

When she came out half an hour later Robin looked like a new woman, body clean, skin soft as a baby's, hair washed and hanging down. Even a small smile on her face, though the brown eyes still looked far away. Sturgis took his plunge in the hot waters and felt in ecstasy. Then they retrieved their clothes—the bellhop had stepped in and picked up from the room for quick cleaning.

They rested. Just rested.

At six o'clock, Sturgis went up and down the hall banging on all the doors getting them up and out.

"Time for din-din, road warriors," he shouted. "And tonight it's going to be more than syrup from some frozen tree—no offense to who found that syrup intended." He grinned at Fireheels who looked quite dapper tonight, with his long dark hair tied back in a knot and his buckskins looking ready for a Fifth Avenue showcase.

They headed down en masse, suitless, creating a stir as they passed other hotel guests and shouted out friendly, but boisterous greetings.

The dining room was just opening as they came in and the waiters led them to one of the white table-clothed banquet tables so they could all be seated. The food was brought in within minutes, course by course and everyone was flabbergasted. They thought this sort of service had died when America got nuked. Tranh whipped out his detachable geiger and swept it over everything that was brought to them. "Just checking," he said; "Don't mean to be rude," he commented to Sturgis who sat next to him. "But I have this strange aversion to eating radioactive materials. Don't know what's wrong with me." But to his surprise there was nothing that was higher rad than just background radiation. The bread, the elk stew, the corn-linguine avec prairie grouse, all were well within the range of human consumption. And with that reassurance they all dug into every course, sending butter and gravies splattering.

Once dinner was over and they were all satiated and quite pleased with themselves, they lit up the cigars that were passed around by one of the waiters. Dixon smoked two at a time, and puffed out clouds of the thick smoke above the table. DeCamp and Robin looked like they were going to send up what they had just chewed down because of the foul smoke, but held their meals. Men like cigars, women don't. One of the mysteries of life, like why women in scanties can lure more than nude women.

"Maybe we should check out some of them gambling halls," Dixon said with a wild look in his slightly drunken eyes. They'd all consumed a fair amount of homemade beer in the course of dinner. Sturgis felt a little nervous about their going off gambling but he knew he couldn't protect them like a mother hen forever. They were men after all, and needed some outlet other than just tramping endlessly through the wastelands waiting to die. Maybe it would keep 'em away from the call girls.

"There's no gambling in the hotel," the maitre'd said as he stood at their table, checking to see that they were all satisfied. "But right across the street is the Bloody Nugget, the biggest casino in town. They have it all—roulette, croupier, and are generally honest folks. As honest as gamblers get," the man added with a raise of his eyebrows. "Will there be anything else?"

Several of the men opted for more dessert, a honey and sweet cactus pie which they ate even as they continued to puff on their cigars out of one side of their mouths.

Robin and DeCamp headed back upstairs—presumably to work out some problem—while the rest of them headed out of the Grand Crater and across the street to the gambling joint.

Sturgis and his men saw a wild scene, a huge floor of gambling machines and tables that seemed to stretch off for acres. Being a two story affair, the place had apparently escaped much of the harm shielded by higher buildings from the atomic blast, and was intact. And it was packed. Mountain men, hustlers, cattle drivers, prospectors, and various indescribable types wearing clothes and hats of every form and color inhabited the place, hard at work losing their money. Here and there a fight broke out, and a few bodies would go rolling around the floor, but basically the place seemed about as peaceful as gambling dens had ever been.

The men each turned in one gold coin, which got them a whole armload of chips and the troopers split up promising to "be good." Sturgis, Tranh, and Fireheels headed over to the poker table, being buffs from way back. They watched the game in progress, ten men seated around a green felt table. And when several of them got up, having lost too much, they took their places and joined in the game.

It was Dealer's Choice, mostly five card draw, which was Sturgis's favorite anyway. The dealer was a very fat man with top hat and a pair of jeweled pinky rings who reminded Sturgis of nothing less than a combination of the riverboat gamblers he'd seen on TV when a child and his old arch-enemy Pinky Ellis. And the shifty eyes and slick card shuffling of the man didn't diminish the impression any. The guy was fast, too fast with his card dealing, making the cards move in a blur as he shot them out around the table.

Sturgis lost a few chips in the first three hands, then hit it big for a few more, winning nearly double his original pile of chips. The deal passed all the way around the table, back to the card shark who was apparently called "Gold Toothed Frankie" by way of the three gold teeth he had implanted in the front of his mouth. This time the hand went really big with everyone betting and counter betting. By the time the last cards were thrown there were hundreds of chips in the center of the table, a small fortune. Sturgis started out with two aces and a pair of tens. But by the time he got his last card he'd parlayed it into a full house, aces loaded, one of the better hands he'd played in a long time.

When all the cards were dealt they showed their hands and somehow Gold Tooth had won. As the man started to yank in his winnings, Fireheels' hand shot out and grabbed him by the wrist.

"Hold it there a minute, pal, I saw a little too much motion in those fast fingers." He gripped the hand and reached up under the sleeve, pulling out five cards, kings, queens, which fell out onto the table. The Indian smiled.

"Son of a bitch," the dealer screamed, jumping up and pulling out a small silver derringer which he let two blasts loose at the Apache commando. But Fireheels was used to facing rattlers that could spit faster than this dude. He ducked down as the shots slammed into the chair behind him. As the dealer reached for a blade hidden in his belt,

118

Sturgis was at his side and bending the wrist back so hard that it broke with a sharp cracking sound. The dealer let out a sharp scream as three of the casino's security, huge beefy fellows in black leather and studs who could have passed for rhinos as easily as men, came rushing over.

"Gold Tooth, I tol' you if I ever caught you messing around here with your extra cards, I'd cut off your goddamn balls and feed 'em to you," one of the bouncers said as he whipped out a long Bowie knife from his side and started toward the man.

"No, please, *God no!* I'll pay up," he looked imploringly at Sturgis who let the broken wrist go and stood back. He'd killed plenty of men in his time, but he wasn't the type to just cold-bloodedly stand back and watch someone get castrated.

"What have you got to make it up?" Sturgis asked as several of the casino patrons gathered around to watch the fun and games.

"Keep the pot—it's yours," Gold Tooth stuttered. "And I have a truck out in the lot, filled with all kinds of valuable items. Take what you want, but please don't let 'em cut my balls off, I need 'em."

"You wants I should cut or let him go?" the bouncer asked.

"I'd rather take a look in the truck," Sturgis replied as he swept in his rightful earnings. He then walked out with Tranh and Fireheels flanking each side of the cheater.

"Gold Tooth, don't ever come back in here, you hear me," the head bouncer said with a sneer. "I mean it. Not even inside the door. Take your games somewhere else, you know we keep things on the up and up in here." Sturgis, Tranh, and Fireheels followed the man around to his truck, a diesel Mack number. He opened the back and they stared in; it was filled to the brim with all kinds of junk, everything from pots and pans to washboards. But what caught all their eyes was a rusty cannon, an immense weapon which must have been over twelve feet long with a muzzle the size of a man's head.

"What the hell is that?" Tranh asked, pointing.

"A 155mm howitzer," Gold Tooth replied. "But you can't take that, I need it for—"

"We'll take *that*," Sturgis replied. "And all the ammo you've got to fit it. I think your balls are worth at least that much, don't you? Fireheels, have Rossiter and Dixon take a look at this damned thing, see what they can do with it. I'm getting tired, going to head back to the hotel. Tranh, keep an eye on our maniac puppies back inside the casino, will you? We need someone on their tail, and I'm fading out fast."

"Will do, Sturgis," the Viet said with a grin. "You go get your beauty rest." Sturgis headed wearily back to the hotel just a hundred feet away and made his way up the stairs one slow step at a time. Running water sure, but no damned elevators! He didn't know why he felt so exhausted, as if he was hardly able to move. The food, the liquor, the cigar. Maybe just having the opportunity to relax for a moment when he was used to being in super high gear all the time. His body hardly knew how to deal with slowing down, even for a few hours.

He had been avoiding too much contact with Robin, ever since he rescued her from the Soviet Brainwash Center. She couldn't stand too much close quarters, too much pressure, even if it was loving.

He knocked softly at the door to his suite and as there was no answer, used the key and opened it. The lights were out and he could see by the few stray streaks of neon street light that Robin was already tucked in.

"Who's there," she blurted out, frightened, as Sturgis knocked over a light chair making his way across the room.

"Just me, baby," Sturgis replied as he took off his clothes. He then washed his face and even his mouth, a luxury he rarely got. He climbed into the bed with her, her body felt hot and scented with delicious woman smells. He reached out for her, wanting her, wanting to break through the wall she had erected around her psyche, her

120

body. She let him touch her with light strokes, but when he reached down for more passionate sport, she said, "Oh God. *No*. No. I can't, Dean. I'm *sorry*. I don't know what's wrong with me. I feel frozen inside, like something's turned dark, like my body's hardly my own. I'm sorry, I'm sorry—" she said the words over and over like a sad mantra, sobbing.

"Don't worry baby," Sturgis said, just holding her tight. "I'm here next to you. That's all I want, to hold you." And he did, tightly. But even as she returned the embrace he could feel something in her very tense, muscles not giving in to him. And he knew that the old saying, "you're never more lonely than when with someone you love, who can't love you back", was just about the truest thing anyone had ever uttered. And the most painful.

Chapter Seventeen

When Sturgis awoke the next morning he found his boots scrubbed and polished to within an inch of their life and a large jug of cool fresh drinking water on a table near the door. He didn't even check to see if it was high rad or not. It looked and tasted like ambrosia of the gods. He awoke Robin who was loathe to come out of sleep, and then dressed. This time he wore the C.A.D.S. suit when he headed outside. In the hotel parking lot, amidst various other vehicles sat the bus which Rossiter and Dixon had apparently driven over during the course of the night from the outer lot. Sturgis found them hard at work when he went down. Their eyes were bloodshot and empty cups of coffee lay around the disarrayed, disassembled bus.

But they'd done well, amazingly well. For welded to the top of the old schoolbus was the 155 mm. howitzer. The bus was rapidly looking less like something that had once hauled kids to classes and more and more like some war wagon. It didn't look too beautiful up there, but it sure as hell looked attached.

"Sturgis, *damn* man, where were you when we needed an extra set of hands?" Dixon asked with a laugh. "This baby was as hard to haul up top as it is to get into a virgin."

"Ain't she a beauty?" Rossiter asked, looking down from the roof, his face the color of charcoal. He patted the field cannon and spat out a gob of coffee-tinted phelgm onto the ground. "Just finished cutting a hole up here, so we can actually operate the sucker while we're in motion. Man can stick his head up and—"

"Did our gold-toothed friend give you any more trouble?" Sturgis asked, although he knew if the fool did he was messing with the wrong pair of dudes. Both had seen their share or street fighting, as well as hard-metal confrontations.

"Yeah, he actually tried to slycock Rossiter here," Dixon laughed. "But junior leveled him with a haymaker that he's most likely still reeling from. Between his broken wrist, mashed-in nose and a few other injuries that we were forced to inflict to find out where he had the ammo and a few connecting parts of the cannon stashed away inside of that junkheap of a truck of his, I think he's going to be needing some heavy Blue Cross intervention."

"How much ammo did you actually dig up from the shark?" Sturgis asked, as he walked up and down the outside of the bus taking in the immensity of the cannon. The sucker could easily blow away a C.A.D.S. suit. That was pretty nasty in his book.

"Only four shells, total," Rossiter replied, looking a little downcast at the question after they'd put so much work into the attaching procedure. "But four of these shells could take out half an army if you aimed 'em right. Besides, who knows if we're likely to run into more ammo? Best deal in Vegas!"

"Yeah, right," Sturgis replied softly, not adding that that was about as likely as Rossiter joining Weight Watchers or Dixon getting religion. He'd bet there was *lots* of weaponry in this town, somewhere. "Good work, boys," he said with forced enthusiasm. It didn't seem like the effort was necessarily worth it. He prayed it wasn't going to throw the balance of the bus completely off so that MacLeish wouldn't even be able to drive the thing. He noted with approval the new double sets of tires.

"We'll be ready in five minutes, Skip," Rossiter said,

smashing at something on the roof with a huge hammer. "Can you bring me a final cup of dark stuff plus whatever you can scrounge up in the kitchen?" Rossiter asked anxiously, afraid he'd missed breakfast by his mechanical efforts.

"Hey pal, I'll get a buffet to go that'll knock you on your ass," Sturgis laughed as he headed back into the hotel. It took about half an hour but at last he had the whole crew, in full suit gear rounded up in the lobby. Per his promise he had the kitchen wrap up a load of goodies and a few dozen two gallon jugs of water. Even some fresh coffee in a steaming urn. He tipped everybody who had helped them out, a gold coin for each of the hops and two for the concierge. He knew it couldn't hurt to keep them in good stead with the whole staff. You never knew when you might be passing back this way again. He'd like to come back.

Then they were loaded up into the bus in much better moods, and about a thousand times cleaner than they had been the day before; a thousand times less hungry. A thousand times less — horny too! At least *most* of the men indulged in the proffered sex.

"I like this crazy burg," DeCamp said from her pole midway down the bus as they pulled through the gambling town. "I won at slots."

"Ah, you're bloody crazy," MacLeish said, sitting hunched up behind the wheel. "Bunch of ripoffs and conmen here make Jack the Ripper look like a Sunday School teacher. Place is a ripoff."

"How much did *you* lose?" Fireheels asked slyly, knowing that the Brit had been hitting the slot machines pretty hard.

"Wasn't the losing at slots, it was the *winning* with the expensive women! Ah, never you mind about that," Mac-Leish harrumphed red-faced as he shifted into a higher gear and put some gas down.

They had to go slowly as early morning gamblers and some drunken revelers from the night before were still lying around the streets. At last they reached the front street barricade and with a wave from the guard, passed through.

"Come again," he screamed out after them. "Next time maybe you'll actually win something."

"Did anyone besides Sheila win anything?" Sturgis asked with a laugh, "other than this big steel pipe we've got glued to the roof."

"I did, sir," a timid voice piped up. It was Timkins, one of the younger troopers, Sturgis could see by the voice ID on his visor screen. "Actually won about three hundred chips. Cashed 'em in for gold."

"All right," Dixon whooped. "I'm glad someone made some bucks while some of us were busting our fucking humps through the cold night. If it wasn't for those two friendly girl mechanics—"

"*Girl* mechanics?" Sturgis asked.

"Well, you don't think *all* we did was work—"

"Blimey, give the kid a *break,*" MacLeish said, with a growl from the driver's seat. "He couldn't have helped but sample the things this town offers. He's good at grease monkey games anyway. Games of put the bolt in the—"

"How's she driving?" Sturgis asked, changing the subject.

"I can feel that bloody doohickey up top, that's for sure," MacLeish replied with a growl. "But so far, she doesn't seem to be screwing things up too much. I guess they actually got the thing centered pretty good. But we'll see, we'll bloody well see, soon enough."

As soon as they were out of town and onto a decent road, he opened her up to thirty, then forty and finally fifty, moving in slow even acceleration so there'd be no surprises for anyone. And the bus went just fine down the decayed asphalt. If anything, the added weight of the cannon seemed to press down on her, helping the balance and spreading the entire weight more evenly over the shocks.

The men were in a good mood as the bus headed into

125

the bright sunshine of the new day. Even Robin seemed
more alive then she'd been for days, commenting once in a
while about this or that as the men kept on a constant
stream of jokes, profanities and insults of one another.
Once they were back out into the flatlands again and
heading straight toward White Sands, Sturgis allowed
himself to relax. Things at least seemed like they were
slightly under control!

It had been basically cloudy for days and now suddenly
it was clear as crystal. The sky above didn't have an ounce
of mist between them and the sun itself. And with the
ozone layer pretty much shot to hell, the heat and rays
and God knew what all that the sun put out by the
megaton was pouring down onto the flatlands — and their
steel bus.

As it grew hotter inside, some of the troopers began to
complain. With their battery packs down to half charge
even with some juice they'd been able to soak up from
generators back at the Le Grand Crater, they couldn't use
their airconditioning units at full blast. Like all ACs that
had ever existed, the things took up a lot of power. It was
changing the very environment to change hot air into cool
air. The suits had been set for Arctic duty! And the
C.A.D.S. suits ACs, without a full charge from their
atomic batteries back at White Sands just sort of huffed
along sending out little puffs of vaguely cool air inside the
suits.

"I don't how long I can take this," Rossiter groaned
after they'd been out in the full baking heat of the sun for
about three hours. The bus was okay, but everyone and
everything else was getting hotter by the second. "I feel
the sweat just pouring out from every cell and it's all
collecting in my boots."

"Don't worry," Sturgis said, trying to calm them down
but starting to get a little worried himself. "The suit can
condense it automatically even without the ACs working

full and evaporate excess moisture out into the air. You'd feel hotter without the outfit."

"I don't know," Fireheels said, "the desert heat is fine."

"So they say," Dixon bellowed out in discomfort from his suit. "But I don't know if anyone told the goddamn suits that." That got a few laughs but they quickly died out. Only Fireheels who sat down in the front stairwell of the bus, without his suit, seemed able to take the intense temperatures. Of course he was catching what little breeze was coming through the missing windshield and the door crack. Sturgis realized they might well have to de-suit and store them all in the back of the bus. The problem with that was that if they were attacked it left them all completely vulnerable to being blasted to hamburger if another attack should occur. On the other hand, if they stayed in them, they were just as prone to being boiled like lobster. Either way they'd end up being chow for vultures. Discomfort was the soldiers' lot. That and death.

But another half hour without letup of the sun's searing eye and the decision was taken out of his hands. Suddenly there was a scream from the back of the bus.

"My suit, it's getting hot, real *hot*," a terrified voice screamed out. It was Timkins, Sturgis's visor I.D.'d automatically.

"What's wrong, son," Sturgis asked soothingly, knowing that heat stroke was at least partly psychological. But not *his* heat stroke. For suddenly Timkins was running up the middle of the bus with smoke pouring out of every part of he C.A.D.S. suit.

"Oh, God," Sturgis muttered as he saw the smoking high tech suit coming straight toward him, where he was holding onto a pole behind MacLeish.

"It burns, oh God it *burns!* I'm on fire, Sweet Jesus, help me, *help me!*" Several of the troopers tried to grab he screaming, running Timkins but he was out of control. The sheer panic and power of the servo assist units inside made him unstoppable. He flew up the aisle, slamming he others aside as smoke was suddenly shooting out of every inch of the thing, filling the bus.

"Stop, stop the damn bus," Sturgis screamed as Mac-Leish threw the brakes on hard. Timkins kept coming in sheer agony as his screams pierced the helmets of every trooper. He reached the front of the bus and couldn't wait for the doors to open but just dove through the glassless windshield and right out onto the hood. They could see him jump down onto the prairie, running in mad circles with a cloud of thick blue smoke pouring out behind him like a jet on afterburners.

"Your *emergency escape!*" Sturgis kept screaming over the mike. "Hit the goddamn *emergency escape!*"

But Timkins clearly was beyond hearing or rational thought. By the time they got the door open and shot outside he was lying flat on his back, the suit smoking and bursting into little tongues of fire along the edges. Fireheels was the first to reach him, being right in the doorway. He reached around the back and slammed the explosive charged blowaway switch. Not a thing happened. The fire and whatever had gone wrong inside the overheated unit had taken that out as well.

"Get him out, get him the hell out of there," Marchi—Timkin's close buddy among the troopers—kept screaming, virtually jumping up and down as they gathered around. But Sturgis could see by the blackened flesh of the face that looked back out at them through the opened visor which had slid down during the course of the fire, that he was dead. Timkins was as dead as you can get, his skin charred and rough, eyes still open but only little black beads of shrunken brown clay.

"He's gone, mister," Sturgis replied softly, resting his arm on the man's shoulder. The dead trooper's friend Marchi stopped leaping and then shook softly with unstoppable tears.

"What a horrible way to go," Dixon muttered, not even realizing he was talking.

"The Model Two suits can't take it," Fireheels said as he looked up at the blazing blue yellow sun, protecting his

128

eyes with the palms of his hands. "You'd better all get out of them—and fast."

"I think the rest of them are actually okay," Rossiter said as he kept glancing down at the blackened husk of a man. The suit continued to burn and now the flames grew higher and hotter so they all had to step back a few yards.

The C.A.D.S. suits, Sturgis knew, rarely went up in flame, but if they did, when the temperatures got to levels where the plastics and internal wiring started melting, the things could actually explode into a bonfire.

"I'll bet you money that one was one of the suits we used the Soviet transistors to patch! I'm not getting any danger readouts on my temp grid from my suit!"

"Everyone, check your internal temp, have the suits do a total checklist right now. Report anything funny at all. We'll see what's what." They all did so, commanding their helmet computers to run through the circuitry, the internal heating/cooling units, the whole shebang. It took several minutes and when all had reported in, it was clear that four of the suits were heading into the same territory as the unfortunate Timkins had entered. Marchi's, Dixon's, Calvert and his wife Robin's suits—all of the ones with Soviet parts—were getting dangerous readings on several checks. He had them get out, fast. Within seconds they were standing there, mortal men and a woman again without the superhuman technology of the C.A.D.S. units to protect them anymore.

"What about Timkins?" Marchi asked.

They quickly buried the dead man.

"All right, back in the bus," Sturgis commanded, relieved to get on their way again. It happened. It was over. At least some of the suits were still functioning. He'd have them make a check every hour. "We'll have to use some of the water supply to keep cool, dousing those with and without suits so—" Sturgis hadn't finished the sentence when there was another scream and he turned wondering what the hell was going to happen next. Half the troopers had already boarded the bus. But Robin was about twenty yards away. She had gone off to look at a particularly beautiful large white blossom growing from the side of a thick cactus. Fireheels shouted, "Skip! She reached out to touch it when from out of nowhere a rattler struck. The ugly thing's fangs attached to her ankle!"

Fireheels was the first one there, able to move faster than the suits in short distance. He whipped out his custom bowie, a good fourteen inches long, and cut the snake free from her with a single slice. The headless body fell away, all five feet of it. Robin fell over on her side like a fallen tree and began shaking, jerking around, the head still attached to the ankle. She had foam coming from her lips.

Fireheels reached over carefully as he kneeled beside her and pried the fangs open, throwing the still venom dripping head to one side. Then even as Sturgis dropped to his knees in the C.A.D.S. suit, Fireheels sliced into the woman's ankle a three inch long gash that went in about a quarter of an inch. He put his mouth to the wound and sucked in hard, then spat out the mixture of blood and amber venom. Then he did it again and again.

The Apache drew out the poison for a good two minutes until his mouth and buckskins and the ground around them both was coated with red. Sturgis kneeled there helplessly, grinding his teeth like ball bearings inside the helmet, cursing himself for not having been more aware of what she was doing, not having warned her to be careful out here in the desert.

"Get me some of that round cactus over there," Fireheels said at last, looking up from his poison removal attempts. "The reddish one."

Sturgis rushed over the sixty feet and sliced off a piece with the instaknife that came out from beneath his metal wrist. He rushed back again as the rest of the troopers formed a circle around the pair on the ground.

"Back, back," Sturgis screamed wildly and they pulled back, seeing that he was in no mood to be trifled with. No matter how you looked at it, Robin was not just one of the other troopers.

"Slice a piece out of the center of the cactus, the white part," Fireheels said as he tied a tourniquet around her thigh just above the knee. Sturgis cut the vegetation open like a mad surgeon, nearly dropping it. He handed the Indian fighter the dripping substance. Fireheels leaned down and applied the cactus to the sliced ankle and then tied a small bandana around it, holding it against the flesh.

"I've done what I can," he said, standing up as she lay there, Sturgis stroking her head with the huge C.A.D.S. glove.

"Is she — is she?" Sturgis couldn't even quite bring himself to finish the question.

"Is she going to live?" Fireheels finished it for him. "I don't know, Skip. She took a lot of poison, that damned rattler hung on like a pitbull. I got a lot of the poison out, and this cactus is a powerful antidote for most poisons. But she's taken a lot. At least the poor woman isn't feeling the pain. The cactus juice numbs the wound. These bites hurt like hell, when the venom starts traveling through the system. I should know — I got bitten too, a long time ago. We'll know within twenty-four hours just what's happening. All we can do now is loosen the tourniquet once in a while so we don't cut off her circulation. And, of course, get to White Sands."

Sturgis looked over at DeCamp who was also a doctor among her various scientific skills. "Doctor — ?"

"I think Mr. Fireheels has done all that anyone can do under the circumstances. I would only add give her plenty of water, for the venom of a rattlesnake causes the body to dehydrate quickly."

Sturgis reached over and picked her up easily in the wide gloves of his suit. As the others watched he walked silently back to the bus. He made a sort of nest for her near the front out of several blankets so the air would cool her as they traveled. The rest of the commando force piled back on and MacLeish started the bus up. They hadn't

131

stripped the dead Timkin's suit when they buried him. It was clear to all that he was melted, fused to the inside of the C.A.D.S. suit. Even the vultures were going to have a hard time with this one, or the coyote's when they dug up his shallow grave.

Chapter Eighteen

DeCamp told Sturgis that the only hospital in America up to the standards necessary to save Robin, no doubt, was at White Sands.

MacLeish drove the armored cannon-topped bus too fast, wanting to get back to White Sands base, still hundreds of miles off, so Robin could get the treatment she desperately needed. They probably wouldn't make it in time, but he had to give it a try.

Sheila monitored her—could do little else. Robin wasn't looking too good; white as a ghost, completely comatose. Her vital signs, thank God, were holding up, her pulse slow, very slow, but maintaining.

"Can't this creaking crate go any faster?" Sturgis demanded of MacLeish for the tenth time in the last hour.

"Don't mean to be disrespectful, sir," the Brit driver replied softly. "But we're off road, and already going sixty to seventy on the straightaways! To be honest with you, I'm just barely keeping the thing under control. Think man; there's a whole busload of men here, not just Robin." He said the words as gently as possible, knowing they sounded harsh. There was a sharp intake of breath from Sturgis's open visor and MacLeish waited for an explosion. But after a few seconds the C.A.D.S. commander's voice spoke low.

"You're right, of course, old boy," Sturgis said with an edge of tension. "There are a lot more people to consider than just her. Don't listen to me. Love makes you crazy, blind to the bigger truths."

"You don't have to apologize, sir," MacLeish replied. "Anyway, I'm keeping her right up there at the edge of blowing up, and if these half decent trails hold out, we should make good time."

"At least the sun is fading a little," Fireheels commented from his crouched position on the stairwell. "Must be about five, soon be dark. And from the high clouds moving in from the west I think tomorrow won't be nearly as hot. If anything, we might get some showers."

"Anything over this damned heat," Rossiter piped up from several poles back, both his huge suited arms wrapped around the pole to keep his large bulk from bouncing into the walls as the bus rocked back and forth on its shocks. "For a few hours there I felt like a snowball in a crematorium."

"You *look* like a fucking snowball in a crematorium," Dixon snapped. He was standing across the aisle from Rossiter. "A big, big snowball and I don't think too much is melting." Sweat rolled down from his tousled platinum blond locks.

Every half hour or so, Fireheels checked the tourniquet, loosened it for five minutes so her blood could circulate, otherwise gangrene could set in. They could see the swelling going right up Robin's leg to the thigh as the poison began its course through her system. And wherever the toxin passed, the skin turned an orange-green color and swelled up a good two inches. It wasn't the most beautiful sight in the world.

"Don't worry about the coloration," Fireheels reassured Sturgis, who could barely stand to see the distended flesh. "Even in small bites, this kind of reaction is common. The main thing is to keep her heart and lungs going. So far there seems no problem."

Sturgis tried to pretend he was reassured by the words, but inside he wasn't. If she died, a piece of him would die with her. A part of his heart, that he knew he'd never find again. And guilt along with it, that it was his fault that she'd had to go through all this. And he wasn't at all sure that wasn't the case. If only he had used common sense, kept an eye . . .

Around five that afternoon with just a half hour of light left, they came over some rolling hills onto a hard packed two lane country road, and then saw a highway ahead. There weren't too many of them anymore. Most had been covered by wind-blown sand. And those that were around were generally so cracked and filled with weeds, their concrete surface so twisted this way and that as if an earthquake had ripped through them, that they were virtually useless. Useless for anything but worms and snails to set up house in. But this highway, a four-laner, seemed in almost untouched shape, except for a few weeds growing through spiderweb cracks here and there.

"All bloody *right*," McLeish exclaimed as they saw the thing extending far to the south. "Look at this gang, we got us a regular L.A. Throughway. If we can hook up to it for even a few hundred miles, should cut our time back to White Sands by half."

McLeish slowed down as he maneuvered the bus from the county road right up the side of a broken embankment onto the highway. The back wheels got stuck and the gear power of the motor didn't quite seem able to push the vehicle up the rest of the way as it hung on the edge, the huge tires just spitting out dirt behind.

"Come on, we'll have to give her a little push," Sturgis said, taking three other troopers with him. They set themselves behind the bus and pushed. The servo mechs of the suits easily gave them the strength to do it and the bus went right up the wash-out slide, and onto the highway.

"Even without E-balls and all that other junk, we can

135

still kick butt," Dixon proclaimed proudly, making a mock bicep inside the suit. They climbed back in and McLeish took off down the highway. The bus seemed to love being on a real road again and he pushed her slowly up to fifty, then sixty, and finally seventy-five, once he saw that the highway was for real and wasn't about to come apart at the seams right under their wheels. After a few major bumps at spots where the pavement had folded in on itself a little, he dropped back down to sixty but was able to maintain the speed.

At first they didn't see a lot other than cacti and prairie dogs. Then they came to a juncture with three other roads, these in much worse states of repair, and they began seeing cars along the sides of the road, all overturned, wrecked. The cars had clearly been there quite a while, as many of them were reddish brown with rust coating nearly every square inch. Whatever was useable in them had long been stripped, but the frames remained, metal skeletons from an era of luxury and waste that was gone and would probably never return.

Here and there they saw human skeletons, all that remained of the drivers who had once used them. Some were lying in broken pieces around their wrecked cars, others still were inside, bony eye sockets staring through shattered windshields, as if they might start the vehicles up again and drive off if they could just find the blasted keys. It gave Sturgis and McLeish the creeps as they stared through the broken windshield of the bus to see the morgue of the past. They couldn't help but wonder if they might somehow have known the dead—those men and women with their bones picked clean of every scrap of digestible cellular material.

Sturgis was just starting to feel a little hopeful as their pace was keeping up at about 60 mph average over three hours. Then McLeish let out a stream of curses.

"We've got some bloody nasty looking company on the road ahead," he said, slowing the bus slightly. Sturgis peered ahead to what looked like some sort of barricade about a mile down the straightaway on the highway. He couldn't see too clearly in the heat shimmer. It looked like a lot of men congregating around.

"Telemode," he vocally ordered the helmet and the grid visor telescoped his view. He had that familiar sensation as if he was actually flying through the air straight at them. Now he could see close up and he wished he couldn't. There were dozens of them, seated all around a makeshift barrier made of cars and trucks upended and piled one atop another. There was a large truck in the center of the barricade that looked as if it could be moved out of the way, allowing access to the highway on the other side, if they chose to let you by.

But it was the faces and getup of the men standing around the vehicular barricade that really caught Sturgis's attention. Pink hair, green hair, blue hair in mohawks, or spikes, and in numerous bizarre geometric configurations. The hair seemed to have been waxed or sprayed with plastic, as it all stood up straight as arrows and had a shining hue. All wore leather, chains, studs. But they apparently believed in more than just bizarre coverings, for many had also pierced pins, forks, knives, right through their faces, their lips, their arms. It looked like it hurt but none complained. And by the weaponry they carried around their shoulders and stacked next to them, these post-nuke-punks had big bites as well as barks.

"Better slow her down a little more," Sturgis told McLeish. "I don't know if we can smash our way through that barricade." He looked quickly back and forth on both sides of the road ahead, but as luck, or more likely, the punks' ahead planning, would have it, there was a sharp embankment that dropped down a good fifty feet on each side. If they tried to take the bus down, chances were good they'd go over. They were already funneled into a trap.

"I think we're going to have a bit of trouble up ahead," Sturgis addressed the rest of the unit over his

137

helmet mike. "So visors down if you got 'em up. And get ready to fire whatever little bit of ammo you got in there. Dixon, you think you can actually fire that elephant sized blunderbuss you and Rossiter mounted up top? Without blowing us all up, that is."

"Bet you right ball on it, Skip," Dixon replied with a laugh, already heading down the aisle with loud thumping noises from his suit boots on the metal floor. "Already got a shell in here. You just give the word and our pals up there in car-city will be in for a big surprise."

"Should I stop?" McLeish asked a little nervously, wanting to just try to ram the bus right through the barricade, though even he could see that would probably do as much harm to themselves as to the barricaders. The blockage of wrecks looked several layers thick.

"Yeah, but not too close," Sturgis replied. "Bring her to maybe a hundred feet from them. And keep the engine hot and your foot ready on that pedal, you hear me, whatever happens." McLeish did as ordered and the bus came to a slightly grinding stop about forty yards from the line of broken vehicles and ugly road-men.

Several of the leather clad uglies ahead waved their arms up and down as they plastered big smiles on their faces as if everything was going to be just fine. Yeah right, Sturgis thought darkly, with faces out a nightmare, hair that could be used in industry. Sure, they just wanted to borrow a cup of sugar for their lemonade, no doubt.

"Howdy strangers, welcome to Arizona, the state of hospitality and wonderful roads," one of them said, the leader, even uglier than the others if that was possible, had a huge obese body beneath his all leather and studs outfit. He had a broken telephone receiver dangling from around his neck by a ripped cord and a fork pierced clean through his cheek, the five prongs aiming forward. Salad fork. He had a half-closed eye that was covered over by a huge purple boil, and hardly any teeth. All in all, he didn't contribute to an appealing picture of post-nuke humanity.

"Thanks," Sturgis shouted out through the windshield frame of the bus as he saw the road-punks start to edge sideways and very slowly begin to come forward in a long line. There were more than he had thought and every one of them was armed with automatic rifles and shotguns.

"Just what's all this?" he asked.

"Oh, the Arizona toll station," the man replied, flashing a hole of a smile. "We keep these roads in good condition so—we expect our due compensation. Now ain't that fair?"

"Sounds fair to me," one of the equally fat slime on each side of him spoke up; one had blue hair cut into a flattop that stood up six inches or so. The other one was bald but for a single knot of hair about an inch in diameter which was quite long, wrapping around his neck and dyed blood red.

"Well, I don't suppose we'd be averse to paying a toll," Sturgis said, wondering if there was the slightest chance of getting out of this whole mess diplomatically. "What'd you have in mind?" He motioned around for DeCamp to hand him a few gold coins.

"Oh, nothing much. Just that there bus you got—and the cannon on top of it. And any wimmen you might have in there. We'll let you walk after that. Ain't gonna hurt no one, you got my word on it."

"His word!" MacLeish muttered through his opened visor, "His bloody word. I'd trust that slime as much as a pimp in a convent. Besides the women—"

"I don't think I can do that," Sturgis replied without sounding antagonistic. Sometimes it was possible to reason with men, even dregs like this. "Got a lot of passengers, including a few wounded. Not that I wouldn't, of course, be glad to let you have the damned thing if it was just me. But I got my own problems, you understand?"

"Oh, understand completely," the leader of the terrible

139

toll-collectors said. "But on the other hand, we got our problems too. We work for Macro-Kill, you ever hear of him?"

He got no response.

"He's the leader of the Killboys, and that's *us*. We're the biggest damned army around these parts. And no one but no one messes with us and lives. You understand what I'm saying? So, if you all would just be kind enough to start unloading the ve-hi-cle of yours, maybe we can get this show on the road. Pay the toll, you can be on your way."

But even as he spoke the conciliatory words Sturgis could see the man nodding to his pals as they began moving forward a little faster, unslinging their rifles and SMGs'. Atop the barricade ahead he could also see a bunch of them slamming a machine gun on a tripod down on top of three wrecked cars piled one atop another.

"Well, now, I suggest you just stop in your tracks, and all your face-pierced pals there as well," Sturgis said, his voice turning icy. "Or I think you're going to be in for a big, big surprise."

"And just what kind of surprise would that be, metal-man?" the leader asked, as he suddenly motioned fast with his hand and the long line of his fellow slugs suddenly rushed forward from all sides of the bus. "These here guns we have are loaded with Teflon bullets. Armor-piercing. You dig, daddy?"

"No surprise, pal," Sturgis answered coolly. "Dixon, *let her rip*." Those were the words that Billy Dixon—up on the roof—had been waiting for. He wasn't quite sure that the huge 155 was really going to work or not. They hadn't tested it. But it was time to find out. Seeing that the cannon was aimed in just about the right direction, Billy slammed the firing lever.

There was a thunderous explosion as the entire bus shook violently. Suddenly the cars and trucks in the center of the barricade ahead exploded out in all direc-

140

tions in a showering rain of glowing red hot metal and large fragments as big as doors that flew through the air, cutting some of the nearby Killboys to ribbons.

Those who weren't knocked from their feet opened fire from all sides of the bus and the passengers inside could hear the pinging shots snapping all around them. They returned fire through the gun-slits.

"Floor it, McLeish!" Sturgis screamed as he threw his body over Robin to protect her from the impacts.

"Hold onto your manhoods, we're heading into hell," the Brit screamed out with a wild kind of glee. He slammed the bus into gear and charged forward into the smoking dissembled wreckage ahead, flames shooting up in a tornado of fire.

The shots continued as all of the remaining Killboys opened up. The bus ripped into the pieces of what was left where the cannon shell had detonated. There were ripping, crunching sounds as the bus tore through the debris. Some of their many new tires blew — but not all.

They were thrown all around inside the bus as it rode up over jagged junk lying on the ground. Smoke poured in through the opened windshield and a tongue of flame as well, which rippled over McLeish's suit in the driver's seat. Fortunately for him he had the visor closed.

Suddenly they were through, smashing whatever was still in the way out of the way. They emerged on the far side with shots ringing out after them. The troopers began stirring from their positions they had fallen into around the floor of the bus.

"We all right?" he asked, standing up behind McLeish. "Keep a look out back in case they pursue."

"The bus seems all right even with all that jarring around," the Brit exclaimed with a laugh. "We weren't in the flames long enough to melt the tires. As far as I can tell from the feel, we only lost a few. Those extra rims were a great idea! She's handling all right."

"Yeah, maybe so," Fireheels said from his crouched position in the stairwell where he had been pulled down like an ostrich trying to avoid being hit by all the flying madness and the flames. "But there's more company ahead, Sturgis, and they don't look any friendlier than our pals back there."

Sturgis stared through the windshield where Fireheels was pointing. Coming down a side road that joined the highway about five hundred yards ahead was a whole fleet of weirdly painted cars and trucks. Perhaps fifty of them. And they were moving, heading to intercept the bus ahead. Whatever type of communication system these jokers had, it worked.

"Damn," Sturgis muttered darkly, feeling his heart sink. They just weren't prepared for this kind of all-out altercation that lay seconds ahead. "Goddamn, unlucky break," he knew the words weren't the most eloquent ever uttered in the annals of military combat history. But they sure summed up his feelings and the feelings of every man on the bus.

Chapter Nineteen

"Move this crate, man, move it," Sturgis screamed at MacLeish who was bent over the wheel with a look of incredible concentration.

"I'm moving it, you bloody loud-mouthed Yank," the Brit screamed back just as loudly. "I told you a thousand times I can't stand people standing over me yelling in my ear when I'm driving." Sturgis didn't even hear the words, he was too busy focusing on the oncoming mechanized armada. He commanded his visorscreen to again telesight him and he got a closeup look at the fleet. The Killboy drivers had bizarre junk dangling from them. They looked like living pincushions. On the fenders of some of the multicolor-vehicles were what looked like a chain of human heads, shrunken and shriveled. He didn't even want to look too closely at them, but he got the idea: Guys who hadn't paid the toll, he supposed.

"Damn, if we just had full batteries and a truck of ammo we could make short enough work of that bunch," Fireheels said bitterly, standing suitless and brave in the stairwell.

"Yeah, but we don't, pal," Sturgis shouted back breathlessly. "Dixon, you still up on the roof?" the C.A.D.S. commander bellowed out through the radio.

"Damn right, and hanging on for dear life," Dixon answered back.

"Any chance of swinging that big gun around and

zeroing in on those bogies coming in from twelve o'clock?" Sturgis asked, hoping against hope for a break.

"No way, José; sorry, chiefie," Dixon answered, his voice quavering slightly as he was lying flat on his chest while the bus bounced wildly up and down. "We did the best we could with the welding, but her gear system got locked to the side. I can't make other than a twenty degree turn in either direction." Sturgis could see that the attack force was breaking off into five smaller groups and spreading out all along the side of the highway.

"Everybody, empty out whatever ammo you have," Sturgis ordered the troopers. "Tranh, you load up and give the rest to Dixon. Get up on the roof with him. When the bastards start getting too close—do what you can."

"Will do, Skip," Tranh said, without another word and headed down the aisle collecting whatever bullets he could from the rest of the men. Sturgis carried Robin to the very back of the bus and had two men stand in front of her. At least she'd be slightly shielded from impending mayhem.

And it came quicker than he was prepared for. Suddenly six of the cars, old beat up Chevy and Fords with metal "ears" and "teeth" welded onto their front ends, came hopping up onto the highway three hundred feet ahead. They were headed straight for the bus. The other units—jeeps, altered RVs—came along each side of the highway in three flanks.

"Cap, they're moving in," MacLeish shouted breathlessly from the driver's seat. "What the hell do you want me to—"

"Coming, man, hang on," Sturgis bellowed as he strode up the aisle half knocking troopers hanging onto their poles out of the way. Sturgis took a quick look out of the smashed windshield and saw that things were rapidly going from bad to much worse. For the Killboys were

144

opening up and this crew had more than just small arms.

As he watched in growing apprehension, Sturgis heard some sharp heavy cracks and saw little explosions rise up in the road ahead. The bastards had artillery too!

"Tele Mode," Sturgis screamed. He could see that some of the trucks and cars with their whole roofs cut away had small cannon, mortars, a bazooka or two. Plenty of stuff to send the bus into hell and everyone on it, if they got pinned down with that kind of firepower coming onto them.

"Like I said, I'm just the bloody driver, what do you want me to—" Sturgis cut him off by reaching out and grabbing the wheel and turning it sharply to the right so the bus careened wildly around on the road. MacLeish barely kept control of the vehicle as it made an almost ninety-degree turn and went bounding down an embankment, this one not quite as steep was what they had just passed.

"Do *that!*" Sturgis shouted angrily, angry at the whole world that they weren't getting a moment of peace out here in the hell lands.

"You crazy Yank," MacLeish muttered inside his helmet as he nearly lost control of the bus which shot down the embankment like a roller coaster starting down its first steep descent. It came down fast and it seemed it would smash into the earth below, but at the last second the bus straightened out and shot forward as if catapulted from a slingshot. Springs popped as it hit a flat field at a good forty, but MacLeish was somehow able to regain control of it.

"Straight ahead," Sturgis screamed, "away from the road. Don't be fancy, let's just get some distance. We gotta get out of range of that artillery." But the words were still hot on his lips when three shells came whistling overhead. They hit and went off to the left and right of the hood of the schoolbus. Geysers of dirt blew up in front of them and swept in through the windshield, whooshing down the center of the bus, bouncing off the C.A.D.S. suits.

"Zig and zag and do every damned thing you ever learned," Sturgis screamed to the Brit driver. "I'm going topside to see what the hell's happening around us." Another set of explosions rocked the bus, bouncing them from side to side.

"Bring me back some tea and cookies," MacLeish snarled as he threw the bus into higher gear and poured the gas on. "I think it's bloody tea time."

Sturgis made his way to the opened trapdoor onto the sheet metal roof. He judged the diameter and then bending his knees about six inches let loose with a jump straight up seven feet. As he exited through the rectangular hole, just scraping the sides, he kicked his feet out to both sides. The moment he felt himself balanced he dropped forward. He fell alongside Tranh and Dixon who were facing backward. They were using a crowbar to turn the frozen-up howitzer, so they could start firing at the army behind them.

"Welcome to the sixth floor," Dixon said sarcastically as more shells whistled overhead. "Bullets, bombs, corpses, heavy mortar are all on sale today."

Sturgis twisted his body around and looked backward. And gasped. Along the embankment down which they had just exited the highway was the pursuing force. They had spread out. There must have been sixty, seventy modified cars, trucks, small pickups, all the way down to souped up VWs. Sturgis swore every one of them had some kind of heavy duty firepower. Even—was it? Yes. *Rocket launchers!*

They had all stopped, right at the edge of the fifty foot descent, content for the moment to watch the bus as it weaved its way across the lower prairie toward the east. The cars rocked back sharply as they fired one after another of their big guns. Then came a dozen rockets—so that the whole line of them seemed to be spitting smoke and fire.

146

And even as Sturgis watched, the shells dropped—short of target. He could see them raising the huge metal barrels now, though, as they got the distance. One shell dropped down just behind them, a mother of a shell, and sent a curtain of hot dirt flying up over them though it bounced harmlessly off the C.A.D.S. units.

"Blue Mode!" Sturgis screamed into the helmet. Instantly a grid map lit up in green digitized image on the right side of his helmet. A map showing their position and motion—and the small geometric shapes representing each of the attacking vehicles. Even as Sturgis watched the screen begin reading out numerous bits of information.

"73 VEHICLES: FIVE FORD'S, 2 ISUZU'S, EIGHT BUICK STATIONWAGONS, FIVE—" It scrolled at high speed every make, model and year of the attack force.

"CEASE ANALYSIS—WHAT WEAPONS?"

Then began with the weaponry they were using. "RECOILESS RIFLE-50 CAL, BLACKARMS MORTAR-50mm, BAZOOKA . . ." It spat out the weapons read so fast that only a man like Sturgis to whom the rivers of information were second nature could absorb them even as he kept an eye on the enemy firing down on them. Billy let loose a 155mm. shell, but it missed by a mile.

"This looks about as close to Custer at Little Big Horn as any of us are ever likely to get," Tranh said with a dark laugh, for he knew and they all knew, they were about to die. There was no way out, the bus was not fast enough.

"Oh, I don't know," Sturgis snapped back. "Custer had a hundred times more men. Load another shell!"

"If we just had some cover out here," Dixon shouted plaintively. "It's like a goddamn shooting range and we're the ducks." MacLeish slammed through a small grove of twenty foot high Saguaro cactuses and pieces of the thorny plants came flying by the three riding atop the metal roof, bouncing over them. They would have been ripped to pieces without the suits; instead the thorns just

147

slid along the surface of the titanium armoring, thwarted in its efforts at flesh tearing.

"P.D. Mode," Sturgis screamed into the suit helmet. P.D. meant Probability of Destruction. The computer could compute, from all its various perceptual modes combined, what their chances were. It was, supposedly, never wrong.

"PROBABILITY OF DESTRUCTION AT THIS SECOND IS 95.67%," the grid read back in stark, green digits. "EVERY SECOND C.A.D.S. UNIT MOVES AWAY FROM FIRING SOURCE, P.D. DECREASES BY. . . 05%."

"Cover, cover," Sturgis muttered. Suddenly he slammed his gloved fist so powerfully down on the metal roof that the two troopers below swore a shell had gone off directly above their heads. "Hold those last shells, Billy. I have an idea."

"Down below," Sturgis screamed into the helmet mike. "Hand up two cannisters of that heavy oil we brought with us for lubing this son-of-a-bitch."

"Will do," two voices replied simultaneously. Within seconds Sturgis grabbed the two cans, opening one up and held it toward Dixon.

"You've got your arc torch still connected to the suit, right? Say yeah, right?" Sturgis screamed, sounding like a crazed man.

"Yeah, I was using it on cannon welding. Ain't much left but—"

"Set the oil on fire. Make it burn, even if you have to keep the torch playing on the surface. Maybe we can set up a cloud of oil smoke. A screen. Burn it man, burn it," Sturgis yelled as Dixon lay there seemingly dumbfounded by the concept.

"MacLeish," Sturgis commanded the Brit driver over the radio. "Move her back and forth about fifty yards from side to side—we're going to set up a smoke screen and get lost in it." Dixon regained his senses and grabbed hold of the large oil can. He flipped the latch to the top and it came off, exposing a large surface area of the dark sloshing liquid. He held his right wrist out to the stuff turning his head slightly away as he wasn't quite sure if the stuff would ignite or explode. It wasn't nearly as refined as gasoline, but accidents happen.

It caught almost immediately and flames licked along the top of the oil inside, sending up a dark acrid cloud just as Sturgis had hoped. Billy crawled to the rear and poured it behind them.

"Good thinking." Tranh said with audible relief in his throat. At least they had a chance, which was more than they'd had a few seconds before. The cloud of smoke produced by the burning trail of oil instantly spread up and out behind them, blotting the view like a sudden thick black fog.

Within twenty seconds they had created a monstrous plume of smoke that began reaching back toward the firing Punker-fleet.

"It's working," Sturgis shouted down to MacLeish on the radio. "Keep it up, keep swerving."

"APPROACHING OUTER RANGE OF THE FOLLOWING WEAPONS:" The C.A.D.S. visor began reading out. MORTAR, M17 BAZOOKA, 89mm TOP MOUNTED FIELD MISSILE LAUNCHER . . . And through the curtain of black and oily gray which rose like a dark stain into the air they could hear the firing slow down, though not stop completely. The smoke poured up all around them into thick patterns in the dust blown air. Still, the infra red mode, could cut right through it. And when Sturgis used that mode he didn't like what he saw. For the auto army had descended the highway embankments too and were spread out coming straight at the bus, slowly increasing their speed.

"What the hell do we have to do to stop these bastards?" Sturgis shouted, frustrated. He was just about to order MacLeish to turn around and stop. They'd at least get off a few cannon shells on target before the end. Though it was suicide.

Suddenly Tranh spoke out. "Look Skip, you'd better see this," the Vietnamese trooper said with a sharp intake of breath. Sturgis turned away from the back.

"Jesus Christ," the C.A.D.S. commander whispered, hardly able to believe his eyes. It was like something out of a Cecil B. DeMille movie, a vast Roman spectacular with Victor Mature and a cast of ten thousand. For ahead of them was a car and truck army filled with the same rotten, face pierced, pink and yellow haired killers who were on their trail. An even larger army of them.

They were parked in rings about a huge sandstone mountain which rose like a volcano out of the prairie. On the mountain were what had to be ancient Indian pueblos, a complex of them that rose up to the very top. To the sides of the mountain were what looked like crude oil wells and smoking refining plants. A series of thick chainlink fences, steel posts and barbed wire spread out from the heavily fortified mountain all the way around. And a wall of fire too!

"Indians," Dixon screamed out in amazement. "I've got 'em on telemode. The craziest Indians you've ever seen are up on that mountain. Covered with feathers and teeth and God knows what all. Even got warpaint. There's even more of them Indians than there are—"

"Oh, this is just *great,*" Tranh bellowed out as he swung his oil cannister over the rear, releasing its canopy of smoke and fire.

Dixon had lost his cool. He shouted, "I've had it! We got an army behind us, an entire invasion force ahead of us, and cutthroat Indians beyond that with barbed wire and fire. And probably what they're all fighting over is which one of them is going to get to kill us. I'm heading for early retirement, right now." Dixon started to rise as if he were going to dive right off the bus.

"Don't be a fool, you crazy redneck," Sturgis screamed as he grabbed his suited arm like a crab claw grips seaweed. "You'll be dead in a second out there."

Dixon stopped.

"MacLeish, stop the zigzagging, head straight for the red sandstone mountain there. If the Indians won't let us in, we'll smash through. At least it'll get us away from these punker bastards for the moment. We don't know the Indians will kill us, we know that these jokers *will!*

Chapter Twenty

They used the last 155mm howitzer shell to smash a hole ahead of them, and drove through the hole in the punk-roadmen's ranks, and through the fire-wall. Fire-heels was protected by the bus's metal shield sections. Thus the bus was able to make its way through the four hundred feet of heavily armored traffic and to the barbed wire that the Indians had erected.

A storm of slugs rained down on the men on top of the bus and even within their C.A.D.S. suits they could feel the ferocity of the attack. But no armor-piercing slugs!

"Open the gate, Indians, we're your friends," Sturgis screamed out, ordering the suit computer to go to Public-Address Mode. His voice boomed out over the metal gates and barbed wire-filled landscape at the skin-clad figures who scurried far ahead.

"Plow through the first gate," Sturgis ordered MacLeish as the bus slowed slightly as it came up to the gate. "We ain't got time to negotiate." The bus speeded up again as MacLeish floored it. Sturgis and the others hung on for dear life on the roof. But even as they flew toward the two gates joined by an upright pole, the fence slid electronicaly apart and made an opening for the bus to enter. Then the next even heavier steel gate, some hundred feet farther inside the first, slid open as well. Behind them some Killboy cars came tearing in toward the opened outer gate. But even as they approached it a sheet of fire roared up anew from one of the hidden gas-gullies. Five cars burst into flame as the mangy occupants became human blowtorches in the twilight. The rest pulled back as the gates closed again one after another as soon as the bus was through.

Then they were up to the last gate and it too swung open. But as soon as they entered the Indian encampment, another set of gates rose up all around them encaging them so that MacLeish had to slam on the brakes.

Sturgis and the other troopers looked down at a dozen or so Indians. They were wearing the most outlandish headdresses made out of everything from discarded sardine cans to gila monster teeth. Their faces were painted with dayglow reds and blues and greens. They were screaming out war whoops as they pointed at the bus and gesticulated with the weapons they were carrying nervously. One of them let loose with a little stream of flame—away from the bus—so Sturgis could see they had flamethrowers. Clearly makeshift but clearly functional. Skulls hung here and there around the poles of the inner barbed wire fencing didn't help Sturgis's stomach any.

"Fireheels, get out there and reason with these fellows fast," Sturgis yelled into the P.A. as the bus came to a total quivering stop. The flamethrowers the Indians carried rose up and aimed at both sides of the bus. It was obvious that if they so much as moved, the Indians were going to open up with liquid fire. Gasoline was their weapon, apparently. And they had damned well learned how to use it in every way to defend themselves, as well as for fuel.

The Indians didn't seem to like the looks of the spacesuited men riding atop it, let alone the armor plated bus itself. Their fingers ran nervously on the triggers of their old M-1's. They looked back and forth at one another as if wondering whether to send the whole bunch of intruders into a flaming hell. Another of them let loose with a stream up into the air just to let them know what they were facing. The jet of burning liquid jetted up fifty feet with a five-foot spread. A lone vulture circling low for food got singed to the bones. Its feathers burned and crackled as the smoking carcass fell directly to earth.

"Okay, okay we get the message," Sturgis snarled over his mike on public address. Behind them the Killboy army pulled back, setting off a few shots along the wire line, shots which landed harmlessly outside the gates. Fireheels walked out from the bus door below as Sturgis watched nervously. The Apache C.A.D.S. man raised his buckskin clad arms, his long black hair falling free behind him. He moved slowly with opened hands high and set in the universal sign for "Peace" to show them no harm was intended.

From out of the flaming shadows a tall, heavy Indian walked. Sturgis could see right away that this one was of a higher rank than the others, a different order entirely. He wore a layered bodyarmor of flattened cans—Budweiser beer cans. They'd been hammered to a flat even texture and interspersed with turquoise stones. His head was endowed with a headdress made of feathers, teeth, and the skulls of small animals all sewn into a crazy quilt. He wore a cape down to his ankles. It spread out to nearly a yard behind him, moving slightly back and forth as he approached the front of the bus. But it wasn't the garb alone that made him important, for Sturgis could see from yards away. It was the regal face, the eyes, the very way he walked. The man generated pure power. You could recognize it anywhere on earth. His face looked like it had outstared the desert. And Sturgis knew he had to play it straight with this man. He was nobody's fool.

He was immense as well as powerful, the C.A.D.S. commander could see as he approached. The chief—he had to be that—stopped about a yard in front of Fireheels and slowly raised his own coppery muscled arm with veins protruding all around it. He looked a good

154

foot taller than Fireheels, who Sturgis swore was 5'10 or 11' and made even the trooper-brave's strong masculature look puny by comparison.

"Hawd whi nakuana," Fireheels said slowly, pointing around to the bus.

"Madua asnapi yikqui," the chief said as the flame-throwers pulled back a few feet to keep the spitting puffs of fuel from landing on their head man. Sturgis was sure none of them wanted to do that.

Fireheels retorted with the words, *"Ikna, mo pihaw. Ina mo linrug."*

The chief seemed to ponder this. Then the chief spoke in broken English after that comment.

"You work for Federal government? Ha. Is no government. Look!" The chief waved his hand out toward the circling army of white-punk killers, and laughed so that one side of his leathery lips moved a half inch or so and then settled back into the stoic stone face.

"You speak English?" Fireheels said with a smile. He was relieved. He hardly knew what he had been saying in the trading dialect of Comanche he'd once learned some words of.

"Yes! Worked as a guide many years ago, before world to PHHHT! and then I become chief here," the man said, stretching his broad arms out as if to indicate his little kingdom. "I am Chief Naktu. He-who-talks-with-the-oil. My people worship me because I have given them all this. Fire. Oil and flame. Protection. Fuel. Life. We are the People of the Black Lake, Naqui, the oil people."

"We come in peace, Great Chief Naktu," Fireheels said. "We want none of your oil or supplies unless you wish to sell to us," Fireheels went on. "That is Col. Dean Sturgis our leader. There are two other C.A.D.S. troopers atop the bus. Inside it are another dozen or so of our men—and two women. We wish you no harm, but were simply trying to return to our base in New Mexico. We were attacked by the same people who seem to have you surrounded."

The chief looked long and hard at him as if trying to decipher the words, or more likely the meaning beneath the words.

"Why space-suits?" he asked, pointing up at the top of the bus where Sturgis, Tranh and Dixon were slowly standing up, arms outstretched to show they held no weapons.

"Suits are made by Federal Government. We are forces that are loyal to the American constitution, flag and way of government. We're the C.A.D.S. troopers, the new law out here. Or trying to be," Fireheels added with a sheepish grin as he realized what an absurd statement that was. After all, they were surrounded by a thousand crop-topped maniacs with enough firepower to take on a battle fleet. "Suits are mechanical, have great power," Fireheels went on. "Can see through things, can fire cannon shells but —" He hesitated, realizing he shouldn't give away the fact that they were nearly out of ammo. It couldn't hurt for the chief to be unsure about their exact firepower capability—"can cause great damage."

"Why *you* not wear suit?" the chief asked the Apache trooper. "Isn't Indian good enough for big suit? Is discrimination!"

"Suit ran out of fuel and was destroyed," Fireheels vehemently answered, taking a chance on that particular truth with the guy, since he was starting to trust him. "These fellows are good. Not against us Indians!"

"We're not gods or anything," Sturgis said softly but with authority from the top of the bus as the chief stared up at him with those dark emotionless eyes. "just men in fighting gear trying to —"

"We talk more later," Chief Naktu said with a sharp yell, cutting off Sturgis's little speech of friendship suddenly, as if he had made the decision to spare them, at least for now. "Enemy of my enemy *may* be a friend of mine," the chief said, looking at Fireheels and then up at Sturgis who had pulled his visor back so the man

156

could see there was a human being inside, could see the power and resolution in Sturgis's own eyes. "Or you fella could also be my enemy. We see."

He motioned for several of the guards to accompany him as he walked off toward a burning well some two hundred yards along the inner fence. The vehicles that had taken a direct hit from the bus-howitzer were burning up, a funneling tower of black smoke that was starting to blot out the whole western sky.

"Thana Suquito," one of the flamethrower-carrying Indians said, motioned them to all come out of the bus. Once they were all lined up outside, they were marched forward with the flamers on each side of them standing some ten feet away. There was just no way Sturgis could risk an assault. They'd all be burned up. Besides, Fireheels was doing okay.

He carried Robin wrapped in several blankets. The Indians looked curious but didn't say anything as they herded them along.

"Take it easy boys," Sturgis whispered over the helmet mike. "Just stay relaxed and—" One of the guards motioned strongly with his flamethrower that none of them should talk. His face was cold, and he meant it. They were led about two hundred feet farther past other Naquis, men and women, many of them armed with flamethrowers around their shoulders. They even had small hand units, children with tiny fuel packs on some of their backs. Sturgis was impressed. This was a tough lot, he could see by their muscular bodies and the stoical desert-hardened faces on every one of them. As many Killboys as there were waiting out there beyond the fences, Sturgis knew they might well have taken on the wrong guys this time.

"Maqui, maqui," they shouted as they came to a cavern entrance dug right out of the base of sandstone mountain which rose above them absolutely covered with pueblo dwellings, levels, ramps. The ancient cliff city rose as far as the eye could see to the top, and to each

side. Condo-city, Indian style.

"They want us to go inside," Fireheels, who was standing next to Sturgis in the lead, said softly. "We better do everything they say, they're really itchy with those fireguns. Apparently—I heard two of them talking—the Killboys have been trying to infiltrate the camp for weeks. Sneak in spies, saboteurs."

"Sure, no problem," Sturgis said with a smile to their captors. The Indians motioned for him again to shut up, pulling the barrel of the flamer across his throat, indicating what would happen if he didn't zip his mouth.

Sturgis walked into the redstone entrance, having to bend down as the suit at 7' didn't make it standing fully up, and holding Robin. Her weight wasn't a problem but didn't make it any easier. Still, it wasn't hard to navigate once he was inside. There were gas powered lamps up on the walls of the tunnel, which quickly widened. The tunnel diverged, spread off in numerous directions. There were rooms everywhere filled with all kinds of pipes and supplies for oil drilling as well as furs, water gourds and other life necessities. The pueblo labyrinth had stepped-corridors rising up to other levels and stairs descending down into the earth. Sturgis and the rest could see that it was a whole city bigger than White Sands Base in there.

As they were herded deeper into the base of the mountain, Sturgis's grid visor kept reading out material assessments, the weight of rock above them, the location of Indians around them. Which was a lot. The place was crawling with the tribesmen. They were like a colony of ants. There were a lot more than one would have imagined from just seeing the outer pueblo dwellings on the face of the mountain. These Indians or their ancestors had dug right into the redstone maybe with their very fingernails. They had secured themselves a rock-oasis in the middle of the lunar-like landscape of the desert!

Chapter Twenty-one

As he carried Robin deeper into the tunnel system, Sturgis began seeing drawings, cave drawings on the red walls of the sandstone mountain. They were clearly ancient, of a different time and culture. Crude representations of bison and braves taking them down; drawings of bull gods and demons with great horned faces and claws. The early artists hadn't held back in their emotional renderings of their feelings, Sturgis thought. He kept looking down at Robin to make sure she wasn't being scraped by his carrying her through the tunnels. She was still unconscious, but breathing well.

They were marched for what seemed like five minutes with tunnels heading off everywhere. He tried to keep track of it all, telling the suit as well to keep a precise map of their path. But Sturgis had his doubts, there were just too many twists and turns, doors right next to one another for even the suit's I.D. computer to keep full track of it all. Up and up they went. At last they came to a large almost circular room with beds and chairs hewn right out of the rock and were guided inside.

Sturgis cleared the dust off one of the rock platforms of hairs and little bits of fabric. It had clearly been slept on before. He put the precious load down and stepped back.

The guards left. Soon after, an Indian with yellow lighting bolts painted horizontally across his face, and bones clanking all around his shoulders and chest came in. He went over to Robin holding a bird skull out in front of him and cawing like one of the feathered flock as well. Sturgis knew he was a medicine man, only trying to help. He circled her once and then reached out and grabbed her, throwing her up over one shoulder and started walking out as if he were carrying an old bear rug.

Sturgis rose and was ready to stop this—then three flamethrower-holding guards, who were standing behind him in the shadows against the wall, moved their weapons toward him.

The chief came in. "No! Sit. Our great doctor must do medicine alone," Chief Naktu said. He rose up even higher than the top of Sturgis's suit. "Must treat bite. sure. Promise she will live. Or you can kill shaman."

The chief folded his arms to indicate the end of that conversation as Sturgis felt a maelstrom of emotions and confusion surge through him.

"Better let them run the show," Fireheels said, from next to him. "I'm sure they'll do their best for her, and it's not any worse than what we're doing. A lot of tribes have herbal treatments for the snake bites that rival anything western medicine could perform. He'll get to that, sooner or later too."

Sturgis sat back down but he was shaking, could feel his entire body shaking inside the suit. He prayed he hadn't just done the worst thing he'd even done in his life by not fighting for her, by allowing her to be taken off.

"Why you pass this way?" Naktu asked Sturgis in a friendly tone, as the others looked on interestedly. A bunch of more stone-faced characters than Sturgis and

160

even Fireheels had *never* seen.

"To return to our home about three hundred fifty miles to the south," Sturgis replied, trying to control the anger in his voice. "We crashed in a plane far to the north and have been traveling for many days."

"No man come from northern desert," the chief said, looking hard at Sturgis, his almond eyes narrowing to lightless wafers.

"We did, sir. The suits are very strong, and can protect against rain, sand, bullets, many things."

"What can do?" the chief asked, clearly not convinced that the C.A.D.S. unit was anything more than a strange buffalo hide arrangement, metal style. That it was all just a front.

"Better show him something," Fireheels said with a lopsided grin. "These guys are from Missouri — you have to show them you're on the side of the gods."

"Right," Sturgis said standing to his full height. He raised his arm and pointed the gloved hand toward a rock formation — a stone lump — hanging down behind the chief on the far side. Without a word he turned his wrist to the right and a quick spray of five 9mm. slugs came shooting out, ripping right into the sandstone. The formation detached from the ceiling with a sharp snap and came crashing down on the ground.

The chief grunted and he talked quickly among the others. That little demo hadn't hurt his side any, Sturgis could see that already.

"It can fire bullets, from .22 long all the way up to bazooka shells. My suit has a computer inside," Sturgis went on, walking slowly around in a circle, as if he were a pitchman at an executive board meeting, showing the vision of the future. "It can sense everything around it, Chief Natku. It has ears, eyes that can see miles ahead. I'll demonstrate." He walked a few yards out toward where the medicine man had carried Robin. To

161

the left was a balcony and Sturgis stepped out on it. The chief followed.

"Infra red mode," he commanded the visor and instantly he could see the barbed wire surrounded land below. And the Killboys, a dozen of them sneaking up on their bellies in the gathering darkness. They had covered themselves with black garments and their faces and arms were blackened as well. They held explosives in packs along their arms meant to rip up all the fencing.

"I can see Killboy nightfighters crawling in through your defenses," Sturgis said with an ironic tone. He checked the computer's supply list for flares and saw that he had one left. He raised the opposite hand, giving the verbal signal and visual coordinates. All Sturgis had to do was look at a spot when he fired, and the laser-guidance did the rest.

A flare shot down the tube on his left sleeve and right out into the night. It flew a quarter mile and then dropped down to about two hundred feet above the attackers. The chiefs rose up on their toes. Chief Naktu exclaimed, *"Ah,"* as the flare lit up.

Now they could *all* see them by the light of the flare. Naktu screamed out orders through a funnel that ran along one stone wall, much like the communication units used in ships, with tubing leading off to other parts of the pueblo dwelling. Within seconds a pool of oil was released right where the twelve nightfighters were infiltrating. They were on fire in mere seconds, every one of them running around in headless chicken patterns, until their loads of plastique began exploding. When it was finished, there were only flaming pieces strewn around the cut-open fencing. Nothing human remained.

"How you see them?" the chief asked, as he walked over to Sturgis and circled the C.A.D.S. unit a few times. He hit it here and there, Sturgis didn't say a word as the not quite 100% functioning shock and recoil system did its best to deal with the gargantuan blows.

"Special vision modules," Sturgis replied. "Like TV rays, cameras hidden inside. It can see into clouds, mountains, even men. I can see in the darkest of darknesses."

"Me try!" the chief demanded suddenly, with a strange smile on his face. "Me try!"

"Well, it's hard to use, and the power's low," Sturgis began stuttering, trying to think of an excuse why the chief shouldn't get into the thing.

"Show me!" the man said, this time more forcefully.

Sturgis knew he was outployed. He put the thing into park and unlatched, until he pushed open the suit's chestplate. It swung open like a mummy's coffin, revealing the greasy, sweat soaked man within.

The chief's eyes widened, as he realized that in fact the leader was just an ordinary man. His confidence grew even stronger. Just a man. He could do it too. "If you friend, you let me!"

Sturgis sighed. "Okay."

"How work?" Naktu asked, as he stepped into the leg sections and then began strapping himself in.

"Oh God," Sturgis whispered under his breath. This could be a disaster. "At least let me help you," he said, walking a few steps and helping the chief with the strappings. He slammed all the weapon's units and self destruction switches into neutral, meaning Naktu couldn't accidentally explode the suit, or take any of his compatriots out. But it *would* move around.

He had the thing all closed up around the chief, who was too big even for a large C.A.D.S. unit. He was all scrunched down inside the thing and the helmet would barely close around the large head, even with the head-

163

dress left behind. But he got in. This was *crazy!*

"How move?" the chief asked as he gingerly tried the right arm.

"It's just like your own body," Sturgis exclaimed, standing before the high tech war machine. "Whenever you move, it will increase that motion, many times. Make you dozens of times stronger than you already are." An idea that Sturgis could hardly think about!

The Chief moved forward, one leg swinging a little unsteadily around. But the servo mechs compensated even for that with their internal gyros. The chief was soon moving faster and faster about the wide balcony, a look of supreme pleasure on his face.

"Feels funny," he said through the opened visor as he raised and lowered both arms, a little jerkily. But then troopers usually worked in mockups of the real thing for weeks, even months before they were allowed in.

The chief suddenly rushed forward laughing like a child. He could feel the extra strength rising out of every muscle that he moved. A small push with his foot, made him rise up a good two feet into the air and move ahead six or eight feet. This was *fun!*

"Like the gods," the chief said, running around the outside of the circle as the other Indians had to pull their bodies quickly aside to avoid his flying metal armoring. "Me happy. I am like the gods."

"Yes, the gods," Sturgis said almost silently. For he had almost forgotten that first feeling he had when he tried the suit. A feeling of being among the immortal ones, with the strength of giants of legend. He had grown used to its capabilities, its tremendous raw power. In a way it made him relax, trust the Indians all a little more, to see the chief's unbridled pleasure in the use of the suit. He watched as the chief strode to the wall and slammed his fist into it. The whole balcony seemed to shake for a second as the gloved titanium hand sank in

164

a good foot. The chief let out with a whoop and slammed the other fist in, making a similar hole and a similar curtain of dust.

"How shoot thing?" the chief asked, turning around and twisting his hands this way and that as Sturgis had done.

"All out of ammo," Sturgis lied, raising his shoulders. In fact there were only a few slugs left, so it wasn't too much of a lie.

The chief jumped around some more, testing the arm and leg strength of the suit and seeming to pick up very fast the operation of the thing. It was as if he wanted to use its power, show his men and Sturgis himself that he could handle its god-energy. After several minutes he stopped and said. "Very tight! Enough—release me."

Sturgis undid the clamps again and the chief stepped out, with a most beatific look on his face.

"We will help you," the chief said, staring at Sturgis so his eyes felt like two dark coals, made of melting sand. "Use these suits against Killboys. We feed you, make girlfriend well. Give you *oil!*"

"Well, I don't think we can. You see, we've got a few problems with the suits," Sturgis said, as he climbed back into his. The chief got a sad look in his eye. "But we'll do our damnedest to fix them. And to help you—friend! Now please, can I see Robin, the woman? I'd like to know what the treatment is."

"Suits," the chief said, staring out over the balcony to the flickering lights of the Killboy's car-army a half mile away. "C.A.S.S. suits," he mispronounced, "will be the 'Hotuli'—Great Weapon—what we have been searching for! We will end forever the madness of the hard-haired ones."

"Oh yeah, a great weapon," Sturgis echoed as he finished snapping the suit closed. Only it wasn't worth a lot more than what the chief had just done, smashing holes in walls. Without ammo, and in the face of high powered artillery, the suits weren't worth more than the Tin Man, the Scarecrow or the Cowardly Lion. But Sturgis wasn't about to let Naktu know that.

Chapter Twenty-two

"Naktu," a voice was yelling out over a scratchy but *loud* public address system from among the cars far away. "Naktu!" it came again, more insistent, as the shelling from the vehicular invaders which had gone on sporadically, ceased. The entire gathering of Naktu and his lesser chiefs, along with Sturgis and Fireheels, made their way to the edge of the stone balcony just outside their fifteenth story level of the pueblo complex. In the darkness, they couldn't be seen. But they could see clearly the armada of vehicles spread out nearly as far as the C.A.D.S. Infra-eye could see.

A bonfire suddenly burst up just beyond the outermost gate as a car, a huge yellow Cadillac with wide tail fins like slicing blades, drove up.

A man got out, stood on the hood, took the bullhorn and began screaming in a gruff voice toward the sandstone mountain.

"Naktu, we well let youse and all your people go, if you just give us the oil," the voice said with an almost pleading tone. "We want only the black gold for our cars and trucks. We have no need of cutting your stinkin' Indian throats." He laughed and the voice and laugh echoed darkly through the smoke-filled but now silent air.

Sturgis had his vision-mode jump to Maximum infra and telemode so he could see better. It was a huge dude, with black and white painted spikes for hair. The hair looked like something that could be found on a mutant cactus, not a man's head. He was very broad and covered head to toe in black leather and black boots. Studs were prominent everywhere, only these were jutting mini-knives and daggers, Sturgis saw, as he did a close-up on the suit. Just banging against the guy accidentally in a hallway would be a death sentence. His face was just formless folds of fat with a bushy beard dyed a vibrant gold. The beard seemed to almost glisten from the rays of the surrounding fires that the besieging army had built for warmth and cooking.

The eyes had no life in them, just dull pools of death. And of course he had the de rigueur Road-rat's kitchen fork pierced through both cheeks, the points facing outward. The white complexion of the man's flesh, not quite an albino, but in the same general family, finished off the appealing picture. Sturgis felt an involuntary shiver race up and down his backbone. If he had ever seen death, nihilism, thanatos, the death-wish personified in human form—*this* was it.

The Naqui chiefs had already made their decisions about not surrendering to the man.

"Macro-Kill!" Chief Naktu spat out with contempt as he stared down at the figure through rusted US Army issue binoculars. He turned to the wall, shouted out commands through the brass voice tube that led to firing stations around the pueblo complex. Even as Marco-Kill continued his poignant speech about why it would be better for everyone involved if the entire tribe just handed over the whole place pronto, a set of flaming gasoline barrels went flying off from immense catapults five hundred feet above Sturgis's head, from the very top of the sandstone mountain. From there they had good trajectories. They were spitting flame as they flew in fiery spirals through the night, headed right

168

for the speaker and his car which was right up to the outermost fence ring.

Macro-Kill only realized that the bastards had actually sighted him up as the cannisters of high-grade kerosene came plummeting down toward the car. At the last possible instant Macro-Kill leaped with a wild burst of blubbery strength from the Caddy. Two of his personal bodyguards didn't have such luck. The barrels slammed into the front and back of the wide yellow ultra-finned luxury car and exploded it. Flying shrapnel blossomed in all directions, burning metal and flesh mixing in the air.

Macro-Kill hit the ground some twenty feet away and was blown another ten yards by the force of the blast, rolling end over end across pieces of debris. But he rose up unscathed, raised his fist at the pueblo mountain screaming out a whole litany of obscene ideas as to just where the Indians could—and soon *would* go.

Chief Naktu watched with folded arms and a most skeptical expression.

"Never surrender," he said to Sturgis just so the suited man would know where he stood. "Other small tribe, the Qusami, a hundred miles from here north. They surrender year ago—were wiped out by these—creatures that call themselves men. Men, women, children, all killed within an hour. The oil ran out there, now they come here. But they lie. They are evil, dark men. We fight the Killboys to the death. And now—you too," the chief added with just a touch of irony in his usually stone face, "fight them."

Sturgis had fallen right into the stone valley of death. But at least he had macho allies.

"Well, hopefully it won't come to all of us having to die," the C.A.D.S. commander replied, trying to add a note of optimism into the extremely depressing conversation. Suddenly there was a deafening roar just yards

169

away. The shock force of a shell had detonated just down the mountain wall from them. Followed by screams which they could hear came from just below them. Someone had gotten hit. The shell must have gone right in through one of the uncovered doors or windows. More of the long-range shells came flying in, all able to go beyond the mile of fences, barbed wire burning streams of oil that protected the tribe.

"They've gotten bigger guns in somehow," Sturgis said, smacking his hand against the stone wall. "Those shells are making greater range." The entire pueblo floor seemed to shake each time one of the shells went off. And within seconds there were a whole storm of the artillery shells coming down around on the sandstone mountain complex. Explosion after explosion lit up the night; dust filled the air. And from above and below, screams came every few seconds. The shells were finding more than stone.

Sturgis telescoped again into Macro and Weapons ID modes. The Killboys had brought in five big M27's, 105mm's. Those barrels were ten feet long and capable of easily clearing the distance to the mountain. Shells roared through the air, filling the sky with plumes of red-like giant tracers. And they hit hard into the face of the mountain, slamming into the outer walls of the pueblo city. The Naqui had built their homes and storage deep inside the mountain just so they could be protected from the outside world. It protected them against sun, rain, even snow from time to time. But even in their wildest dreams, they and their ancestors who had begun the excavations had never envisioned anything like this.

But the Killboys stopped firing after ten minutes. Out of ammo themselves — for now. But wherever they got it, they might be able to get more.

Sturgis was allowed to return to his men. They had clearly all been accepted as "friends" at least for the moment. The guards had been taken away and they were free to roam the place, with a guide, Laughing Elk, Naktu's son, a youngish brave who couldn't have been over eighteen. Unlike many of the Naqui this lad had a sunny disposition and seemed interested in Sturgis, his crew and the C.A.D.S. units. He wore an odd combination of Indian garb and hammered out pieces of Americana as armoring over his body. The armor seemed made of smashed-in aluminum pots and pans, though it was hard to tell, with everything flattened and attached by wires through holes. He was surrounded by the dangling armor which gave him a sort of walking junkheap look. His face was streaked with blood red stripes that started at each side of his mouth and went in an upward angle giving the appearance of whiskers, bloody whiskers. And yet he was friendly enough.

"You guys need more food?" he asked after he'd been introduced to the team, most of whom had taken off their suits which stood standing but driverless along one wall. Only MacLeish and Dixon kept theirs on, saying they felt more comfortable inside them. Sturgis could sense they didn't yet trust the Indians, and wanted to have a little bit of armoring between them and their captors as well. Sturgis took his off. It was almost impossible to get through some of the narrower passageways. He just didn't like the idea of getting wedged in somehow like an overfed sardine in a tin, having to be blasted out of the stone walls.

"Could always use more food," Rossiter answered Laughing Elk's question, patting his ample stomach. Laughing Elk grabbed some of the service squaws who were rushing by the large room the C.A.D.S. unit had been given as temporary home. He spoke quickly to them. The comely maidens in leather tassled skirts and blouses nodded and went running off.

"Will bring more," the young Indian replied gruffly. "You just tell me. What you need—I get. My father says to treat you all with respect due those who the Oil-god sent!" He bowed slightly toward Sturgis.

The colonel was just going to demand to see Robin, but suddenly two braves brought Robin in through the door. They laid her gently down on one of the straw beds.

Sturgis could see that she was alive, her chest rising and falling slowly. One of the braves spoke to Laughing Elk, who listened intently, then translated. "He say. Medicine Man has done what he can." The chief's son addressed Sturgis as the C.A.D.S. troopers gathered around Robin, looking down at her with drawn faces. They all knew what she meant to their commander. "Medicine man has given her herbal treatments, steaming the wound to get rid of poison. We have own antibiotics made from petroleum," Laughing Elk said with pride. "Not just savage Indians like it might appear." He laughed, somewhat contemptuously. "Much modern stuff here—machines, medicine. You get to know us—you'll see."

"I believe you, pal," Sturgis said as he stroked Robin's sweat-soaked hair. Whatever they had just put her through seemed to have generated a lot of heat. He'd have to trust them. He had no choice.

"Come," Laughing Elk said to Sturgis, "make grand tour of La Mesa, our mountain."

"I'd like to come too," Rossiter piped in, "see if there's anything we can use for power generation acceptable to the C.A.D.S. battery inputs."

"Come," Laughing Elk said, looking the chunky trooper up and down. "I show you power stations."

"I'm going to take a look around," Sturgis addressed the rest of the crew. "You all stay cool, and I'd appreciate it if you basically stayed inside here. The shelling was intense. I don't need any accidents that could be avoidable, if it starts up again."

"Will do, Skip," Tranh replied. He automatically took over as number two when Sturgis was off; not that the rest of the unit necessarily loved the idea. Billy for one, felt he should have the honor!

Laughing Elk led them down the passageway. There was tremendous activity everywhere around the place, Indians running around madly, carrying all kinds of supplies. First stop was four levels down where they came to a large generating room. Four heavy duty gasoline powered electric generators were chugging away as electric cables spread out of them heading into different areas of the pueblo city.

"All *right*," Rossiter said as he spied the equipment. He got down on hands and knees and begin trying to make heads or tails of the connecting junctures. The supervisor of the power plant, a large broadchested Indian who was stripped to his loincloth—as the heat was quite intense in the large power chamber—came over. Laughing Elk introduced him to the C.A.D.S. men and told him to give Rossiter whatever help he needed. Many of the older Indians spoke English, at least enough to make basic communication possible. Rossiter ripped out a pad and pencil and began drawing diagrams of how the units were linked up and figuring the kind of interface he needed to charge the C.A.D.S. batteries.

Then Sturgis was given the tour. It was as if the brave wanted him to see just how grand the city really was, how many people and different elements were involved.

The C.A.D.S. commander was impressed. Level after level of housing, supplies, schools for the children, a

173

hospital, several large cooking chambers where meals for the entire complex were on the gas at all times. They had cleverly used the electric power they generated to run just about everything in the place. It was a miracle of engineering. Crude, but effective.

As they traveled to different levels, the shelling began anew outside. Just where the Killboys had gotten hold of so many shells was beyond Sturgis's ken as the stuff was very hard to come by. Most heavy stuff had been used up in the 'Psycho-Days,' the year after the nukes had fallen. But they were using it up with a vengeance. It seemed endless. The place rocked and dust began falling from the ceilings through the complex. Sturgis just prayed it was all going to hold up. Dying inside a giant Indian sandbox was not one of the C.A.D.S. commander's favorite choices on how he wanted to leave this earth. Though when he thought about it for more than a few seconds, there was no way he wanted to leave. Not right now. Not with the thousands of Killboys out there!

Chapter Twenty-three

It was clear to Sturgis that Laughing Elk was showing him all this to let him know that the Indians were as powerful as Sturgis and his armored unit. Men feel more like equals when they know the other is fully aware of their strength. A balance of power, even in friendships, makes for better relations.

What the Naqui had done with very primitive conditions and raw materials was astounding. And the colonel let the man know it, complimenting him on their many accomplishments. Laughing Elk took these compliments with great pride. Sturgis could see that pride mattered greatly to the man and to all of them.

By the time they headed back to the chamber where the C.A.D.S. team was bivouacked, Rossiter was feeding electricity from a thick cable into one of the suits.

"I've got this doohickey already hooked up to our suits, Cap," Rossiter said as Sturgis walked over. "These guys are ingenious. They don't have plugs or whatever in each room, but they do have long cables on coils on each level, four of them. As you can see, they can be unraveled on a coil cable to wherever it's needed. We rigged up some voltage transformers and power circuits using some spare parts I had along, and some junk the Naqui let me use—great guys, by the way. Had a stimulating talk about electrical engineering in sign language and drawing figures in the sand. Should try that some time when you're trying to express amps and resistances with a twig."

"So what's the diagnosis?" Sturgis asked. "Are we actually going to get some of these tin cans up to full power?" The idea of fully functioning suits again, even without full ammo was most appealing.

"Let's say I can probably jam us up to seventy, maybe even eighty percent. Maybe even get jump-modes working again. With the oil—they have it in the right refined quality—we can fuel up just about everything—except—can't make *ammunition* out of oil or electricity!"

"What's the EFT?" Sturgis asked. Using the initials for Estimated Fueling Time, as it was commonly referred to by the C.A.D.S. techs back at base.

"Maybe all night. I'm using a jumper to do two at a time, but it's a slow process," Rossiter said as he leaned over and looked at a gauge on the side of one of the suits. He slammed it hard with his hand and then smiled as the arrow moved up to the 75% battery storage reading. "Maybe have four, at best six of them up to par by midnight. All of them by morning, if we go in teams."

"Good work," Sturgis said, slapping the thick armed Rossiter on the shoulder. He walked over to Robin who they had rigged up a real bed for in the back of the chamber. She looked pale as a Victorian ghost, but her breathing seemed deeper and more rapid than when he had left. He felt helpless, and hated that. What if the Indian treatment didn't work?

"The signs are good," Tranh said, as he sat down next to her. "Sheila was giving her water from a gourd earlier. Some of the liquid just trickled down her lips, but some got inside. The shaman warned that dehydration was one of the main dangers and asked Sheila to keep the fluids going."

Sturgis nodded. He could hardly stand to look at her,

so corpse-like did she appear. Tears kept welling up in his eyes as he couldn't help but think that's how she would look if she were dead. But he swallowed hard, stroked her face a few times and then turned away. There wasn't time for emotion, not with half the artillery in America coming down on him and his men.

"Skip, got to talk to you," DeCamp said, coming over. She looked as bad as they all did. Her sweatshirt and slacks were coated with sand, dirt and flecks of leaves and twigs — as if she'd been rolling around in a meadow. But her firm strong body was clearly visible beneath the clothes and an occasional leer from some of the C.A.D.S. team showed that the doctor was all woman. "MacLeish and I decided to see what kind of shape the computer of the first of the suits Rossiter juiced up was in. So we fed in our coordinates and — follow me — "

She led him over to one of the already-juiced suits with an 85% reading showing on its storage gauge, standing like a robot with both arms out by a wall. MacLeish was standing alongside it, pressing buttons on the outside on a little pop out computer keyboard. The information was projected onto the outside of the helmet visor, a recent innovation by the White Sands tech boys, one could use the computer info system without being in the suit.

"Commander," the Brit said, his ruddy face glowing with excitement. "We're getting some hot intel over here. We started playing with the computer trying to see just how much was linking up to internal mega memory."

"And we found," DeCamp spoke up, cutting off MacLeish as she wanted to get in on the action and get the credit. After all, it had been her idea. "When we asked it for all US Government facilities within a hundred mile radius, we learned that there was a combination airfield and supply dump not twenty miles to the north

177

of here. It was top secret, and according to the C.A.D.S. map coordinates was supposedly blown off the face of the earth by a small yield nuke. However—" she grinned at Sturgis, taking a deep breath, "when we pulled up the plans of the base out of Level 3 memory, it showed that the place, Fort Collins, was super-hardened. It was made to withstand a ten meg hit almost dead on. And all it took was maybe a twenty kiloton field nuke."

"Hardly enough to cook lobster," MacLeish broke in with a dark grin.

"It's quite possible, this base having all kinds of steel doors, and twenty foot thick concrete walls and being largely built underground, that it's been undiscovered ever since. Could be filled with a warehouse of ammunition. Stuff that would fit the C.A.D.S. suits, or close enough with the Variable Caliber Mode of the firing mechanisms to work."

"You're right, that's damned interesting," Sturgis said, looking on as they punched in the keyboard asking for the coordinates of the base in relation to the pueblo's mountain. A grid map flashed onto the outer tinted surface of the visor and Sturgis watched with rapt attention.

"It even still reads 'INTACT' " DeCamp pointed out as the green letters flashed alongside the small pyramid shaped symbol representing Fort Collins. "Now that doesn't necessarily mean a whole lot. But at least it's not among the bases and fields that White Sands *knows* were destroyed, by satellite observation."

"Could we even get in there?" Sturgis asked, "even if we found the place under the sand?"

"I think so," DeCamp replied. Aside from being a full-fledged field trooper she had also worked in the Intel and and in the Engineering sections of White Sands, absorbing a lot of information along the way.

"We've worked out a code system that runs through a million possible code sequences a minute. Even if the whole place was wired up for Top Security access, I'd say we have a real shot at getting in. Of course I can't promise anything but—"

"But it's worth a try," Sturgis said with enthusiasm, the first time he'd felt any in days. "You're sure of those map coordinates?"

"Checked 'em and doublechecked 'em," DeCamp said with a firm voice. "Unless the nuke that hit there moved the whole place a few miles—we're right near it. It would appear to have been hit with a neutron bomb or the equivalent, high gamma radiation, low heat and blast. The Reds apparently used a lot of the little buggers on small isolated bases around the country, rather than the big meggers. After all, they had plans for colonization until we, among other counter-strike groups, put some dampers in their plans."

"Amen to that," MacLeish added, slamming his fist into his hand.

"Then let's get the show on the road," Sturgis said. "I'll need three suits, as juiced as you can get them within, say an hour. Can do?"

"It's going to be hard, Skip," Rossiter said, who had been listening to the whole discourse. "I'll do my best," he mumbled. With a big wrench in the palm of his hand, he headed back and began fiddling with the circuits to speed up the juicing operation even more.

Sturgis and Laughing Elk headed up to the council room where Laughing Elk told their plan to the pueblo's hierarchy. There was a heated debate for several minutes and at last Chief Naktu spoke up.

"My people—and I—are unsure," the chief said as he looked fixedly at Sturgis. "We *want* to believe you will help us. Yet the ammunition for your robot suits would give you tremendous firepower, would make you most able to destroy us from within."

"Chief, if I had a thousand years, which I don't," Sturgis said, with all the sincerity he could muster, "I couldn't prove to you that we don't mean harm. But we want to help you. We will go and bring the ammunition back, load our C.A.D.S. suits—and fight *with* you, not *against* you. Somewhere along the line, men must trust each other. I beg you to trust us. It could make the difference between life and death for all of us. We both know that the shelling is just the start. Those Killboy cars up there aren't going to wait forever."

"Yes, you are right," Naktu said with deep solemnity. He looked deep into Sturgis's eyes as if trying to gauge the depths of the man's soul. Then over at his son, Laughing Elk who had spent several hours with the C.A.D.S. commander. The young brave nodded slightly. A *yes*. His father trusted his judgment. And his own intuition as well, which told him that Sturgis, unlike most of the white race, was an honest man.

"I believe that what you speak is what you mean," Naktu said. "All right. You may go. Laughing Elk will accompany you to lead. The way out the back is very hard to follow. May the gods be with you. And may I not have made the mistake that will wipe my tribe from the face of the earth." He didn't speak anymore. Just felt a trembling in his heart.

At midnight, one hour later, they assembled in the C.A.D.S.-occupied chamber. Sturgis had chosen Tranh, Dixon and Fireheels to accompany him. And DeCamp as well. He felt trepidations about bringing the woman doc on such a clearly dangerous mission. But only one suit was going to be completely functional in time, and she was the expert. She had to go about decoding locks and electrolinking the suit's computer system into the security system of Fort Collins, if it really did exist. He had no choice. So, armed with detached pistols, each

180

holding only a dozen or so 7.2mm slugs, DeCamp in a C.A.D.S. suit and Laughing Elk with one of the mini flamethrower handguns with fuel pack around his waist, they set off down into the lower levels of the pueblo complex as the shelling sporadically continued to rock the very foundations of the place.

They reached the lowest level of the mountain, headed back about a hundred feet where Laughing Elk lifted a large wooden door that looked as though it hadn't been used for decades.

"Escape hatch," he smiled at the others. "Not that we will leave here. All stay, all die if need be. The Killboys will *never* get our oil! Indians no longer flee from white men, like in the old days. Now, we hold our ground."

Sturgis felt a surge of respect for Laughing Elk and his people. Whatever subservient interactions they and other tribes had had with the white men, with the government in the past, those days were over. In the future, if there was one, this tribe would meet with the white men only as equals, with full shares in the new America and all that it might offer. And Sturgis wouldn't have it any other way.

"Going to be a tight squeeze," the brave said as he started down the stairs. Sturgis followed behind him, then DeCamp. Tranh and Dixon looked around warily as they went right down into the earth. Fireheels took up the rear, eyes scanning all around them.

"It's very old down here," Laughing Elk said as they started forward through the circular shaped tunnel. He held a small battery operated lantern that illuminated the tunnel ahead, though even as they walked they began stirring up dust that tasted like it was eons old and the air became obscured.

"Your people have always lived here?" Sturgis asked as he made his way a yard or so behind the brave.

"First ancestors moved in a thousand years or more

ago. Then fled here in early 1950's, to avoid the fallout from nearby atomic tests. My people reclaimed it after the Great War. Fixed it all up, good as new," he laughed, slapping a piece of wall so a whole chunk came out and dropped to the ground. There were more of the cave drawings down here, these even more primitive than the ones up in the higher levels. Crude scrawlings of things that were barely discernible as animals. They looked like some of the first paintings ever made, as if men were still learning how to draw.

"I'm having a little trouble here," DeCamp spoke through her opened visor. Sturgis turned to see that she had wedged herself in slightly at the shoulders since the tunnel narrowed at the top. But Tranh and Dixon, right behind her, gave a few hard pushes and she was free.

"Better bend down more," Sturgis advised her, "the servo's should take the strain off your knees." She followed his advice and quickly seemed to get the hang of it. They walked for what felt like miles, the tunnel system getting more ancient feeling. Far behind them they could hear the shells making their holes in the pueblo. But even that fearsome sound died out and they were alone in the deep darkness, with only their breathing and footsteps.

"Lord, I'm feeling even more claustrophobic than I did upstairs," Tranh said after they'd been marching about half an hour. "When does this termite tunnel come to an end?"

"Soon, soon, impatient one," Laughing Elk let out with a little laugh and they could see where he got his name. For the laughter was filled with a kind of joy and fullness of spirit as if everything was amusing. It made them all grin slightly. The man had *something,* like his father. A vitality. Just when it seemed that they must be heading into the lobby of hell itself, Laughing Elk slowed them down and cut the lantern.

"Outside, just ahead," he whispered to Sturgis. "Maybe Killboys waiting." He took out a long machete-like blade from his belt, not wanting to create a ruckus if there was a way to avoid it. He led them around a twist in the tunnel and then up a straight corridor that rose steeply. They rose perhaps fifty feet over a hundred foot length, giving DeCamp a little trouble again at the steep angle. But suddenly they were there.

Laughing Elk and Sturgis got their shoulders behind a boulder that had been pushed into place and quickly rolled it free. The whole barren desert lay before them, the stars shining down like a billion knives, ready to fall to earth and impale those who dared walk through such hallowed grounds.

Chapter Twenty-four

They shot out into the night, knives in hand just in case there were enemy forces waiting out back. But no one awaited them. All the Killboy forces were behind. A mile off, they could see the end of one of the siege lines of cars, too far to be noticed by them. At first they moved at half speed, getting used to the desert, the night. They let their muscles stretch out a little, let the cool oxygen-rich night fill their lungs, sear their throats with an icy electricity.

But soon they were moving at full speed. The men, Sturgis, Tranh, Dixon, Fireheels, and Laughing Elk were all in excellent shape and hit a stride that would have made an Olympic marathoner envious. DeCamp, as well, fell into the motion of the servo mechs on the full powered C.A.D.S. suit. She took great leaping strides ten, fifteen feet at a time. Once she was in full gear and feeling in control of the suit she surged ahead of the men. DeCamp felt a thrill of female pride that at least inside this high tech marvel she could outrun them forever.

She and MacLeish had programmed in the coordinates of Fort Collins and by merely looking at the grid map on the visor she could see where the place was and their proximity at all times. The rest of them ran a game of catch-up just yards behind her.

The moon was a razor-thin edge of white which kept

slicing through high green strontium clouds. The stars and the eerie whiteness of the prairie itself seemed to take whatever light there was and reflect it in all directions. At any rate they had little trouble seeing, once their eyes adjusted to the ghostly dimness. An occasional lizard or snake slithered by as they ran and Sheila stepped on something soft which made a dreadful sound and went diving off out of the way.

They all ran with a kind of joy, their minds for the moment forgetting why they were out here and feeling only the sheer pumping of their lungs and chests, the oxygen rushing into them like a drug. Cactus and scrubby yucca trees grew more prevalent as they got ten more miles away from the sandstone mountain. Sturgis thought he saw other structures on some smaller sandstone mountains—what looked like pueblo dwellings here and there as well. On macro-powerscan they appeared lifeless. Whoever had once lived in them was long gone.

DeCamp surged nearly a quarter mile ahead though they could see her by the high profile of the suit. She was way ahead of the boys and for once in her life she wasn't about to allow them to catch up, Sturgis realized.

They tore through the chilly night though once their bodies were covered with sweat they didn't feel the cold. Running in a mindless stride for nearly three hours. At last they came to a rise and as they reached the top found that DeCamp had stopped 20 feet down the far slope and was looking ahead intently. Two small craters stood about a half mile apart with a big dome of sand rising in the space between them. They had reached their goal. But it looked like little more than prairie, not a piece of metal sticking up, not a building visible.

"You sure this is it?" Sturgis asked as the men came alongside her huffing and puffing, their faces red.

"No question about it. In fact I'm getting a very very faint automatic distress radio signal. Repeating over and over on 2 MZ band! No, it all fits, the neutron bombs on each side created the small craters. It's all just as we deduced," she said with a twinkle.

"Damn, if there's weapons or ammo down there, we're going to need a fleet of bulldozers to get it out," Dixon said with disgust. "Hope we didn't run all this way just to see these picturesque little craters here. And by the way, I've seen bigger and better ones than those two anthills in my back yard back home."

"Right," Tranh said with a smirk. "Everything's bigger down in Georgia, right?"

"You got that right, No. 1 Asian son," Dixon replied sarcastically.

"Oh, knock it off, you two," DeCamp said through her opened visor. "This isn't the time to play super-macho. We have work to do." DeCamp was taking charge of the expedition. Before they could say a word, she was already bounding down the slope, taking great jumps so that her boots slammed a good six inches into the top soil as she landed. They reached the floor of the valley created by the two bomb craters, each about a hundred feet across, rim walls forty high, their tops long since smoothed out from the unceasing winds.

"What's the rad readings around here?" Sturgis asked as they approached with looks of awe up to the sand-covered base. "My readout is kaput."

"Not too bad right around where we are right now," DeCamp replied, reading the rads measurements on the visor. "But ahead, under the sand is still hot. Maybe ten times hotter than these outer sands where the winds have moved the topsoil around.

"Just where is the doorway?" Dixon asked, kicking arond at the dirt with his boot as if he might find it.

"I'm checking that right now," DeCamp said. "We'll

find out fast enough .Spread out and let me know if you see any building materials, pieces of metal, anything. The first thing is to figure out the configuration of the complex. Then we can try to get in."

They did as she requested, spreading out around the raised mound of slightly greenish dirt which stretched hundreds of yards. They kicked and poked and prodded and found nothing other than pieces of broken antenna, half collasped concrete blocks. It was Laughing Elk who found it first, the top of a concrete wall, which still seemed in one piece, just a foot or so beneath the surface. He called the others over and they dug out about a yard down until they reached a sign, faded and pockmarked with indentations from the sand which must have blasted into it when the two neutron antipersonnel bombs went off.

"Excellent," DeCamp exclaimed. She reached down and touched the metal door, the top of which stood in view. They heard the computer system inside the helmet chugging and beeping away.

"What she doing?" Laughing Elk asked in amazement at the technological churnings of the suit.

"She's touching the metal," Sturgis answered as De-Camp's attention was a hundred percent on the readouts she was getting on the visor. "The sonar probe finger of the suit sends out a minute electrical charge which circumnavigates the entire complex. It gives us a general image of what lies under the sand. Read your manual, you can work miracles."

"All right, we're in business, boys," DeCamp said with gusto as she raised one suit arm in a victory fist. "I've got the whole thing roughly mapped out now. The main entrance, where we have the best chance of getting in, is on the far side."

Without another word she began trotting over the sand as the others followed her. They reached the far side and began digging where DeCamp pointed out. She helped as well, taking wide kicks with the C.A.D.S. suit boot which sent whole little storms of sand flying off. Using several I-beams they found as shovels, it still took nearly half an hour for them to dig down the six feet. They uncovered a thick steel door. On the outside of it was what looked like a series of sockets and electrical inputs.

"This is *it*," DeCamp said with growing excitement. "The outer code-and-command controls. They built this sucker so that in the event of an attack, rescuers could get in from outside. Let's just pray that the code system is still functional." She kneeled down and pulled a small cable out from the side of her suit, reaching forward and plugging a five pronged futuristic looking plug into the opening.

"How could the generators, computers, or anything for that matter still be working after a half-dozen years?" Dixon asked with skepticism, starting to think that this whole nighttime run had been a wild goose chase.

"Works on a very different system," DeCamp muttered through her helmet as she had a little trouble getting the plug into the door. "Doesn't use a whole lot of power, at least this part of it. But we'll see. I never made any promises."

She put the plug in and then ordered the computer to send out combinations of electrical impulses. The access code had been changed daily years before so the computer began sending out combinations of possible numbers, a ten digit code, one after another. Since it could generate a thousand of them a second, it went through over a hundred thousand before there was a sudden satisfying beep coming from both the computer and the door itself.

"We're in, gentlemen," DeCamp said with satisfaction

as she looked up at them. They all watched in a kind of stupefied amazement as the door slid sideways into the concrete wall with a grinding sound, as if it didn't really want to go. Loose sand came pouring down into the opening so they had to jump back or be swept in. And the entire sandpile right in front of the opened door dropped about four feet so more of the steel frame was visible.

"Let's go, gentlemen," DeCamp said stepping gingerly into the darkness and then disappearing inside as they slid down the small dune surrounding the entrance behind her. DeCamp threw her helmet, lantern on and a bright beacon shone out from the top of the C.A.D.S. helmet lighting up the darkness within. The blast effect clearly hadn't penetrated the underground base, at least on this side. Though the high neutron radiation had, and surely that had killed the men inside.

"Getting higher readings here," she told them all. "In fact quite hot. But suit says should be okay, even unprotected for maybe up to an hour. After that—" They walked forward along the concrete block passageway. Another door, steel, and as thick as the first, blocked their passage.

"This isn't supposed to be here," DeCamp said with frustration as she looked around the thing for another set of interfacing plugs. There were none. She tried the handle on the thick steel door but it appeared stuck. The men gave it a few kicks and teamed up trying to shift the thing, but it wouldn't move for them either.

"I've got an idea," DeCamp said after a good five minutes of fruitless efforts. "It could be that the thing rusted up a little, is just jammed. Otherwise there would be some kind of electrical interface. Laughing Elk, why don't you spray your flamethrower over the joints, around the edges. Maybe—it will help loosen it up." The Indian looked over at Sturgis, not quite wanting to take orders from a woman. The C.A.D.S commander nodded almost imperceptibly, not wanting to get DeCamp riled up.

The Naqui heir to the chiefdom took his flamenozzle from its holster. Motioning for them all to stand back, he sprayed the entire door and the handle with gasoline flames. He moved the tongue of fire back and forth so that every inch of the sides and the handle got a good dose.

DeCamp reached forward to try the handle and Laughing Elk gasped as he blurted out, "No, too hot, don't." But the gloves of the suit were armored to take higher temperatures than the several hundred degrees of the door. She grabbed hold of the handle with both gloved hands and gave it her all.

Alone she never could have done it, but with the servo-assist mechanisms of the C.A.D.S. suit, the steel handle turned with a croaking, heavy sound. She pulled with all her strength and the steel door came slowly open, groaning like the door to a crypt locked for a thousand years.

Chapter Twenty-five

Inside the second door, they walked down a corridor, moving slowly, cautiously, DeCamp in the lead. The men would have had to admit that they felt a little chagrined at following a woman, had they questioned themselves very deeply. But she was batting a thousand so far. So they followed. There was a smell in the air, not at all pleasant, but familiar. Perhaps meat in a butcher shop, meat that had been allowed to sit around for a long, long time. They came to another door at the far end of the corridor and DeCamp tried the handle. This one swung open as if it had just been oiled.

They walked in and stared at a vision of hell. They were at one side of what had been a war room. Maps, computers were everywhere. And seated in front of them, still in the chairs they had occupied at the moment the neutrons had struck, were the officers of Fort Collins. Dead. Long dead. Only they hadn't disintegrated, hadn't decomposed down to their skeletal remains. Their skin had a leathery look, creases on the faces, eyes hard flesh marbles. But they looked basically the way they had died, some with red burns from the high stream of radiation.

"They look like creepy mummies," Dixon blurted out, breaking the many-yeared silence. They all had the creeps, all had shivers coursing along their flesh.

"Whatever happened here?" Tranh asked, getting the

most nervous of all of them, as he had a thing about ghosts and demons. He swore they all looked like they were about to start moving. There was something so lifelike about the way hands still rested on controls, the way a coffee mug sat still full in front of a few of them. The way one's mouth was open as if he were about to finish a sentence that would never be finished.

"I think I can explain it." DeCamp said as she walked a few steps, feeling as if she were entering a sanctuary that had best not be disturbed. "The neutron bomb, the different washes of electromagnetic rays it sends out — can go right through concrete by the way — killed them all on the spot, but basically left the base alone, their flesh untouched other than these burn marks."

"But why haven't they decomposed?" Sturgis asked, as he came up alongside her.

"Because even the bacteria down here are dead. Everything inside here was irradiated. They could stay this way for ten thousand years without changing at all except —"

"Except what?" Dixon asked, as he joined the rest of them inside the immense high tech chamber that must have been two hundred feet long, a good hundred wide with twenty foot high ceilings.

"Except that we've allowed bacteria in. We've let the outside world into this burial tomb. Now, it will all begin rotting, decomposing. It is already. Now its disintegration is inevitable."

"Jesus," Dixon said, covering his mouth with his hand. They walked along through the center of the war room looking from side to side, noting the last moments of every man there. It was like a frozen sculpture of several hundred air force officers. It was simple enough to see just what each had been doing, or trying to do in the last seconds.

"Probably didn't even know what hit them," Fireheels commented as he shuddered deeply, his own tribal ghosts being conjured up in his mind. Even the bravest man can face the living, it's the dead that bring nightmares.

"Oh, they knew it was coming," Sturgis said. "Look, you can see right here on the computer screens. Some of them are locked in to the final warnings. He pointed out a few of the monitors which read "IMMINENT DETONATION TWO WARHEADS." And "IMPACT ONE SECOND." And other such telegrams of destruction.

"Look, a—a dog," DeCamp said as she passed the center point of the War Room. It was lying on its side, the fur blackened all along one side, the other half virtually untouched. "The gamma rays must have caused its fur to catch on fire. Poor little pup."

"What's the rad readings now?" Sturgis asked as he felt his skin seem to warm up, though he knew it must be psychological.

"These deceased fellows are hot as ovens," she said, pointing the geiger built into the glove of the C.A.D.S suit at various of the seated inhabitants. "But away from them much of the radiation seems to have dissipated. The concrete, metal, plastic of the computers doesn't retain it for all that long. It's living things that sponge it up."

"Oh damn," Dixon suddenly blurted out and they all turned fast as his voice sounded terrified. He had bumped against one of the sitting dead and it had fallen from its chair. Upon hitting the concrete floor the head, arms, everything sort of just came apart and fell off in separate directions. They all stopped in their tracks looking like they were about to gag. It was DeCamp who spoke first, her voice calm, considering what it was she was describing.

"The neutron bomb rays cause cellular destruction on a massive scale," she said. "Actually makes the cell walls collapse, turned to jello. They're all being held together by the outer layers of skin which have semi-petrified from the initial blast rays. I wouldn't touch any of them. Not only will they fall apart like Dixon's friend there, but their flesh might not come off so easily from your own flesh. It's like glue if I remember my molecular atomic biology 101." If any of them had any doubts about a woman having leadership abilities, DeCamp's attitude was changing all that, though none would say a word out loud about it.

They walked on through the center of the room, not wanting to look but being unable to turn their eyes away from the ghastly apparitions that sat everywhere. It seemed that in spite of their leathery brown ugliness any of them might rise up and begin talking or come toward the C.A.D.S team, arms outstretched, mouth spitting black powder. And if they had, it's possible that every one of them would have turned and run. But though it was a chamber of horrors, there was nothing supernatural about it. Gamma rays kill. This was the proof. Science, the technology of science, not of ghosts, was responsible for every dead man here.

They reached the other side of the room and De-Camp opened a steel door so that a whoosh of dank air swept over them for a moment. A few of the bodies tumbled from their seats at the pressure change and crashed into pieces on the floor like ancient chinaware. Already the smell was becoming stronger as the outer world let in its bacteria, viruses, funguses, and countless other microbes that were going to have some fine feasting down here.

DeCamp led them through a series of corridors where they saw more of the dead in awkward, absurd, even comical positions. Two men had been having a conversation face to face. They still stood face to face, their rubber-soled shoes vulcanized to the floor, and one man's arm was raised as if he were making a point, his black hole of a mouth opened wide to say a word that would never come out. The other listened, hardened eyes staring blankly into the face of his pal.

"Wonder what he was about to say," Dixon said with a mischievous grin.

"Oh shut up, Dixon," Tranh snapped out. "It's not smart to mock the dead. Their ghosts can hear even if the bodies can't. You might wake up one night and find one of these dudes staring down at you and he might not be too happy about being made a joke."

"Hey, lighten up, Asian buddy," Dixon said, holding his hands up as if to ward off Tranh's words. "I was just—"

"Both of you shut up," Sturgis snapped. "I don't want to hear any talk at all down here, okay, unless it has to do with the mission. Let's show some respect for our honored dead."

"It's this way," DeCamp said as they came to a juncture of three passageways. "They must have stayed pretty close to the original blueprints. Thank God," she added softly, not even wanting to think about what it would be like to have to search the miles of tunnels and storage rooms down here without the computerized plans. They walked another two hundred yards or so seeing more bodies, then another door. This one also was stuck tight and wouldn't budge even under the force of the DeCamp's servo arms.

"Use your Zippo lighter there," Sturgis suggested to Laughing Elk who pulled out the oddly configured pistol and let a stream of flame lick its way around the hinges, lock and handle. Still, it wouldn't budge.

"We don't have time to fool around down here forever," Sturgis said. "You've used the suit a lot in combat in Moscow—right DeCamp?"

"Well, had some practice, But I don't want to—"

"*Kick* that sucker down. Just plant one foot on the floor and let go with everything you've got. We'll have to try the brute force method." He could see by the look of confusion on her face that she didn't really want to do it, if only because so far everything had been done so scientifically and controlled. "Move it doc, we ain't got time," he said again brusquely.

"All right, stand back," she replied sharply to them. "I don't want any of you getting hurt from the flying shrapnel." She planted her foot and both arms against each side of the cinderblock walls and then swung the other leg back as far as the C.A.D.S suit would allow. Then she slammed it forward, the booted foot hitting right into the door just below the handle which they had turned to opened position. The entire steel door flew right off its hinges and fell inward with a loud clank that echoed like thunder along the narrow corridors.

"Son of a bitch," Dixon said, with grudging respect. "This broad can kick bukanky."

"Thank you Dixon, I'll take that as a compliment," DeCamp said, "though I'm not sure what 'bukanky' is." She walked into the corridor, stepping over the flattened door which had come free from the wall, dust filtering down where the cinder blocks had been ruptured. It was Laughing Elk's turn to be a touch overwhelmed at the power of the suit. He hadn't realized even yet just what the C.A.D.S unit could do when it was fully functioning. They followed her in down another hundred feet or so and came to a door that opened easily. Then stepped through.

Their mouths all dropped open. For they were at the edge of an underground warehouse that looked like it extended for acres. And it was filled to overflowing with munitions. Steel shelving floor to ceiling, a good twenty feet high was absolutely loaded with boxes of cartridges, shells, grenades, equipment of every make and description.

"Man, you could start a war with this pile of junk," Dixon said, impressed.

"And win it too," Tranh added as they stepped inside. Dim lights were still burning here and there so there was enough light to see by.

"All right, we're here," Sturgis said, taking over the controls of the operation from DeCamp, who seemed to relax a trifle as she realized she had done her thing and it was all back in Sturgis's hands. She had enjoyed the role of leader even for a few hours but had felt the stress as well. When you were leading you were also responsible for the lives of all who followed you. It was a weight she wasn't used to and was just as glad to have it off her C.A.D.S-suited shoulders. "Now, let's spread out. We're looking particularly for stuff compatible with the suits—we've been over the list. But anything interesting—grenades, bazooka shells, whatever useable you can find, grab it. Any questions just yell out, don't come running back and forth to me, we've got to move."

They spread out up and down the different aisles, undoing the large duffle bags that the Indians had given them and they had been carrying around their shoulders. They walked around inspecting just what might be useful. All were trained in the capabilities of the suits, including its multi-calibration ammunition capability. Which meant the stuff didn't even have to be exactly what they had been using. Within a range a lot of ammunition, even small artillery shells could be stuffed into the suit's firing chambers—and it would adjust. It was one of the prime features of the suits, as the designers had known that if there really was war that getting what you wanted would become increasingly unlikely, and ultimately non-existent.

It took over an hour but at last they rejoined at the main door to the room, their duffles loaded to capacity. Just about everything that Sturgis had been hoping for was on the shopping list, including ten 65 mm's.

Each trooper carried between seventy-five and a hundred pounds of ammunition. Sturgis strapped two of

197

the bags to DeCamp's suit and she turned and walked for a few moments to test if she could handle it. She could. The suit computer increased the gear ratio of muscle to machine, and she hardly felt off balance. They made their way back out, passing through the corridors, the war room of the dead.

"I took video pictures into memory of all this computer equipment, along with the munitions," DeCamp said to Sturgis. "They're going to love this information back at White Sands. Forgetting the ammo—I guess there's enough computer parts and wiring, chipboards and whatnots to outfit another thousand suits. This could be a goldmine for the whole C.A.D.S. operation."

"Excellent," Sturgis complimented her, not at all sure they were going to make it back to White Sands base. But he kept such thoughts to himself. Always to himself, the curse of leadership. They made it back outside, all of them letting out a deep sigh of thanks to be back in the real world, the real air, out of the mausoleum of the past. The old world was down there, under the sands. And the old world was dead. Sturgis stopped as DeCamp closed the main outer door and they all piled sand to cover it over again. It took ten minutes but it was worth it. He didn't want anyone finding this shopping mall of ammo. Then he stood up on the dune that looked down over the burial site and spoke softly but firmly so they could all hear him.

"We thank all of you who served your country so well. Who made the ultimate sacrifice so that others might live," Sturgis said as they stood around the outer door, the sands swirling around their feet. He saluted the buried base and the dead. The rest of the team did so too, even Laughing Elk, who didn't quite know how to make the salute correctly. But he brought his hand up to his eyebrows and held it there as the others did. Respect goes beyond national—or tribal—loyalty. It's

something as deep as a man's soul. And all inside this
place of eternal death had earned it.

Chapter Twenty-six

It was hard going heading back. Very hard. The loads the team was under, which at first had seemed tolerable, added on pounds every mile that they traversed. Though they started out running at just about the speed they had come toward the base, they quickly began slowing, losing speed every mile. Sturgis kept shouting encouragement, cajoling, threatening them, just making them move, making them forget how terribly heavy the loads were around their backs and shoulders. DeCamp didn't say a word, even with two hundred pounds plus attached to the suit. The servo mechs seemed to be functioning even with all the extra weight, for she was able to keep up the lead, which if anything pulled the others forward, unable to accept that a woman could outcarry and outrun them, even if she was wearing a C.A.D.S. suit.

The first ten miles were hard, the next five seemed like hell itself. Above them the sky was slowly moving from black to a slate blue gray. The sun would come up soon and Sturgis had a feeling that the attack would begin before noon. They had to make it back in time. In his mind his worst fears were that when they arrived all would be dead, his men and the Indians. He used that particular nightmare to make his legs pump, his lungs suck in the cold air against their cellular will.

As they reached a rise and could see pueblo-filled mesa, the sandstone mountain reflecting the far rising sun off its peaks, a flock of flapping bats came tearing by. There must have been a hundred thousand of them and all the men felt a deep revulsion course through their veins. But even as they prepared to dive to the ground the cloud of bats flew on overhead. Insect catchers! They had no interest in flesh.

They had gone another three miles, two more left to reach the pueblo city when the shelling began in earnest. The jig was up. The Killboys were moving in. As tired as they were, the sounds of the scores of shells coming down and the engines of hundreds of vehicles, motivated them that little extra. They reached into their very souls and pulled up the strength to keep on. The commandeered ammo felt like it weighed a ton now.

As they approached, the sun rose up over the far off mountains. The world was suddenly thick with pastel shadows, colors oozing along the prairie, lighting everything with a rainbow of hues. And the sound of the explosions was coming louder by the second.

"We must, of course go in the back way with all this ammunition," Laughing Elk said to Sturgis, who was running alongside him. "Can't take a chance and go around in front of the invading forces."

"Sounds like a great idea," Sturgis said, rolling his eyes, thinking about the tight spots in the tunnel. There were just a hundred yards of open ground to go. They tore ahead, but suddenly a bulldozer came through the smoke and flame, its multi-steel-toothed shovel leveled straight ahead at them. It moved fast for such a bulky and immense piece of hardware coming at them at a good thirty miles an hour. Laughing Elk saw it first and pointed. Then DeCamp, right behind him, turned without hesitating, rushing toward the dozer to protect the rest of them. "Get the stuff into the tunnel! She yelled. "I'll delay—"

"No!" Sturgis screamed out in horror as she charged ahead, her arm outstretched like a linebacker trying to fend the 'dozer off. A trained man in a hyped up Model One suit, coming at just the right angle might have had a chance to move the thing. But though her attempt was heroic it was futile. For as she sidestepped and came in from the right firing small calibers, the dozer operator, obviously a pro, turned fast. He sent the dagger-tipped teeth flying straight ahead at waist level.

She took the blow right at mid-suit. The C.A.D.S. suit could take a lot but the sheer mass and momentum of the dozer forced the teeth right through the titanium armor—and probably through DeCamp as well, Sturgis realized.

She didn't scream and somehow, in her last conscious seconds, she managed to swing her feet around and under the dozer, getting the thick armored legs stuck in the treading of the industrial earth-mover.

It thus came to a screeching halt with sparks and grease flying out everywhere as her suit leg got entangled in the tread. It ground to a full halt turning around as if nailed to the ground. It seemed to grind her in deeper between the machine and the huge treads. Suddenly Sturgis understood. Then the dozer came into contact with the two hundred pounds of explosives she had been carrying.

There was a massive explosion aimed mostly backward at the advancing Killboy army! The dozer and DeCamp and about a dozen punk-weirdos within fifty feet all went up in an explosion of metal, dirt and red flesh.

She had given Sturgis and the rest the precious seconds to reach the tunnel. They couldn't waste it!

They flew through the stone opening in the mountain rising above. More shells kept dropping as the smoke cleared a little. Flaming oil barrels came flying down on the advancing ranks of dozers, just behind Sturgis and his men, allowing them to make it.

"Damn," Sturgis shouted as they tore through the tunnels. They made time despite their loads, straight to the combat chambers on the second level where Laughing Elk knew the other C.A.D.S. troopers would be waiting.

"Goddamn it," Sturgis yelled again, his words echoing off the painted red stone walls. "Why did she have to die? It's not fair."

"She got us *in,* man," Tranh, yelled from behind him. "Men have sacrificed their lives for centuries, eons, so that their fellow might live. I think Sheila was proud to go out like that, Skip."

He huffed breathlessly as they rounded a corner and tore up a ramp, half banging into the walls with their loads of ammo. "She wanted to be a good fighter, a real fighter, a trooper as tough as any man. And she sure *was!"*

"That was the bravest thing I've ever seen," Dixon coughed out, coming up behind them with his load. He had a new respect in his voice for the deceased, wishing he hadn't been so snide with her when she was alive.

Sturgis tore the left arm off his suit in a tight spot and had to abandon it. But not the ammo.

At last they saw light ahead: *"Here,"* Laughing Elk screamed as they came off the second level ramp and turned a corner. They tore into a large room with high ceilings where the team was already suited and standing in lines, ready to be parachuted out the window.

"Sturgis, thank God you're here," Rossiter screamed as they entered the room, their faces red as beets and breathing so hard their lungs rose in and out like balloons ready to pop. "You got the ammo?" he asked hoping beyond hope it was true. For through the wide window opening carved through the sandstone they could see the Killboys close below, the faces of the mohawked-haired, leather-and-stud-wearing psycho army clearly, leeringly visible!

"Load them up," Sturgis yelled to the others as he dropped his pack in front of the man on the far right. It was Henderson, one of the newer recruits.

"Listen Henderson," Sturgis screamed as their visors were opened. "I'm going to load you up with several different calibrations of small shells. These things will have maybe half the power of our depleted E-balls, God bless their souls. So you got power, plus a whole load of 7.2mm Nato which I'm pouring into your side feed here." Sturgis pulled back a hidden slot just around the backside of the metal suit's waist and poured the stuff in. The suit would sort it automatically and load it into VSF firing chambers.

"Now left wrist is lower calibers, right turn is higher. You got that? If there's a jam—"

"Colonel, with all due respect," the young, firm-jawed recruit spoke up. "I've been through a lot of training in the suit. Been in combat operations already in Moscow, remember? I can handle it."

"Just flip the caliber mode switch on auto," Sturgis shouted as he finished the loading, slapped the thing closed and slammed the man on the shoulder. He felt the salt of his tears reach his lips. Crying as he shouted orders. Sheila, *Sheila* was *gone!*

"Rossiter has equipped us all with jury-rigged jetpacks," Henderson shouted through the growing thunder of explosions galore. The air was thick with dust and smoke. "Says we may get blown to pieces—but what the hell. Anything's worth a try."

"Kick ass," Sturgis screamed as the man walked through the doorless frame carved out of solid rock, slammed his jetpack on as soon as he reached the farthest point on the balcony outcropping. He suddenly shot up into the air, as white flame fueled by Indian high-test whooshed out the back of the suit. He flew off as the shelling grew even more intense.

They tore down the row loading each man and giving him quick battle instructions. The troopers were anxious, but eager to get into battle with *real* ammunition, with *loads* of it!

Rossiter came tearing down the center of the room toward Sturgis. "You did a great job, man, getting these rocket packs burning again," Sturgis said. "We can make jumps in and out of battle, one of the suit's main tactical advantages. How'd you convert for—"

"I fiddled with the combustion nozzle. Usually, we use more refined forms of fuel, mixed with all kinds of catalysts and what not. But, hell, I tried some of the Indians' most refined stuff, tested it out on a pack—and it spat pure kinetic reverse power for a good five minutes, no flameouts, no—"

"Don't have time for a treatise right now," Sturgis snapped, opening the long ripstop bag at his feet. "Load up some of those middle guys there," Sturgis pointed, as he moved onto the next man. It was MacLeish. Evidently, no one had noticed that Sheila hadn't returned. So they were feeling good.

"Throw some bloody ammo into this computerized garbage pail, will you, the Queen's waiting," MacLeish smiled, slamming his visor down.

"Take care, old friend," Sturgis said in a whisper and slammed closed the quick-feed as soon as he had him loaded.

"I'll be back in time for dinner," the Brit shouted out. "Tell them no more of that corn gruel. I want chicken tonight, thank you, bloody chicken." He walked ahead as the suit vibrated with energy now that it was almost fully powered. Small red lights blinked on and off at the ankles and elbows. He walked out to the sandstone terrace and instantly disappeared in a rush of fire which seared the stone terrace. The things were burning fuel like a 747. But they flew.

"Sturgis, there's a suit here, a makeshift we threw together overnight from parts," Rossiter yelled over the din of battle outside. "Maybe—"

"Where?" Sturgis asked, burning to join his men. Rossiter double-timed it back across the wide room and up to the wall where two suits stood, their clamps undone, so they were opened out like high tech iron maidens. Sturgis jumped right into one and sealed it all shut and snapped onto full combat systems.

"Load me, baby, load me," Sturgis shouted out but Rossiter was already feeding the precious ammunition into the loading chambers.

"I'm giving you everything that's left," Rossiter yelled out as the battle sounds grew so close they were almost deafened. "There's all kinds of crap in here—grenades . . ."

"Just pour whatever will fit into the salad," Sturgis shouted back "and give the rest to the Indians. I'm sure they can find good use for it." He slammed down his visor and read with satisfaction the diagrams and charts and moving 3D maps twisting along the edges of the screen. It felt good to be in a C.A.D.S. suit again. To be a warrior.

"Loaded," Rossiter shouted out, slamming the suit on the titanium rump. Sturgis grimaced inside, his heart pounding as it always did when he headed into battle. He walked to the terrace and peered with electromagnetic rays into the smoke and fire, and horror of the scream-filled killing grounds. And he took off on a tail of blue-white fire.

Chapter Twenty-seven

"Battle Modes—*all systems*," Sturgis screamed into his mike as the C.A.D.S. suit shot up through the smoking curtains of fire. "Human Interface Linkup full manual. Firing Selection full automatic," Sturgis shouted out, giving the computer guidance combat orders. It had to know just what aspects of the fighting he wanted to handle, and which it would take over automatically—as much as it could.

"ALL COMBAT MODES 100%," the panel read out in dancing green digital letters. "ROCKET FUNCTION 87% . . . FUEL CONSUMPTION 1% PER SECOND. TAKING OVER DEEP RECON, BEEPER WARNING, MANUAL OVERRIDE CIRCUITS . . ." Sturgis looked away and down, ignoring the readouts, he knew enough. The jetpack was burning it up like an early NASA rocket. He had a minute, maybe a minute and a half of use at most. It would do. *"For Sheila,"* he muttered. Then he commanded:

"MODE RED." The visor cut through the chimneys of smoke which covered the vast battle below. Suddenly he could see them all in infra-red, heat and magnetic imaging and sonar-probe, all simultaneously formed into one image, giving it depth and shimmering levels of color.

He saw two of his men zoom down out of the smoke and fire several rockets out of their right firing tubes. Three heavily armed stationwagons and a pickup truck filled with ammunition went up with a thunderous blast that he felt from two hundred yards away. They flew off back into the rising smoke before the Killboys could get a bead on them, sending up withering hails of slugs. But the air was already empty!

The nuke-troopers made jump after jump and then vanished quickly before anyone knew what was going on.

"Good boys," Sturgis muttered as he saw a big tank-like vehicle covered over with so much armoring it looked like a steel armadillo come out of the smoke fog. The men were using the suits right. Quick strike and out. Maybe it wasn't fair and doubtless the Killboys would accuse them of not fighting like "men." But from the Revolutionary War back to time immemorial outnumbered guerrillas and freedom fighters had always had to use their wits—and their speed. Don't have to get macho "stick-to-your-post" about war—Just have to win!

Sturgis aimed the suit straight down like a hawk coming in from a hundred feet and soared over the top of a thirty foot long armored truck/tank with large 105mm cannon mounted right on top of the makeshift warwagon. He raised his right arm and released two of whatever was in there. Two anti-tank shells, each one a good six inches long, thick as a man's wrist, came flying out, separating as they flew the hundred and thirty six feet to the target.

The first shell blew half the outer wall off. The second made its way inside through the smoke hazed opening and took out the thirty mohawk-haired killers ready to come out like marines off a landing boat when they hit the first of the pueblo walls.

Sturgis felt the shock waves hit his suit and he tumbled over sixty feet higher in the air, letting himself go with it instead of panicking.

The first thing raw recruits did when stuck in a roll situation was throw on more power. Which more than likely meant destruction. You had to ease into it, like going over a wave at the beach, then add a little power as you straightened up again. He should know, he had taught "rock and roll" as they termed it, for two years before taking over as primary field and combat commander of the C.A.D.S. White Sands base. That "hard" base was now devoted completely to support, production and innovation on the suits, and doubled as the new U.S. White House.

Sturgis regained his mid-air balance and settled down fast on the ground to get a worms-eye view of the battle. He landed right between two Killboy cars which came to a halt, sure they had one metal man at least, surrounded. Automatic fire opened up from the windows of each as red and green spiked haired punks screaming "death, death", their eyes bulging with madness and drugs. Sturgis could feel the stream of slugs rocketing against the outer layers of the suit like a hard rain. Some made dents.

He jumped quickly, not even needing the jet pack, and came down on the far side of the right flank car. He grabbed hold underneath and with a surge of servo-assisted power lifted up.

The car, passengers and all, turned over on its side and as he pushed out hard like shoving a boisterous drunk at a bar, the car went flying end over end right into the second car. There was a crackling of sparks as the engine wiring and fuel tanks ripped free and then a blinding explosion as the gas tanks of both cars suddenly went up in a single roaring eruption of fire and screams.

"Jet boost!" Sturgis yelled to the suit as a warning light flashed urgently on the visor readout. It had read: "IMMINENT DESTRUCTION, PATTON TANK CLASS A, RADAR FIXING ON—" But the suit's jet pack was already firing, even as it read out the fact that he had 1.07 seconds to live. The rockets flamed on and he shot up into the air as if launched from a giant spring.

A *real* tank, a modern job that the killer army had somehow dug up fired. Its long cannon spat out two shells aimed right for Sturgis. He rose just above them, could feel the steel projectiles vibrate the air just past his boots. Finding nothing, they flew past and slammed into two Killboy pick-up trucks about a hundred feet off, both of them erupting into hot shrapnel and cold flesh. Sturgis actually laughed. "With friends like *that* . . ."

"C.A.D.S. Commandos—make sure Blue Mode is on," Sturgis screamed, slamming his headset into auto-link. The airwaves were suddenly abuzz as he could hear all of them screaming at once.

"Tranh, three o'clock," Dixon's voice yelled out, "a buzzard with heavy jaws."

"Conrad, a joker's on your tail, look out, *look out.*"

It was hard to even distinguish what was going on, everything was moving so fast. On the grid maps of Sturgis's visor screen the C.A.D.S. computer tried madly to keep up with the incoming combat info, scrambling it across in a waterfall of numbers and charts. The video-game of "Life and Death."

"That you, Sturgis?" a voice screamed through the ethers.

"Yeah, dammit, go to blue mode—blue mode. Don't shoot your own man." He didn't know how many had heard him and didn't have time to ask. He had come down just ahead of three jeeps rigged up with machine guns on their opened backs. The jeeps had sighted up some Indians. The gunners all saw him and opened up with all three 50 cals swinging them around to make target acquisition. They poured out with such power that for a few seconds Sturgis was actually pushed straight backward as if a nose tackle had just plowed into his guts. He steadied himself as the gyro's helped to maintain balance. He ripped up his right arm. No way were these guys gonna cut down any Indians.

"Fire," he screamed, and the arm bucked back a fraction of an inch as the shocks took the recoil of the two mini bazooka shells that the autofeed had selected as being worthy of a try.

The seven-inchers tore through right into the front of the middle jeep, disintegrating it. The whole engine, burning like a mini-sun spun through the air and slammed into the jeep to the left. The two of them seemed to fuse in flame as burning men went jumping off in all directions, their howls of pain louder than the battle all around them.

Sturgis jumped a fast ten yards to the right and as the third jeep came tearing up trying to sight him, he sent out a stream of 7.2mms. They ripped through the windshield of the jeep taking out the driver, then scythed their way down the back where they sliced the machine gunner nearly in half, red holes appearing everywhere across his black leather jacket.

There was a series of explosions behind him and Sturgis turned as his visor cut through the smoke fog. It was the lead bulldozers and cars—they were reaching the base of the pueblo mountain. From above, barrel after barrel of gasoline came flying down. The final remaining gasoline troughs dug into the ground at the mountain's base erupted flame as well. A wall of steel met a wall of fire. And the steel melted. Even the armored dozers under the intense double flames couldn't take it. Or at least the men inside them couldn't. They came flying out as the bulldozers smashed into one another or buried themselves in the outer sandstone walls digging their teeth deep into it but stopping.

And as the gasoline cannisters flew, Sturgis saw that

Rossiter had actually loaded up the huge 155mm on top of their bus. He pulled at the firing mech and the bus shook with a primeval roar and spat out a huge shell. Aimed almost horizontally it ran about a hundred and fifty feet before hitting a large yellow razor-finned Caddy.

The car and everything within thirty feet of it turned into splintered metal and flame. Between the cannon and the Indian's fireballs, the flames burned heaven and earth, demolishing the first hundred feet of invading dozers, cars, and armored vehicles.

Suddenly out of the pueblo doorways and windows all along the main and second floor rushed and jumped hundreds of the Naqui, stripped down to battle gear, warpaint coating their faces, chests, arms and legs. They carried flamethrowers and bandoliers of grenades that Sturgis and his team had brought back from Fort Collins. They flew like the wind moving out fast in all directions. They crouched and ran, weaving back and forth like running backs heading past the hailstorm of gunfire and right into the advancing cars.

"Go, go," Sturgis screamed with excitement as he saw that the Naqui had stopped the first wave of the invasion in its tracks. Indians still fell from multi-levels up and down Mesa Mountain as the Killboys continued their heavy firing. But the attack was slowing down, stopped by the lack of forward progress.

"C.A.D.S. team." Sturgis shouted into the mike. "Fall back behind the invading force. We will form a second front on the battle."

It took another minute to get the fourteen of them who were left in a long line nearly six hundred feet across to match the width of the invading force which they were now standing behind.

"Concentrate firepower, especially on the big stuff," Sturgis told them. "Move fast, like those Naqui. Speed, that's our strength." They suddenly went charging forward, the huge suits jetpacking down among the back ranks of the slowed invasion cars. They unleashed murderous sheets of slugs left and right, ripping through metal and flesh alike of all they passed. Return fire came back at them from countless vehicles, but the small shells just ricocheted off the suits.

The counterattack was as merciless as the Killboys had been in their attack of the pueblo city. The Naqui braves rushed around with their spurting flamethrowers and throwing grenades through car windows tearing the attack-lines apart. And from the rear the C.A.D.S. force wouldn't allow retreat but fenced the enemy in along the entire rear flank, firing at every piece of steel, every head with dayglow-spray-painted plumage of polyurethaned hair.

Confusion began tearing through the ranks of the Killboy army as they saw their ranks getting thinned out in large numbers, men on fire and missing limbs running in terrified retreat. Many of the top leaders in the most fortified vehicles were attacked hard and that only added to the confusion as the Killboy ranks began breaking formation and turning around trying to find the enemy.

Here and there Indians were taking shots and going down in their own mini-explosions as their flame-throwing pack fuel tank went up on their backs. Sturgis saw a C.A.D.S. trooper take a direct hit from a tank cannon right into his helmet. The helmet protected his head all right, but the detonation ripped the whole thing free from the body and it went sailing off slamming into a slug-holed cactus.

"You," Sturgis suddenly heard a voice scream, bellowing out from behind him. His helmet showed trouble, some big guns bearing down fast. He turned—it was Macro-Kill, the huge bloated-belly general of the psycho army. He hadn't been in the yellow Caddy when it was hit! His brown cracked mouth was grinding hard as if trying to chew down Sturgis's soul. "You die, bastard!" the man shouted again as he sat at the controls of a Super Harley MaxiCycle 1500 with mini-luchaire 89mm rocket launchers mounted on each side of the metal frame. Not to mention machine guns, grenade launchers, spikes on the wheels and various other accoutrements that any self-respecting motorcycle battlewagon wouldn't be seen dead without.

"*You* die, pal," Sturgis whispered back though he knew the slime couldn't hear him through the closed visor. The helmet suddenly did a closeup in one quardrant of the screen showing a video telemode of Macro-Kill's hands tightening on the firing mech's for the missile launcher.

"Jetpack up, fucking up," Sturgis screamed as he jumped with all his strength to add momentum to the takeoff. He timed it, but nearly too late. A two-foot-long missile trailing a tail of white smoke tore just inches under his departing heels and slammed forward nearly a quarter mile into the side of the pueblo mountain. It took out a dozen Naqui who had been firing a large cannister-catapult.

Sturgis did a full spin in the air as he leaned and came down hard on the other side of the warbike about thirty feet back as Macro-Kill swung his cycle around on a dime, flooring it as he held one huge leg to the ground. His twin machine guns started firing before he had even swung the full 180°.

Sturgis aimed ahead and fired with his big stuff. And nothing came out. A jam, from one of the Ft. Collins shells.

"MALFUNCTION IN MAIN FIRING TUBE," a right visor monitor read out in digital letters. "0% FUNCTION ON SHELLS AND ARTILLERY SHELLS. ONLY SMALL ARMS CALIBERS NOW FUNCTIONING. FIVE 7.2mm BULLETS REMAINING."

"Great," Sturgis snarled. The damn auto-sort wasn't worth shit. He'd have to complain to the techs back at White Sands. *Right*.

Suddenly Macro-Kill found his range with the machine gun and a stream of slugs ripped across the suit's chest. Again Sturgis was pushed backward and could hardly keep his balance from the sheer energy of the slugs. He threw his body to the ground, falling forward as the following slugs poured overhead. And the instant they stopped he pushed off and kicked up with everything he had. The motorcycle came speeding right toward him, the huge spikes and hooks on its sides ready to grab hold and chew him up. Sturgis flew right up in the air from the kickoff.

The cycle flew by below him and he could see the bulbous tumor-ridden head of Macro-Kill. Sturgis came down boots first, yelling, *"Die,* cockroach!"

The heels of the descending C.A.D.S. boots came down right on top of the skull of the death-general. They smashed through the skull and then through the brain inside pounding down all the way to the neck. Sturgis looked down and saw that the general had no head anymore. It was enough. "Cockroach smashed," he intoned. He stood savoring the moment for a few seconds. Then decided to move. "Rockets on," Sturgis commanded the suit almost gently.

The suit shot up with a weakening jet blast and he hovered for a few seconds at fifty feet sacrificing the last of the precious fuel for a look at the war.

The good guys were winning. *Had* won. The Indians had decimated the front ranks of the cars. Burning and burnt wrecks of blackened frames were everywhere around the fields. Their fences and barbed wire were all knocked down now. Bodies, their flesh turned to crisp black beef jerky, their bones poking through where some had been consumed in intense heat, were everywhere. It was a rout.

The C.A.D.S. troopers, coming from the rear, met the Naqui's, cheering. Their grenade packs were gone, their fuel tanks were reading empty. But it was over. They met and embraced and cheered, two armies victorious.

The Indians slammed the suits with good cheer though the C.A.D.S. men couldn't return the favor of they might kill their new-found friends. The very very few Killboy cars that were capable of still moving went tearing out of the valley of death, their wheels spitting up sand behind them. They left the Indian lands with far less sound and fury than they had come in.

Chapter Twenty-eight

"I can't stand the thought of leaving her," Sturgis whispered, looking down at Robin's comatose form. She lay flat on her back on some elk hides, long and thick, that cushioned every part of her. Lay there like a sleeping beauty, her face oddly at rest, at peace. Her color was slightly better, her pulse too. But she sure wasn't moving.

"Can't take her," Laughing Elk translated as the buffalo-horned medicine man stood on the far side of the bedding. "He says she's doing good, but can't travel now. She must lie very still while her body absorbs and distributes the herbal remedies, so that her cells can excrete the poison. Take a few weeks, even a month. Then she will come out of coma. The coma is actually helping her, helping her heal." Laughing Elk said this all softly, trying to comfort Sturgis, the man he now felt incredible gratitude to. His intervention had clearly saved the Naqui lands and their pueblo and their oil operation as well.

"Anytime, you and your men need gas, need to refuel those big tin monsters of yours," Laughing Elk said smiling, "come back."

Chief Naktu beamingly handed Sturgis a feathered and multi toothed headdress. It wasn't nearly as long and complex as Naktu's, but it would do. Sturgis took it with thanks and held it up for the other men to see.

"I accept this SuperBowl trophy for the whole team. We'll mount it on the warroom back at White Sands." The troopers cheered as they stood patiently in their suits, visors open, ready to move out through the dirt and the sand, the grit and grime and hell that awaited them outside the protecting sandstone walls.

"We will take good care of her, I promise you," Laughing Elk said, looking at him with clear brown eyes. "You know you can trust us. As we can trust you. We are brothers."

"Blood brothers," Sturgis replied softly. A lot of blood had been spilt. Nearly fifty Indians dead and five more of his own men gone. Tranh had taken an armor-piercing machine gun slug through the suit's arm. The rest of his team were okay. "For both of our people gave their blood."

"If you are representative of the new America, the new government," Laughing Elk said with solemnity. "Then we can respect you and even swear you allegiance. Our relations with the *old* government were never good. But we can try, try again. We try or the world will forever sink into the desert of white buffalo bones, where all things to go die."

"To a new and better world then, even out of all this," Sturgis said, nodding toward the death field just outside the window ledge where they stood.

"Skip, we have to get moving if we're going to get a jump on the day," Tranh said, gently reminding his commander that emotions would have to give way to grim reality.

"Yeah, you're right," Sturgis said. He leaned down and gently stroked Robin's spread locks with the huge gloved hand. Beauty and the Beast.

"Take care baby," he said, with tears glistening in his eyes behind the visor. You never knew if you'd ever see someone again in this age of mega death. "I'll be back for you, I swear," he whispered low. "I'll be back in a month."

He was a commander of a unit of fighting men. And they had to return to White Sands and report the find of computer parts and ammunition depot at Fort Collins. It could speed up the development of more C.A.D.S. suits, many times over. And, God knew, America needed lots more of them. To sort out the good from the bad, the beautiful from the very, very ugly. To win the final battle.

"Let's move 'em out," Sturgis said, walking to the ledge as the rest of the strike force checked that everything was latched up on their suits and that they were all sealed in like babies for the long dark night. He turned and bowed slightly toward the chief and Laughing Elk and they returned the gesture. Then Sturgis faced the coming dawn and hit his jetpack button. He rocketed up, a sliver of crimson flame against the circle of the ghost white moon.

THE SURVIVALIST SERIES
by Jerry Ahern

#1: TOTAL WAR	(2445, $2.95)
#2: THE NIGHTMARE BEGINS	(2476, $2.95)
#3: THE QUEST	(2670, $2.95)
#4: THE DOOMSAYER	(0893, $2.50)
#5: THE WEB	(2672, $2.95)
#6: THE SAVAGE HORDE	(1232, $2.50)
#7: THE PROPHET	(1339, $2.50)
#8: THE END IS COMING	(2590, $2.95)
#9: EARTH FIRE	(1405, $2.50)
#10: THE AWAKENING	(1478, $2.50)
#11: THE REPRISAL	(2393, $2.95)
#12: THE REBELLION	(2777, $2.95)
#13: PURSUIT	(2477, $2.95)
#14: THE TERROR	(2775, $2.95)
#15: OVERLORD	(2070, $2.50)